MISS DASHING

MISCHIEF IN MAYFAIR—BOOK EIGHT

GRACE BURROWES

GRACE BURROWES PUBLISHING

Miss Dashing

Cover design by Wax Creative, Inc.

DEDICATION

To Jen, plot-stormer extraordinaire!

CHAPTER ONE

"I am a curiosity." Lord Phillip Vincent paced from the pianoforte to the French doors and on past the great harp. "I have no wish to become a laughingstock."

"Has somebody derided you to your face, my lord?" In Miss Hecate Brompton's opinion, only a fool would make fun of Lord Phillip. He stood several inches over six feet in his riding boots and moved with the brisk vitality of a wild creature in roaring good health. His hair needed a trim, and his clothing, while well made, was clearly borrowed. The fit across those broad shoulders was a trifle too snug to be Bond Street's best work.

And yet, those rough edges made him all the more imposing. In a fair fight against Mayfair's dandies and Corinthians, Hecate would put her money on Lord Phillip—not that Mayfair fights were usually fair and not that she gambled with her wealth.

"You lot don't insult a man openly," his lordship replied, straightening an unlit taper in a wall sconce. "You find it more diverting to whisper about him behind your fans and chortle over his missteps in the clubs."

"Perhaps we seek to spare that man embarrassment?" *You lot.* He made polite society sound like a secret club for naughty children. Not far off the mark.

"Nothing so considerate as that." He prowled back to the pianoforte and took a seat on the bench, which creaked under his weight. "You seek to embarrass him to the maximum extent possible, humiliation by a thousand cuts, and all of them delivered by unseen hands when his back is turned. I travel a dark forest rife with snares, and I am the most ignorant of prey."

The analogy was all too apt. Hecate had taken her own turn as the most ignorant of prey, which was why she didn't change the topic to the weather, pour his lordship a cup of tea, and send pointed glances at the clock on the mantel.

"Learning any new terrain takes time, my lord. You are a marquess's heir, and the fools will twit you on that basis alone."

He glanced around the music room. "I cannot help that my brother holds a title. I can do much to foil the fools, though, provided I have proper guidance."

Had Hecate been in that dark forest, she might have experienced the same uneasy sensation when a twig snapped in the dense thicket behind her.

"I can recommend some etiquette manuals."

He was back on his feet, retracing the same path he'd just trod. "I've read them. They are for a cit's daughter who has bagged a baronet's nephew and now must entertain an MP's cousin. I'm to be introduced *at court*, God help me, and my brother... Tavistock was to the Great Nonsense born. He doesn't even grasp how much he knows about proper deportment. The whole business goes beyond good manners—which we have even out in Berkshire—to mysteries too numerous to name."

"I can solve one mystery for you," Hecate said. "A gentleman does not pace."

He stopped, heaved those muscular shoulders in an audible sigh, and returned to his piano bench. "There, you see? Another snare closed 'round my ankle. I've probably paced the length of three ballrooms, four guest parlors, and two conservatories in the last week alone. Why doesn't a gentleman pace?"

"Would you like some tea?"

"Please. Cream and sugar, but this is Mayfair, so you probably have only milk. Don't bother if that's the case."

"You put cream in your tea out in Berkshire?" Who knew the shires were home to decadence?

"I can't speak for all of Berkshire. At Lark's Nest, we have plenty enough cream for our butter and cheese, so yes, I can have cream for my tea, porridge, and bread pudding, if I prefer, and I do. I also ensure some of my heifers freshen in autumn. Thus we have ample supplies in the dairy year-round."

He looked at his hands. Broad, capable, calloused. A white scar crossed the knuckles of the left hand. No signet rings, no lace draped over his wrists. Not the hands of a gentleman.

"I have just committed another six breaches of decorum, haven't I? Now I want to pace again, but a gentleman doesn't, and you've still not told me why."

"A gentleman also doesn't make his hostess hike across the music room to deliver his tea. Come sit over here, and I will explain about pacing and fidgeting."

"I do not fidget." He crossed the room and settled beside Hecate on the sofa, which dipped the cushions and nearly had her pitching into his side. "But sometimes I want to pace all the way back to Berkshire."

"One lump or two?"

"In that thimble? One will do."

She obliged and passed him the cup and saucer. "A gentleman does not pace or fidget because it betrays a lack of self-control. A lady is to behave at all times with similar composure. She never touches her face or hair in public either, lest she convey anything other than serene calm."

The tea disappeared in a single swallow. "Whyever not? If she's frightened by a mouse, will her serene composure impress the little fellow into scurrying off posthaste? If she's set upon by foot-pads, will serene composure keep her reticule from their grubby mitts? If a curl comes loose, is she to ignore it bouncing in her eyes?"

Hecate had offered similar arguments to her finishing governess, though Lord Phillip's baritone rumble made the same logic more convincing.

"The lady with an errant curl is to withdraw to the nearest retiring room to repair her coiffure. Next time, wait until I've served myself before you enjoy your tea, and try to savor it. Sip rather than gulp."

He glowered at his empty cup. "I knew that. We have tea trays in Berkshire. But I'm so blasted unsettled, I forget basic manners. What else?"

Lord Phillip was determined, and he wasn't arrogant. "A gentleman never sits close enough to a lady to risk inadvertently touching her person, unless the relationship is one of friendly familiarity."

Lord Phillip wrinkled his nose—a good, lordly beak—gave Hecate an inscrutable look, and moved a foot away on the sofa. "Don't stop there. We're just getting started, I'm sure."

Hecate sipped her tea and pointedly did not glance at muscular calves lovingly encased in gleaming leather. "A gentleman removes his spurs before entering a dwelling."

"I vaguely recall that one too. No sense in it, though, when the mud is on his boots rather than his spurs. But then, I rarely wear spurs at home. A horse should go when you tell him to without needing a jab in the ribs to remind him. These are for show, and a ridiculous show it is."

Hecate grasped only too well the sense of bafflement that Mayfair Society could cause in those new to its peculiarities. Lord Phillip was right to trouble himself to learn this dark forest and find all the hidden snares and mantraps.

She wanted to spare him those mocking smiles and smirking

silences before they escalated to pranks, wagers, and worse. And yet, he was not her debutante to launch.

"Wearing a fancy uniform into battle is thought by some to be ridiculous," Hecate said. "On campaign, that fancy uniform will get dusty, dirty, bloody, and torn."

Phillip passed her his empty cup and saucer. "But that uniform tells all and sundry to which regiment the fellow belongs. It proclaims him to be a soldier, a hero, rather than a bandit, though he's engaged in many of the same activities bandits are prone to. You are saying I need to learn to wear the uniform, and I agree. Will you teach me?"

Hecate refilled his cup with a steady hand, though the blunt request took her aback. Nobody asked Hecate Brompton for anything anymore, except to prevail on her to dance an opening quadrille with a spotty, bumbling nephew.

She had worked for years to make it so. "Why me? Why not ask Tavistock to appoint you a finishing governess? I'm sure among his army of step-relations and acquaintances, he knows somebody who could see to your Town education in due time."

Lord Phillip wanted to pace again. She could feel the restlessness in him, even from a foot away. Instead, he accepted his refilled cup, took one sip, and set his drink aside.

"Anybody Tavistock chose would jolly me along, overlook three-quarters of my bungling, and pronounce me fit for Almack's. I'm not stupid, Miss Brompton, but I'm ignorant. I'm the slow top younger brother kept out of Society's view by decree of the late marquess. He's dead—thank the Deity—my brother acknowledges me, and now everybody is entitled to have a gawk at the bumpkin spare. For the sake of my brother and for the sake of my own pride, I need to make a good showing."

Family loyalty was a trap Hecate understood only too well, and pride was both her besetting sin and her saving virtue. "Did you pay me a compliment when you implied that I'd call out your bungling?"

He retrieved his tea for another sip. No slurping, no gulping. "A drill sergeant bellows at his recruits because he wants them to survive battle, not because he's an overbearing, foul-mouthed brute by nature. Bellow at me, Miss Brompton. Whip me into shape. Please help me survive the battles I'll face in Mayfair's ballrooms."

Lord Phillip wasn't begging, but rather, asking for help. He was also issuing Hecate a challenge. She hadn't had a challenge in ages—other than how to manage her family—and the Little Season was still weeks away. She had time to make a silk purse out of...

Wrong analogy. Lord Phillip was intelligent, shrewd, physically impressive, and willing to apply himself to his studies.

With the right tailoring...

But no. Hecate had enough on her plate dealing with her rackety family. "I am not well liked," she said. "If you are looking for somebody to show you the basics of charm and flirtation, I am the wrong resource."

"You are respected. You are formidable. A woman who does not suffer fools and who hasn't succumbed to the blandishments of the fortune hunters. You are my first and last choice of finishing governess."

How she would have rejoiced to hear herself described thus ten years ago—respected, formidable—and the words were still some comfort, though the finishing governess part...

Nobody had warned her that not suffering fools left a woman with little company in polite society.

"A lady doesn't raise her voice or use profanity," Hecate said. "My drill sergeant qualifications are sadly lacking."

Lord Phillip saluted with his tea cup. "A gentleman is doubtless such crushingly dull company that he ensures a lady is never inspired to colorful language. I have excellent hearing, however, so we can hope you won't have to raise your voice to me in truth. Putting the manners on me should be nigh boring for one of your accomplishments."

His eyes were dancing, though his expression remained otherwise solemn, and Hecate realized what about this man had drawn her notice.

Lord Phillip seldom looked anybody in the eye. His gaze was invariably on his surroundings, on his hands, his boots, the nearest painting, but not on the people in his ambit. The same tendency in another man might have come across as furtive or shifty. Lord Phillip was neither—far from it—and she was sure in her bones that he wasn't arrogant either.

But quite possibly, he was *shy*.

He'd be torn to pieces and tossed to the tattlers.

Until Tavistock and his new marchioness were blessed with sons, Lord Phillip was the heir presumptive to a marquessate. He was a landed gentleman in his own right, young, attractive... The matchmakers would make a meal of him if the gossips left enough to snack on.

"Mayfair will undoubtedly bore you witless," Hecate said, "if it hasn't already. I don't suppose you're wealthy?"

Lord Phillip took up a visual inspection of the great harp. "Is that question rude?"

"Very. Also pertinent."

"I'm happy to pay you."

Holy angels defend him. "I will not accept coin for spending time with an agreeable social connection."

Lord Phillip again swung his gaze in her direction. "You should be compensated. Your time is precious, and I'm a quick study, but I have much to learn, and agreeable comes close to a falsehood, Miss Brompton."

He was sure of his strengths and honest about his weaknesses. That lack of prevarication left Hecate at a loss for how to respond. Lord Phillip was also the first person to inform her that her time was precious.

She should say no. She should politely decline. She should recommend him to some agency that specialized in deportment instructors, though none immediately came to mind.

"Very well." Phillip rose and bowed. "I'll wish you a pleasant rest of your day. I can see myself to the door. My thanks for hearing me out."

He'd said *please.* He'd been respectful. He was facing a pack of wolves and had sense enough to know it.

He was about to leave the room without offering her a bow, for pity's sake. "Coin of the realm is of no interest to a lady, but if I'm to take on your education, I need an idea of your means."

Lord Phillip sent a longing glance at the French doors. "I'm not in your league, but I'm well fixed. I own Lark's Nest thanks to Tavistock's generosity, and the estate prospers. I've invested a bit here and there, and I'm patient. I patented a plow design a few years back and some wool shears for use in the left hand. My tastes are modest, my needs few."

Hecate considered that recitation. "Ten thousand a year?"

"And a bit more, most years."

What had Tavistock been thinking to leave his brother tethered in Town like a goat set out to tempt the matchmakers?

But then, Tavistock hadn't been thinking. He'd been dreaming of wedded bliss with his Amaryllis.

"You'll need funds," Hecate said. "Funds for a wardrobe, cattle, a curricle or phaeton. We have time for that, but if you want to make a good showing this autumn, we'll need to get started."

"You'll take on my education, then? Break me to harness?"

Still not the right analogy. "You are on probation, my lord. Try my patience too far, exceed my tolerance in any way, and I will toss you to the penny press."

"I am duly warned."

"Then do stop looming over me. I have more questions, and I have it on good authority that my time is precious."

"So it is." He resumed his place on the sofa and poured himself a third cup of tea.

∽

Phillip had put off calling on Miss Hecate Brompton for a week, until it was almost too late, until most of the best families had left the sweltering confines of London for the green and restful shires. He would have decamped for Lark's Nest with them, except that home was Crosspatch Corners, where Trevor, Marquess of Tavistock, and his darling Amaryllis were embarking on their honey month.

"I suppose I should not have served myself. Is a third cup of tea beyond the pale?" Phillip asked. He knew it was, but he liked hearing Hecate Brompton talk. Her words trickled past his ear like a bright, splashing brook. Full of light, purpose, and energy, but never hurried.

"A third cup is occasionally permissible. Appropriating the pot is generally not done. If you are among true friends, rather than mere acquaintances, and nobody has an eye on the clock, the rules are relaxed. The worst sin a guest can commit is overstaying his welcome. Perhaps you'd care for a tea cake?"

He'd like a cold tankard of Pevinger's best ale, served by a smiling Tansy Pevinger in the common of the Crosspatch Arms with a side of steaming cheese toast.

"No, thank you, but neither am I ready to leave. Give me some assignments. Let me embark on a curriculum of manners, and I will be less inclined to pace."

The pacing had been about getting free of her scent, which was light, rosy, and brisk. Probably blended specially for her, a failed attempt at convention. The little spicy note—nutmeg and pepper—turned the fragrance intriguing instead.

The severe bun piqued his curiosity as well. How long was that lovely chestnut hair? Did it ripple to her hips, or swing in a soft curtain halfway down her back? When had she adopted the style of governess, and why?

"Can you dance?" she asked, eyeing him critically.

"Not well. I've seen the country dances enough times to stumble through them, but the fancier ballroom dances haven't made it to the local assembly in Crosspatch."

"You'll need a dancing master, then. I can recommend several.

Can you ride?"

"Passably." He *rode* quite well, but he hadn't the knack of turning a mounted outing into a fashion exhibition.

"Do you read the *Times*?"

"The financial pages. The rest is tripe."

She gave him a sharp look. "No, it is not. You will add *La Belle Assemblée* to your reading list, and I will quiz you on the contents. Read the political articles, don't just sneer at the patterns and fashion plates. Can you read French?"

"Competently. My pronunciation is atrocious, because I've never heard the language spoken except by our local liveryman. Dabney hails from the Caribbean, and his French is mostly profanity."

"No profanity, my lord, not in the company of the ladies, anyway. Gentlemen consider colorful languages something of an art, one I am unqualified to teach."

If so, profanity was the only aspect of polite society's curriculum Miss Hecate Brompton avoided. She prattled on, about tailors (Bond Street), boots (Hoby), handkerchiefs (always carry two, one for show, one for necessity), cravat pins (gold for every day, discreet jewels for evening), gentlemen's clubs (the grand equivalent of the snug at the Crosspatch Arms, having the sanctity of the confessional and the comfort of unlimited libation), and horseflesh (always know the bloodlines before you purchase, as if Phillip gave a donkey's fart for bloodlines when a beast's conformation and gaits were obvious to the eye).

All the while she interrogated and lectured, Phillip pondered his own list of questions. Did Hecate Brompton ever laugh? She had a rare, pretty smile. He'd seen it once, when she'd caught him studying her at the only formal dinner he'd so far endured.

The array of cutlery and glasses had baffled him. One did not use any old fork to eat lobster. One used the smallest implement on offer, because that made no sense whatsoever. One did not partake of every dish and vintage the footmen brought around, lest one be comatose by the end of the meal.

Phillip had survived the ordeal only by closely watching what Miss Brompton did, and when the ladies had withdrawn, he'd been assigned to escort her to the parlor. Ladies, for reasons unknown to mortal man, were incapable of navigating a half-dozen yards of carpeted corridor without a gent to show them the way.

At the parlor door, Miss Brompton had smiled at him, thanked him, and swanned off. Tavistock had seen the exchange and for once kept his big, handsome, insufferably competent mouth shut.

"And a ladybird," Miss Brompton said, "may be driven in the park during the carriage parade—you acknowledge only gentlemen when she's at your side—any day except Sundays."

"Because?"

"Because it's the Sabbath."

"And thou shalt not take the air with thy mistress on Sundays? I missed that one."

"It's *not done*, my lord, and if you think to thwart convention in this regard, you can find somebody else to explain the mysteries of Mayfair to you."

She wanted to pace. How Phillip knew this, he could not have said, but the martial light in Miss Brompton's lovely eyes told him so.

"Somebody flaunted his mistress before you."

The martial light died, not without a fight. Miss Brompton sipped her tea, which had to be tepid, and topped up her cup with a fresh splash from the pot.

"My lord, I grasp that you are perceptive, astute even, but one does not blurt out one's every insight. One exercises discretion and kindness. If you suspect that I was slighted in the manner you describe, the gentlemanly choice would be to ignore the possibility. Such an occasion would have been an insult to me, had it taken place, and would have spoken poorly of the fellow at the ribbons."

The tea cup when she replaced it on the saucer settled without a sound. Her heart had apparently been broken with nobody the wiser either.

"Did some lady snatch the bachelor you'd chosen to be your

own?" Phillip asked. "You mustn't tell Tavistock, but his marchioness was at one time the object of my fondest fancies." Not particularly erotic fancies, but fond all the same. "Amaryllis DeWitt was the perfect wife for me. Sensible, kind, well bred without being high in the instep. Tall enough that I would not look ridiculous partnering her if I ever did learn the wretched dance steps."

Doubtless a gentleman kept such maunderings to himself, but did Hecate Brompton truly believe she was the only person to stumble on life's dance floor?

"Does she know?" Miss Brompton asked. "Does Miss DeWitt— does her ladyship know you harbored a *tendresse* for her?"

"No, and she never will. I've lately concluded that if I was so keen to marry her, I should have proposed. That's how brilliantly astute I am. Our estates march, she was of age and then some, and she needed a husband."

"But you let the moment pass?"

He'd let the *years* pass, always finding another excuse. Amaryllis's family was in mourning. Her family had just emerged from mourning. Her family was back in mourning. Her family needed her. She deserved to take her place in London Society.

All valid considerations, not a one of them insurmountable to a devoted swain.

"One wants to marry for something more lasting than expedience," he said. "Amaryllis and I would have rubbed along tolerably well. We were and are friends, but that friendship would have been a casualty of matrimony. I have so few friends. To reduce their numbers by even one would be a shame."

Miss Brompton studied him. "Was that the real reason you did not offer?"

Phillip had given the matter considerable thought, and Miss Brompton could be trusted with the truth—the rest of the truth— perhaps even comforted by it.

"Amaryllis would have married me for good reasons—to ensure her family's wellbeing, to ensure *my* wellbeing, to silence the unkind talk about spinsterhood and antidotes. We aren't fancy in the shires. We understand and respect pragmatism, but if a fellow truly cares for a lady, he wants more for her than practical solutions. He wants her dreams coming true. Tavistock can do that for his marchioness, while I could not. Ergo, all is as it should be, and I am pleased for her."

Miss Brompton's scrutiny became specific. Her gaze drifted from his brow, to his nose, to his lips and chin. He had the sense she was seeing him for the first time, and though he loathed visual inspections of any kind, he bore up without flinching.

"You are a gentleman," she said. "The dancing and cutlery and handkerchiefs are trappings of the role, but the reality is in here." She tapped her sternum with her index finger. "All the deportment instruction and dancing masters in Mayfair can't make a true gentleman out of a selfish bore. They can only provide him a handsome and expensive disguise."

"A costume," Phillip said, "and 'the apparel oft proclaims the man.'"

He'd hoped to lighten the moment, but Miss Brompton's gaze narrowed. "You've read Shakespeare?"

"I'm familiar with the plays and sonnets." How else was a country lad to endure English winters? "The Bard was paraphrasing Erasmus, *vestis virum facit*, who was doubtless paraphrasing the ancients. I had an adequate basic education, Miss Brompton, though classical literature never interested me half so much as farming."

"Farming is good," she said. "Gentlemen who take care of their acres are well received, but don't prose on about it."

They were back on safer footing, which disappointed Phillip inordinately, though his call had been, on the whole, successful.

"I should be going, shouldn't I? I've had my polite two cups plus one, and I must not overstay my welcome." He rose rather than put her through the effort of a polite demurral.

"Offer me your hand," she said, gazing up at him. "Assist me to rise."

Phillip stuck out his paw. "You are marvelously vital, fit, lithe, in the very pink, and capable of standing without assistance, and yet, I have been remiss..."

She took his hand and stood and shifted her grip to lace her arm through his. "Some women do need assistance. Their apparel is confining, they are weary, their high-heeled slippers render their balance questionable. A gentleman offers."

"You mean they've been laced too tightly. Foolishness, that. Gratuitous torment. If a lady enjoys robust dimensions, then let her dress for her own comfort and to blazes with *La Belly Ass Whatever*."

He'd barely recognized the French words when Miss Brompton had uttered them earlier, and he'd defaulted to his own pronunciation. Close enough.

Miss Brompton dropped his arm. She stared at his boots, which were the work of old George Deevers, not to be confused with his parent, Grandpa Deevers.

Her shoulders twitched, and Phillip feared the tea might have disagreed with her. His worry was relieved when a peal of laughter rang out over the music room, followed by a hoot and more laughter.

"Repeat after me," Miss Brompton said when her merriment had subsided. "*La Belle Assemblée*. Never that other thing. The whole French language is cowering in terror at your pronunciation."

Phillip composed his features into his best imitation of the marquess about to hold forth in damnably flawless French. "*La Belle Assemblée*."

"You're a good mimic. That will come in handy." She tried for a return to her usual starch and decorum, but the citadel had been breached, and Phillip had peered over the walls.

Hecate Brompton was beautiful when she was on her dignity, but she was *captivating* when her tiara slipped. Phillip resolved to compensate his new finishing governess for the Sisyphean labor of turning him into a lordling by giving that tiara the occasional friendly nudge.

Or maybe frequent nudges. The least he could do for her, being a gentleman at heart and all.

CHAPTER TWO

"Mrs. Charles Brompton to see you, Miss Hecate." Selwyn held out the silver card tray. "I put her in the family parlor."

Blast and bother. "Is Mrs. Brompton composed?" Eglantine usually showed up on Hecate's doorstep bearing problems.

Selwyn was too good at his job to grimace. "Happily agitated, I'd say. I've asked the kitchen to send up a fresh tray."

"Thank you. Some sandwiches would be appreciated as well. I'll just be a moment."

Hecate put aside the list she'd been making—dancing masters, French instructors, tailors— tucked it into the escritoire and locked the drawer, then slipped the key into her pocket. Nobody thought to snoop in the music room, but Hecate had become cautious of necessity.

She stopped before a pier glass and rummaged up a polite smile. The effort looked tired, as all of Hecate looked tired. The social season did that—wore a woman out, even a woman firmly on the shelf.

"Eglantine, welcome," Hecate said as her guest squeezed her hands, beamed, and squeezed her hands again. "Sweet of you to call."

"Oh, I just had to, Hecate. I had to, had to."

Eglantine did everything in triplicate. Well, almost everything. Only two children so far, both of them boys. Given Charles's nature, another child was bound to come along soon.

"You are in good spirits." Which often boded ill for Hecate. "Shall we sit?"

"Yes, we shall. A cup of tea will settle my nerves if anything can. I am so excited."

Eglantine was so *young*. Barely twenty-five, the mother of two, and married to an earl's heir. That Cousin Charles would one day be a peer was proof the Fates occasionally took to tippling.

Hecate led her guest to the tufted sofa and situated herself in the wing chair across from her. The tea service arrived, sandwiches doubtless to follow, and Hecate resigned herself to having her ear talked off.

"Charlie has had the best idea," Eglantine said, stirring her tea vigorously and tapping her spoon on the saucer. "My Charlie is so clever. Nobody gives him enough credit."

Rather the opposite. *Everybody* extended credit to Charles Brompton on the basis of his expectations, despite the fact that Great-Uncle Nunn was in excellent health.

"Have some cakes," Hecate said, holding out the plate. "They go down so well with good China black."

"No sandwiches?" Eglantine made a face and put three cakes on her plate. "Cakes will have to do, but with supper so far off, you'd think the kitchen..."

A footman paused at the door, nodded, and deposited a tray heaped with sandwiches on the low table. "Anything else, miss?"

"No, thank you, Timmens, and my compliments to Cook for her prompt work."

Timmens bowed without so much as glancing at Eglantine and withdrew.

Eglantine added a pair of sandwiches to her haul of cakes. "You will die, Hecate, simply expire of envy when you hear Charlie's idea. I am so proud of him."

Eglantine, bless her loyal heart, was a good wife. She'd been all of seventeen and in anticipation of a scandalous event when Charles had offered for her. Her settlements had gone a long way toward rewarding Charles's supposed gallantry. Their firstborn child was no relation to Charles, a complication Charles had been willing to overlook before he'd become Great-Uncle Nunn's heir.

Let it be said, Charles was not mean. He'd made his bed, feathered with the last wealth Eglantine's family had had to offer, and he'd lain in that bed more or less contently ever since—albeit with myriad opera dancers, widows, and light-skirts.

"What wonderful idea has Charles come up with now?" Charles's wonderful ideas invariably involved spending money.

A racing stud—as if those were not thick on the ground, and every one of them bleeding coin.

A charitable orphanage—always profitable, if well run, in Charles's vast and deep experience. When Hecate pointed out that charities should not *be* profitable, Charles had grumbled about details.

A finishing school for illegitimate young ladies with wealthy, titled fathers, and—of course!—Hecate could be its founding patroness.

Even Eglantine had winced at that notion.

"Charlie says we must have a house party," Eglantine pronounced around a mouthful of cake, "and Mama-in-Law supports the notion. Technically, she'd be the hostess, and nominally, Great-Uncle Nunn would be the host. London is so unbearable in the summer, and Nunnsuch will be Wharton's home one day. He and Winston should be spending time there."

Wharton was Eglantine's eldest, Winston his toddling younger brother. They were delightful children, thus far, having their parents' cheerful dispositions and an innocent sense of fun. Hecate gave it about five years before public school and the insidious Brompton talent for mischief ruined them both.

And now the boys were to have their first, nursery-eye view of a house party?

Hecate sipped her tea and mentally counted backward from twenty in Latin. The Brompton family had two main branches. Papa was a cousin at a remove from Great-Uncle Nunn, while Charles had the great good fortune to sprout from the titled side of the tree. Papa resented his titled relations, resented Hecate, and would probably resent a pot of gold if it had the temerity to land on his foot.

The titled Bromptons, by contrast, were a frivolous lot, frequently pockets to let and wits gone begging, and their numbers were legion. They were always scheming, always looking for a way to turn deviousness into coin, usually with disastrous results. Great-Uncle Nunn, the Earl of Nunn, cast a dim and disapproving eye on his dodgy relations and mostly ignored them.

He'd likely show up for the final day or two of this bacchanal, harrumph down the room with the highest-ranking female guest, and declare the whole thing absurd. Of all her Brompton relatives, Great-Uncle was the one whom Hecate respected.

"It's rather late to be planning a house party, Eglantine. Most of Society has already decamped for the shires."

"But grouse season is still weeks and weeks away—weeks, I tell you—and Nunnsuch is a lovely property. If we invite a combination of friends and family, with a few neighbors thrown in, we'll have plenty of guests, but here is the best part..."

She popped another tea cake into her mouth and chewed vigorously while Hecate steeled herself for disaster. What fool had decreed that ladies did not use profanity?

"We shall invite,"—Eglantine's eyes took on a gleam of triumph —"Lord... Phillip... Vincent!" She clapped her hands like a small child. "It's brilliant, Hecate. My Charles is brilliant, positively brilliant. Nobody has invited Lord Phillip much of anywhere, and we shall be the first. The matchmakers will be eaten up with envy. A marquess's brother, his heir for the nonce. We will be the talk of Mayfair."

The Bromptons were frequently the talk of Mayfair, and for all the wrong reasons. "I wasn't aware Charles and Lord Phillip were connected."

"Yes, you were. Don't be coy, Hecate. Charles still feels badly about Miss DeWitt's early experiences in Society. A regrettable misunderstanding. She would agree, I'm sure, but no harm done—she married the Marquess of Tavistock, didn't she? Now pour me a second cup, there's a dear. These sandwiches look a bit dry."

Hecate poured the requisite second cup and passed it over. Perhaps a lady was permitted slightly colorful language in French? A few quiet curses?

"Charles abused Miss DeWitt's trust, Eglantine. Don't distort the facts. You feel guilty because he offered for you instead of for her, and that was strictly a matter of your settlements being larger than hers."

In one of his many drunken moments, Charles had confessed to taking liberties with Miss DeWitt. In Hecate's opinion, Miss DeWitt had had a narrow escape, despite the drubbing Charles's defection had delivered to the lady's standing.

Charles opined that he'd had no choice in the matter, given the state of his mother's finances.

Eglantine slurped her tea and commenced sniffling and blinking. "Why must you be so hateful, Hecate? Nobody will marry you because your disposition is so sour. You can't let go of the past, and you want everybody to be as miserable as you are. Charles comes up with a brilliant idea, one that could go a long way toward smoothing over any lingering hurt feelings with the new marchioness, and you find fault. Why must you always find fault?"

Because I want you to survive the battles still ahead. Because your firstborn son will face yet more battles and because Charles is a philandering idiot. That side of the family excelled at producing philandering idiots.

"If we see the flaws in our plans," Hecate said gently, "then we stand a better chance of achieving success. When you invite a man of Lord Phillip's standing, for example, your guest list will need a few other courtesy lords and ladies. Whom did you have in mind?"

Eglantine's inchoate tears underwent a miraculous remission. "Mama-in-Law said we must leave those details to you. You would criticize our efforts past all bearing if we even attempted to create a guest list without consulting you first."

The problem with the Bromptons—the other branch of the Bromptons—was that they believed their own press. Charles had doubtless convinced himself, his mother, his wife, and his horse that this house party would brilliantly patch up all bad feeling between him and his former intended—now the Marchioness of Tavistock.

From there, collateral justifications had doubtless multiplied in his handsome head like baby rabbits:

London was so boring for Eglantine and Mama in the summer— and unhealthful for the children (and devoid of merry widows and opera dancers).

Great-Uncle Nunn rattled around the family seat all by himself, and one must take pity on lonely elders (with whom one needed to curry favor).

Mrs. Rose Roberts lived not five miles from Nunnsuch, and a widow of such wealth and great good looks would always be a welcome addition to a social gathering. That Mrs. Roberts might have been one of Charles's romping partners last autumn was of no moment.

And—this argument likely topped Charles's list—poor old Hecate could always use another little project to while away the tedium of her pathetic existence. *We must do our part to enliven her dull days. We are her family, after all.*

By the time Eglantine had donned her bonnet to make this call, Charles's house party had become—in his mind at least—the most benevolent, inspired notion ever hatched in the mind of man. Though in all likelihood, the notion had been hatched by Charles's mother. Not a Brompton by birth, but Edna certainly fit in well with her in-laws.

"What if Lord Phillip declines your invitation?" Hecate asked.

"Then you will beg him to reconsider. You've been introduced. You know the marchioness. You can make this happy occasion come true for us, Hecate, and Lord Phillip will be in your debt."

The sense, not unfamiliar, of an iron door swinging closed on a dank cell of family intrigue and expense rose up in Hecate's heart.

"Do you expect me to be present at this gathering?" she asked.

Eglantine bit off the corner of a cake. "Of course we do. The guest list will be mostly your doing, after all, and you should be on hand to ensure all goes well."

That was Brompton family dialect for: *You should be on hand to blame if everything goes to blazes.* "The first thing you will need, Eglantine, is a budget."

Eglantine beamed at her tea cake. "Oh splendid! We were hoping you'd help with that too."

~

"I am homesick." Phillip confessed this sorry state of affairs to his horse. Herne was a sturdy lad standing about seventeen hands, blessed with his plow horse dam's calm mind. He'd grown into his sire's pale gray coat as the years had passed, which was devilish inconvenient when the horse had a propensity for rolling in mud.

"You are doubtless homesick too," Phillip went on, because Hyde Park was blessedly deserted now that Town was emptying out. "No decent mud to be had in these surrounds."

No billing and cooing newlyweds either, but that was London's only attractive feature, other than Miss Hecate Brompton. The same day Phillip had called upon her, she'd sent him lists in a tidy, elegant hand. "A few suggestions" that rang with the authority of royal decrees. He was to report to this tailor and that bootmaker, then to a jeweler, watchmaker, glovemaker, and a purveyor of gentlemanly sundries.

In the intervening three days, he'd called at perhaps half of the establishments she'd listed, though he'd yet to look in on the purveyor fellow.

"What the devil is a sundry in polite parlance?" he muttered as Herne navigated a bend in the leafy path.

"My lord, good morning." Hecate Brompton sat upon a gleaming chestnut mare who had probably taken tea in the royal stables as a filly. A groom on an equally elegant bay gelding waited several yards back.

Do not gawp like the bumpkin you are. "Miss Brompton, greetings. A fine morning, is it not?"

"The best part of a summer day for a hack. Shall we?" She nodded in the direction of the bridle path, and Phillip wished himself back in Crosspatch Corners. The paths in Berkshire went on for miles, many of them with a provenance that predated the Romans.

Hyde Park would barely make one decent-sized farm, and the city was encroaching on three and a half of its four sides.

"I got your note," he said. "Much appreciated. I won't be hiring a French instructor, though."

"You really should, my lord. Proper French pronunciation matters almost as much as proper English diction in certain circles."

Snooty, highfalutin circles the very thought of which gave Phillip dyspepsia.

Miss Brompton, the sight of whom did *not* give him dyspepsia, wore a riding habit of imperial blue trimmed with black. The cut was severe and devoid of the enormous draping skirts fashionable women seemed to favor for horseback outings in London. Her toque sported two peacock feathers—the barest nod to whimsy—and sat nearly straight on her head.

"I have taken more comprehensive measures to learn my French," Phillip said. "Tavistock has traveled much on the Continent, and his language skills are impressive, particularly his French. He has often remarked that London's émigré population numbers in the tens of thousands. I've hired French house staff for the summer and instructed them to speak to me in only their native language."

"You might well starve ere the summer ends."

"The result has been much hilarity, and that provides sustenance too. Then too, my new staff members know the Continental dances and are willing to walk me through them. I fear the quadrille will be the end of me. Too blasted long and complicated."

Miss Brompton made such a pretty picture on her mare, but even in the summer glory of Hyde Park, birds creating a racket in the canopy overhead, water fowl honking and quacking over on the Serpentine, she conveyed seriousness of purpose.

"Your approach, while unconventional, is commendable for its expedience. Mind you caution these émigrés to discretion."

"The person who needs such a scold is the same person who will ignore it. I am brushing up on my dancing and my French pronunciation. What of it? My French staff know how it feels to be parted from all that's dear and familiar, and they will either guard my dignity or not. They have no loyalty to your *certain circles*, Miss Brompton, but they might well be loyal to another stranger in a strange land."

Miss Brompton flicked a glance over him. "An unusual strategy. I wish you luck with it, but one wonders if you are trying to compete with your brother."

"Compete?" Did a donkey try to compete with bloodstock? "What would be the point? He is the marquess, a lovely fellow, full of charm, Continental élan, blond good looks, and affable bonhomie."

"You'd be within your rights to hate him."

The day was so pretty, so peaceful, and Phillip did not want to spend this unlooked-for encounter with Hecate Brompton discussing dear Trevor, much less the temptation to hate him.

"Resent, perhaps," Phillip said, "but not for the reasons you assume. Tavistock is welcome to the title and the properties and all the lordly whatnot. Before we met, though, I was happy. I had a few frustrations, but many consolations and joys. I was simply Phillip

Heyward, a quiet, retiring fellow who immersed himself in yeomanry."

Herne stopped abruptly at a mud puddle and rooted at the reins.

"Oh, very well," Phillip said. "Take a moment to play, you great lout. Miss Brompton, you will want to put some distance between my noble steed and your skirts."

Before Phillip had finished speaking, Herne dabbled a sizable front hoof in the water. Much pawing and splashing followed, though Phillip curtailed the festivities before Herne could develop truly mischievous intent.

"He's tried to roll in the mud with me on his very back," Phillip said, urging the horse along the path. "Damned near ruined a good saddle. Town does not agree with him, but he's bearing up as best he can."

Damned was profanity, alas.

"You were saying that Tavistock has disrupted your life," Miss Brompton replied, and Phillip had the sense she was ignoring Phillip's cursing and Herne's bad manners all of a piece.

"The marquess has definitely turned my life top hat over teakettle," Phillip said. "While part of me longs to get to know him better, to ask him all manner of questions and learn his every particular, another part of me is overwhelmed by the whole notion and longing for a quiet stroll along the River Twid. Life was simpler before my brother acknowledged me."

"Less lonely?"

What an odd question. "I was lonely in a manner so familiar to me as to be almost comfortable. Now Tavistock is in my life, but he's not part of my days, and yet, I must learn to *chassé* and *glissade* through polite society because he is my sibling."

"I'm about to complicate your life further, my lord."

"I refuse to be presented at Court until autumn, Miss Brompton. Call me a coward, but my courage has its limits. Besides, Tavistock must be on hand to nanny me at any royal levee. If I'm to sport about in satin knee breeches, then he must as well. Only fair." Trevor had promised to present him, and Trevor was preoccupied with being a newlywed, though that condition would likely persist for the next twenty years.

"Do you own satin knee breeches, my lord?"

From any other woman, Phillip was sure the question would have been scandalous. "I'm having the requisite articles made up. You sent orders, I followed them, and my exchequer will be considerably lighter as a consequence."

"And you are working on your waltzing?"

What was she about? "Not until I master the rubbishing quadrille. I want to get the worst ordeal behind me."

"I'm afraid the ordeals are only beginning, my lord. If you haven't received it already, you will find in today's post an invitation to a summer house party out in Hampshire. The Earl of Nunn is the nominal host."

Phillip had done his homework, at least where Hecate Brompton was concerned. "He's related to you, a cousin at some remove."

"Second cousin, though everybody calls him Great-Uncle Nunn, or Uncle Nunn. Not a bad sort, but hands-off when it comes to his side of the family. Charles Brompton, another cousin of sorts, made the Marchioness of Tavistock's acquaintance when she was plain Amaryllis DeWitt. Charles is hoping to mend fences with the marchioness by inviting you to the family seat."

Phillip let Herne plod along on a loose rein. The horse was pouting—he did so treasure his mud puddles—while Hecate Brompton was executing a strategy of her own devising.

"How many lies did you just tell, Miss Brompton?"

He expected her to stiffen and descend into lecturing. Instead, she kept her gaze straight ahead. "No true bouncers, a few prevarications."

"Are you feeding me to the lions so soon?"

"The Bromptons aren't lions, though they fancy themselves as such. Charles is up to something, of that I have no doubt. Perhaps he wants to invest in Tavistock's beer-making scheme, or he's decided you should marry one of his sisters. I'm not entirely sure what's afoot, but I've been managing the Bromptons for years. If you agree to attend, I'm fairly confident I can keep them from troubling you too sorely."

"And if I refuse this gracious invitation from virtual strangers?" At least one of whom, Phillip suspected, had toyed with Amaryllis's affections, if not her virtue.

"If you refuse, they will try again when the shooting starts in August, or they will mutter and whine about your rejection."

"I'd best get it over with?"

She nodded, and that single, terse gesture yielded an insight. The Bromptons were relying on Hecate to get him to this house party. If he refused, their muttering and whining would be directed against *her*, the one family member he knew.

"I have two conditions," Phillip said. "Well, three, though I assume you will attend for the duration?"

"I will."

"Then my other two conditions are as follows: no quadrilles, and Mr. Gavin DeWitt will attend with me."

"Miss DeWitt's younger brother?"

"A lifelong friend, a gentleman, and an accomplished charmer. He'll be a credit to the gathering." Also a towering pain in the arse some of the time. Needs must.

Miss Brompton studied Phillip as the horses plodded along. "Mr. DeWitt will be a decoy, distracting everybody from your presence by spreading his peacock feathers at your command."

"He'll also be my second if I have to call this Charles Brompton out. I'd do so, Miss Brompton, not because your cousin offended the marchioness long ago. She has her own champion to fight that battle. I will call Brompton out if in any way he shows the least inclination to disrespect you."

Miss Brompton gathered up her reins. "Violence is not on the list of entertainments I'm devising, I assure you. One other question: Why did the old marquess insist you be raised in obscurity?"

She'd been bound to ask, sooner or later, and yet, Phillip still wished she hadn't. "Is that truly relevant?"

"The gossips will find it very relevant. Forewarned and all that."

"I did not resemble the mardy old poltroon, and he used that evidence to question my patrimony. I was slow to speak, clumsy, and could play for hours with the simplest toys. Papa added mental deficiency to my store of sins and washed his hands of me."

"You are not mentally deficient or noticeably clumsy, and you speak as well as any man, if a bit too honestly. Are you legitimate?"

"In the biological sense? Haven't a clue, nor does any other living soul. I am legally legitimate. I am of a height with my brother, we have some mannerisms in common, and we seem to be in sympathy regarding our view of the world generally. Are you legitimate, Miss Brompton?"

He asked the question merely to be impertinent, but her posture acquired yet another increment of rectitude.

"That is nobody's business. I wish you good morning. If you'd like to ride out again the day after tomorrow, I'll acquaint you with some of the dramatis personae."

He'd offended her, and that dimmed the very sun in the heavens. "Miss Brompton, I apologize. I meant no insult."

"Until the day after tomorrow, my lord. Good day."

She cantered off, her groom trailing a respectful half-dozen yards behind, and Phillip resisted the urge to call after her.

A pointless display, of course. Some varieties of loneliness admitted of no comfort, and it broke his heart that Miss Hecate Brompton suffered at least one of them.

CHAPTER THREE

"A spare hiding in the shires." Miss Betty Blanchard checked the strength of the tea. "How marvelous. One doesn't envy Lord Phillip his patrimony, but the brother seemed a decent sort."

The tea would be weak, no matter how generously Hecate had seen Miss Blanchard pensioned. "You know Lord Tavistock?"

"I've had occasion to observe him when he first abandoned university. Companions do a lot of observing and comparing notes on what we observe. Now tell me about this house party."

How Hecate longed to pace, but Miss Blanchard's parlor would allow for about three steps in any direction. And on three out of four walls, Hecate would be confronted with sketches of herself as a girl, then as a young woman. The fourth wall was reserved for Miss Blanchard's regiment of nieces and nephews.

"If I'm to believe Eglantine," Hecate said, "Charles was the inspiration for this disaster. He treated Lord Phillip's sister-by-marriage ill when she made her come out, and I suppose Charles is trying to ingratiate himself with Lord Tavistock. If her ladyship ever gets to dredging up bad memories, Lord Phillip will be on hand to report that Brompton really isn't a bad sort, and the family is very congenial."

"Charles all but left Miss DeWitt standing at the altar." Miss Blanchard poured two cups and stirred a drop of milk into Hecate's. "She was better off without him, but then Charles became old Nunn's heir, and I'm sure the lady knew a pang of envy."

Hecate sipped to be polite, but nursery tea would have offered more sustenance. "Her mother and grandmother doubtless harangued her with if-onlys and why-couldn't-yous?"

"If Miss DeWitt had a chorus of only two to sing those laments, then she had it a good deal easier than you did, my dear. I gather you are to attend along with Lord Phillip?"

"Even Edna Brompton wouldn't expect me to pay for a house party in absentia. His lordship refuses to attend unless I'm on hand."

"Shrewd of him. Would you like me to have a look at the guest list?"

How Betty Blanchard, retired companion living out her years on a quiet lane in Chelsea, knew Society's goings-on, Hecate did not care to speculate. On the one hand, Miss Blanchard's information was useful when Hecate faced yet another London Season. On the other hand, why did Miss Blanchard bother? Why remain attached to a world that hadn't treated her all that well?

"This is my first crack," Hecate said, extracting a list from her reticule. "If Charles is to have his merry widows, then I've recruited some bachelor uncles to partner them at whist."

"And a half dozen of the titled cousins. Edna doubtless hopes to snabble Lord Phillip for Flavia or Portia. Is Lord Phillip frivolous?"

"One look at him, and you'd know the term could never apply."

Miss Blanchard perused the list. "Dour, then?"

Lord Phillip had an off-putting quality that made Hecate uncomfortable, even though she understood it.

"Reserved," she said. "Brusque. No need to announce himself with horn blasts and fluttering doves. He'll lurk by the potted palms and manage to look perfectly content doing it."

Unlike Hecate in her years among the ballroom greenery.

"Doesn't take after his father, then. The old marquess was full of his own consequence. His poor wife was entirely cowed. I wonder if Lord Phillip wasn't a little rebellion on the part of the late marchioness."

All of Society would wonder the same thing, if they hadn't already. "He claims not to know, and I suspect he doesn't care. Lord Phillip describes himself as a farmer, and he has a plowman's physique and a yeoman's interests."

Miss Blanchard wrinkled her nose. "Clodhopping sort? Bull in a china shop? Lord knows you've stood up with plenty of those."

"He doesn't know how to dance, but I wouldn't call him clodhopping. He will sit out every waltz until he can give a good account of himself on the dance floor." And Hecate understood that too.

"How would you describe him, my dear?"

A puzzle Hecate had been considering for days—and nights. "Prudent enough to know that his rural ways need some polishing, smart enough to know Society will find fault even with perfection. He will make a reasonable, dedicated effort, then get back to his plowing and pamphlets."

Miss Blanchard passed over the guest list. "He sounds tedious, but then, to the average suitor, Miss Hecate Brompton is tedious."

By design. Hecate had spent years being tedious to all suitors under all circumstances. The strategy had worked, though the price was a life that had become tedious in truth.

"I'm content," she said. "The Bromptons thrive for the most part, and that is all Papa has ever asked of me."

Miss Blanchard was the picture of the fading spinster. Past her half-century mark, graying hair in a tidy bun, hands still those of a lady, but wrinkles showing that lady's age. Her dark eyes missed nothing, and her hearing was sharp.

"Do you ever wish you'd married your Johnny?" she asked.

Hecate hadn't heard the name in forever, hadn't thought about the man for months. "I'm told he's happy. Canada's gain is our loss. We both had growing up to do."

"But the whole family hoped you two would suit."

Hecate had begged Johnny to take her to Canada with him, but he'd smiled, hugged her gently, and declined to put his foot in parson's mousetrap for her convenience. The only Brompton on that side of the family with any sense, and he'd talked Uncle Nunn into buying commissions for him and his devil-may-care younger brother.

"Being an officer's wife would have been challenging," Hecate said. "If John's letters were to be believed, a Canadian winter lasts forever and makes the ninth circle of Dante's hell look cozy." And yet, Johnny had written of the vast wilderness with a sort of enraptured awe—and never used his leave to return to England.

"You were too young to marry," Miss Blanchard said, "but when has youth ever stopped a Brompton from pursuing a goal?"

I'm not a Brompton. "Lord Phillip asked if I was legitimate."

"Ye gods and little fishes. I hope you pinned his ears back."

"He wasn't being unkind. I'd asked after his antecedents. I suspect he was trying for levity in the face of homesickness."

"An odd sort of levity. Your tea will get cold, dear."

Hecate sipped again, though the tea had gone tepid. Her life was tepid tea, ledgers, and newspapers, leavened by the occasional charitable committee, but what had Lord Phillip's life been in that time before his brother had acknowledged him?

Happy, according to him. *Free.* Hours in the out of doors, rambling the countryside. Probably a friendly hound or two at his side. Fishing in his beloved River Twid, the occasional pint at the local inn shared with merry old fellows who'd watched him grow up. Lord Phillip likely knew each acre under his care, every fox's covert and badger run, just as his neighbors knew him.

"I felt as if his question were a snare," Hecate said. "He'd know how to set a snare, know exactly where to place it to catch an unsuspecting rabbit. One moment, I was prattling on about French pronunciation. The next, I'm caught fast and struggling to keep my balance."

And laughing. Truly, honestly laughing.

"Was he threatening you?"

"No. I've been threatened. There's no malice in Lord Phillip, but a man that perceptive doesn't have to be unkind to see too much or say something too insightful."

An enormous orange cat leaped into Miss Blanchard's lap and commenced purring at the first stroke of her hand on his furry head.

"And Lord Phillip came to you for help?"

Hecate nodded. "Offered to compensate me for being his finishing governess. I wanted to smack him, but he was trying to be respectful. Said my time was valuable." *Precious* had been his word.

"He interests you," Miss Blanchard said as the cat began to circle on her lap. "He has won your notice."

The purpose of this call had not been to discuss Lord Phillip Vincent. "One ignores a titled caller of sizable dimensions at one's peril."

"Nonsense. One can do the ignoring while smiling across the tea tray and remarking on the dreadful heat, or the dreadful drought, or how quiet London can be in summer. You haven't noticed a man in years, my girl. I suggest you take this fellow to Nunnsuch and enjoy the fresh country air with him."

Perhaps that was the real purpose for this call. To hear Miss Blanchard suggest what Hecate's imagination had dared only to whisper.

"I promised I'd attend the house party, and I am not about to allow Edna and Eglantine a free hand with my exchequer in any case. They'd like nothing better, but Papa would never forgive me."

"Your papa's forgiveness is beside the point. You gave Lord Phillip your word, and you will keep it, but he's right—you deserve some recompense for your efforts. The Bromptons owe you more than they will ever admit or repay. If you don't seize a little fun and frolic now, you will find yourself white-haired, slow-moving, and talking to your cat."

"I'm not... Romping is not for me." Hecate had learned that much in the only way there was to learn such a lesson.

"So don't romp, but flirt a bit. Laugh, stroll the garden by moonlight, and let a marquess's perceptive and interesting heir stroll at your side. He wanted to make a bargain with you, a fair exchange to assuage his dignity, so put him on escort duty. If he shows you some attention, the rest of the family will be a bit more respectful of you. Would that be a bad thing?"

"I'm not a scheming Brompton." And yet, what had Lord Phillip said about loneliness that became almost comfortable? Nobody else could have made that remark, much less have expected Hecate to grasp its significance.

"Then don't scheme. Propose an enjoyable bargain." Miss Blan-chard finished her tea and set the cup and saucer aside, the cat having snuggled himself into a feline circle of contentment on her lap. "You see me as an old woman who lived her life on the fringes, a poor rela-tion, a paid companion, never fitting in, no children to comfort my old age. That's all true enough, but I also had the occasional adventure, and those memories are more comfort now, Hecate dearest, than any pious social halo could ever be."

To have Hecate's suspicions confirmed... Miss Blanchard had never lacked for dancing partners. Older fellows mostly, and they had regarded her with genuine respect and affection.

Was there a Brompton on the face of the earth who regarded Hecate with either?

Hecate stashed the guest list back into her reticule. "I'm sick of being the sensible Brompton, the solvent Brompton, the dutiful Brompton. I've done all that has been demanded of me, asking for only a certain degree of independence in return, but the importuning never ends."

Perhaps that had been half the appeal of running off to Canada with Johnny. He'd certainly felt the need to escape. Maybe he'd real-ized if the family heiress escaped with him, then his reprieve would be temporary.

And he'd been right. Ten years on, and Hecate was still paying for every stupid gambling debt, overdue coal delivery, and house party the Bromptons saw fit to drop in her lap.

"Go to Nunnsuch," Miss Blanchard said. "For once, enjoy yourself. Ride neck or nothing over the countryside, wade in the fountain, stroll barefoot through the park."

Wading in the fountain sounded... lovely. "You did all those things, didn't you?"

"I did, and in the most luscious company."

~

"A house party." Gavin DeWitt imbued three words with a tinker's barrow full of dubious connotations, but then, DeWitt knew how to make his lines count. He'd spent two years on various provincial stages and had rejoined his family in Berkshire on the recent occasion of his sister Amaryllis's nuptials.

As brother to Tavistock's wife, Gavin was thus family to Phillip by the reckoning of Society, as were all the DeWitts. Such were the marvels of matrimony among the Quality.

"A house party," Phillip said, opening one of three wardrobes gracing his dressing closet, "is a perfectly harmless method of whiling away a few weeks of summer, or so I'm told." He surveyed his collection of new attire with a sense of bewilderment. So many clothes, all made to fit his exact proportions.

In London, they'd been delivered box by box, and Phillip's staff had sent the lot on to Lark's Nest. To see the entire hoard all at once, neatly pressed and ready for duty, put a few things into perspective. Phillip's old favorites from before, from his Mr. Heyward country squiring days, hung limp and shabby in their corner.

Phillip refused to surrender them to the rag-and-bone man. Not yet.

Nonetheless, he'd eschewed his worn breeches and frayed shirts since returning to Berkshire, and he felt vaguely disloyal to his home for doing so. Disloyal to the hardworking squire he'd been.

The new clothes were a seductive reward for taking on the new name. The handiwork of a Bond Street tailor created a handsome, confident fiction of a man. From broad, symmetrical shoulders to a tapered waist, to muscular legs, and everything in between, the tailor's customer became more wondrous, more masculine, more attractive for donning his plumage.

His peacock feathers, to use Miss Brompton's term.

"Why me?" DeWitt asked, fingering a pale gray waistcoat embroidered with bluebells and violets. The lining was satin, and the thing fit Phillip like a favorite glove. *Not for church*, the tailor had said, doubtless because any angels in attendance would be envious.

"You will accompany me," Phillip retorted, closing the wardrobe, "for the simple reason that you have a place to take in Society, just as I do. The DeWitts are wealthy, your years of vagabondage are behind you, and you owe me."

"Where is your lordship's valet?" DeWitt imbued the honorific with the irony it deserved.

"In the kitchen, flirting with my housekeeper, I suppose. Why?"

"It's his job to pack up all this finery and get it sent down to Hampshire. You snap your fingers, indicate that packing must commence, and he sees it done. From airing the trunks, to choosing the sachets, to folding each cravat and stocking, the job is his."

Phillip closed the doors to the wardrobe. "How do you know that?"

"I had a father, a man of means who knew how to prepare for travel."

Phillip sat on the bed. "I had no father worth the name. My means haven't a patch on yours, and I know how to get two pea crops in during one growing season. But I also know you owe me."

DeWitt lounged against the windowsill. He made a lovely picture silhouetted against the afternoon sunshine, and having been an actor, he'd know that.

"I am aware of no debts outstanding between us," DeWitt said, folding his arms across his chest.

Before DeWitt had literally run off to join a traveling troupe, Phillip could have dismissed him as an insolent puppy. Everybody liked Gavin DeWitt and probably believed that DeWitt liked them too. Maybe he did, or maybe he'd adopted the role of charming bon vivant early in life, because an only son born to wealth could pull that one off fairly easily.

In any case, DeWitt had avoided taking over the family businesses—his womenfolk were appalled to think of their darling fellow dirtying his hands in Grandpapa's trade—and he'd indulged his own whims for a time.

"If you see no obligations between us," Phillip said, wondering when his mattress had grown so lumpy, "then frolicking on the stage has turned you into a dolt. Would your family have enjoyed limitless credit at the livery during your absence if I'd not had a quiet word with Dabney three months after your departure? Would Deevers have kept your sisters in new boots without my willingness to pay down his bills by three-quarters before they were presented?"

DeWitt scrubbed his hands across his handsome face, then brushed dark curls back from his forehead. Stage business, no doubt.

"How much?"

"I didn't keep track, and I'm not asking for repayment. One assists neighbors in need. Now I'm a neighbor in need, and you will assist me."

"I haven't accepted the invitation yet. Mama is in alt, Lissa isn't saying much, and Tavistock suggested I discuss the matter with you. I don't care for house parties."

"Neither do I, and I've yet to attend one. There is bound to be dancing, at which I am hopeless, and people speaking French, another forlorn hope in my case, and fribbles dangling after merry widows, when I've no patience with fribbles and no experience with merry widows."

"None?"

"With merry widows? Only a little." Though all of it lovely.

DeWitt pushed away from the window. "I was one of the fribbles. First, because I was a fribble—between terms at university, finished with university and available to make up the numbers—and then because I was among the actors hired to entertain the guests. At house parties, we assisted with theatricals, ran scenes, did recitations, filled out the sets on the dance floor, and so forth. Anything for a square meal."

"Anything?"

DeWitt colored up like a small boy caught purloining a pie. "Don't be insulting."

Good God. And the memories made Gavin DeWitt blush. Interesting. "Did you meet any Bromptons in your travels?"

DeWitt settled on the vanity stool. "The house parties I was dragooned into were mostly up north, far from the blandishments of Town. No Bromptons, though you should know that as a family they have a reputation for self-indulgence."

Save for Hecate, the lone beacon of sense and probity among a passel of wastrels. "Dueling?"

"One heard rumors."

"Does one pack his favorite pair of Mantons?" Not a question Phillip could put to Miss Brompton, and that was half the reason for demanding DeWitt's company.

"No. The Earl of Nunn will have a lovely pair gathering dust in his armory, if the occasion arises. Do you truly want me to come along, or are you trying to keep me from running off again?"

"If you run off again," Phillip said, rising and smoothing out the wrinkled coverlet, "you will take me with you. I have acquired a deportment instructress in the person of Miss Hecate Brompton, but at a house party, I will encounter circumstances she cannot foresee, venues beyond her ken—male venues. Your job will be to keep me from falling on my arse before an audience of fribbles and dandies."

"A thankless and Herculean task."

Phillip regarded DeWitt with the same patience he turned on Herne when that good beast was helpless to resist a mud puddle.

"I didn't know," DeWitt said. "I had no idea my mother and sisters would encounter such financial difficulties in my absence. The bank notes and bills all just wafted about me. Amaryllis told me what to sign and what to send on to the solicitors. I could use some instruction myself, you know. A lot of instruction."

Ah, youth. Youth and masculine pride. "You don't want to ask your sister for a few pointers?"

"Tried that. Lissa says the ledgers are very straightforward, then goes back to rhapsodizing about Tavistock's beer-brewing schemes. I want to like the fellow, but honestly, Heyward... I mean, my lord. Amaryllis is obnoxiously happy to be his marchioness, and the ledgers don't tell me *why* an expenditure was made, or if it was the *correct* expenditure for a given need."

"Then we have a bargain," Phillip said. "I have a thorough grasp of estate ledgers, and you know how to manage the merry widows. Fetch the ledgers, and I'll have my valet see to my packing."

DeWitt grinned and stuck out a hand. "A bargain, my lord. Well met. No Mantons necessary."

~

Lord Phillip Vincent had made an entrance, and likely without realizing it. He'd walked his horse—*in hand*—up the manicured Nunnsuch carriage drive. When a worried groom had trotted around from the stable, his lordship had insisted on seeing the horse situated himself.

The same groom had told the head lad, who'd told the head footman, who'd told the butler, who'd told Hecate that the horse hadn't been lame. His lordship had walked the beast the last mile to *stretch his legs and enjoy the view.*

Nunnsuch was a lovely property, dating back to a time when successive sound matches had resulted in the earldom's coffers being if not full, then at least consistently solvent. The house sat in whitewashed neoclassical splendor on a gentle rise, the requisite Capability Brown landscaped park adding to its air of bucolic repose.

Hecate had never regarded the family seat as home, but she had enjoyed her visits.

Until now.

"My lord, you came in through the *terrace door*," she said, beholding a slightly dusty version of the Tavistock heir. "This is *not done*. The host and hostess or their supernumeraries are deployed to the *front door*, where they hope to offer arriving guests a *cordial welcome*. Instead, you... Are you laughing at me?"

His eyes were dancing in that subtle, I-know-something way that made Hecate want to smack him.

"The day is lovely," he said. "Might you give me the benefit of your wisdom out of doors, Miss Brompton?"

The main foyer was deserted, but that didn't mean privacy was assured. Far from it. "Very well. We'll stroll the garden if you are so determined to enjoy the pleasant weather."

He winged his left arm—the correct choice for keeping his saber hand free—and Hecate held her fire until they were perambulating between beds of mostly spent roses.

"I made good time down from Berkshire," Lord Phillip said. "I considered that arriving early might be gauche. DeWitt chose to take his traveling coach, which is commodious but lumbering. I didn't want to put anybody out, and I did want to reconnoiter the property."

"You were stalling," Hecate said, feeling an unwanted stab of sympathy. "Putting off the inevitable."

"Girding my mental loins. I nearly turned back at least once a mile. What am I doing here, Miss Brompton?"

"Learning the opening steps of the quadrille, which do not include putting away your own horse or strolling up the drive."

When they reached the end of the roses, his lordship kept walking straight down the steps into the park.

"Which is the worse offense? Seeing Herne rubbed down or walking up the drive?"

"Walking your horse might have been necessary if he'd picked up a stone bruise, but comporting yourself like a groom... Why do that? Surely even in Berkshire you rely on the occasional stable lad?"

"For the carriage and plow stock, yes, but for my personal riding horse... Don't you have a mare to whom you confide all your troubles, upon whose back you gain a loftier perspective on the cares of mere pedestrians?"

"I do not." Bellona had gone to her reward three years ago. "I grasp the concept, though. You sought to remain in friendly company, which suggests that Mr. DeWitt stands below your horse in your esteem."

"Gavin DeWitt delights in reading plays," Lord Phillip said. "*Aloud*, voicing all the characters. Fine entertainment for a winter's evening, but for hours on end, trapped in a bouncing coach with mad kings and scheming witches... No, thank you. Herne, by contrast, is a horse of few words. Shall I introduce you?"

"Is Herne the gray gelding you rode in Town?"

"The very one."

One could tell a lot about a man from how he kept his cattle. Lord Phillip apparently doted on his gelding.

"Because you have arrived early, and I'm not desperately needed in the house, and you likely have questions about how to go one from here, I will accompany you to the stable."

"Let me guess. Visiting the stable is not done? The horses are not receiving until after three of the clock? Must I leave my card with the head lad?"

"Visiting the stable is done. I should be wearing a walking dress, though, or a riding habit. A carriage dress would also suffice."

He looked over at her, then at her afternoon dress. Whatever judgment he was pronouncing on her wardrobe, he kept to himself.

"Herne won't tattle," Lord Phillip said. "One of his many fine qualities. Will both of these paths take us to the stable?"

They'd come to a little arched bridge over a stream that watered a park. "That way is more roundabout," Hecate said, gesturing to the left, "but shadier."

"Because I inveigled you into the out of doors without giving you time to fetch a bonnet, much less a parasol, we will take the shadier path."

The shadier path was also more private. With a younger woman, a more eligible woman, his choice would be daring.

"Do you have questions?" Hecate asked as they crossed the bridge. "Now is the time to ask. Once the other guests start arriving, I will be pulled in six different directions by the hour."

"Why?"

"I beg your pardon?"

"Why are you stretched on the rack of the overtaxed hostess? You are a guest, as I am, and I doubt I will be pulled in even three different directions. You've traveled farther than I have to get here. Your journey was as fatiguing as mine, and yet, you face a forced march. Why?"

Because Edna sprang this wretched house party on me with too little time to prepare. Because the nominal hostess lingered in Town buying out the shops with Eglantine, using her own house party as an excuse to refurbish an already lavish wardrobe.

"House parties require thorough planning, done right. Cousin Edna, our hostess of record, has deputed me to assist her."

"Why you? Does Cousin Edna have no daughters? No daughters-in-law? No goddaughters?"

Why me? Hecate had asked that question so many times during her first Season, it ought to have become her personal motto. "I am experienced at planning and managing social gatherings."

They passed into the short portion of the path that cut through the woods proper, a blessedly cool, shadowed hundred yards where both house and stables were obscured from sight by towering oaks and a thick understory of encroaching maples along with a precocious birch or two.

"Your tone tells me I should drop my line of inquiry, Miss Brompton, but my motive is concern rather than curiosity. You look knackered, in need of a respite. I certainly am, and I merely spent a few hours on horseback, which I'm likely to do any given day. Shall we sit?"

They'd come to the bench somebody had carved from the trunk

of an oak claimed by the royal navy in the third earl's day. He'd cut the tree down, burned the stump, and sworn that lightning—rather than the need for wainscoting in the foyer—had claimed the tree.

The Brompton propensity for scheming had a lengthy provenance.

"I can't tarry long," Hecate said, though the prospect of getting off her feet was pathetically welcome. "Do I need to tell you that one doesn't remark critically on a lady's appearance?"

"One isn't critical. One is compassionate." Lord Phillip handed her onto the bench and took the place beside her. Not touching, but not half a yard away either. "You put me in mind of Amaryllis DeWitt, lately the Marchioness of Marital Bliss. You will have heard that her brother, Gavin, scion of the house, left his womenfolk to make shift while he indulged his thespian talents. He thought he'd arranged sufficient provision for them, but alas..."

"Avaricious solicitors, misfortune, miscommunication. I am familiar with the tale."

"Amaryllis became the unpaid house steward, land steward, manager of the home farm, accountant, leader of hymns, finder of misplaced spectacles, designer of altered bonnets, and head gardener. We neighbors did what we could, but beyond a certain point, the ladies were on their own. You strike me as very much on your own."

"I like being on my own." Why had a firm statement of the obvious come out sounding plaintive?

Lord Phillip patted Hecate's hand. Because she'd been arranging the centerpiece for the evening's buffet when the butler had informed her of Lord Phillip's arrival, she wore no gloves. Lord Phillip had likely removed his riding gloves out of habit, and thus the brush of his fingers over her knuckles was real, human contact.

"You pay dearly for it, don't you?" he said, craning his neck to look straight up into the canopy. "Whatever rebellion or misstep your mother might have taken, or did not take but could have taken, you are made to pay for it."

This again. Hecate had tried to put his casual, foolish question aside, but he apparently recalled the moment, contrary to every dictate of good manners.

"One doesn't... That is, I have no idea to what you're referring, my lord, and I must be getting back to the house."

He caught her hand before she could rise. "Miss Brompton... Hecate. My mother was blamed for my backwardness, for my dark hair, for my slowness of speech. Clearly, she'd disrespected her vows, or her lineage had harbored undisclosed defective tendencies, else I would have been born with my father's blond hair and excel at drawling bon mots in French."

His grip was warm and firm, and yet, Hecate could easily have broken free. "You were treated unfairly, and so was your mother. I'm sorry."

"True, and so are you treated unfairly. Between thee and me, you need not dissemble. I am troubled that your family imposes on you, and I trust you have your reasons for allowing it. Even so, I am not in the habit of ignoring ill usage when it's right under my nose. Provincial of me, I'm sure, but there you have it. Would civilization truly cease to function if you took an hour's nap?"

She needed a nap. Craved a nap. Longed for a nap. Had barely slept for all the preparations requiring attention. The journey out from Town earlier in the week had been stifling and interminable.

"We should be discussing the weather."

Lord Phillip rose and drew Hecate to her feet. "For years, for all of my life until Tavistock came along, I was forbidden to leave Crosspatch Corners on pain of losing the only thing I valued. Now I am allowed to roam the earth at will, to see, and do, and investigate any activity that catches my eye. I am not wasting the next twenty minutes discussing the weather with you, when you should be dreaming of the perfect waltz. Away with you, mademoiselle. I will manage until supper."

He kissed her knuckles, truly kissed them, which was terribly forward and truly not done and also lovely of him.

"Come, I'll walk with you back to the house," he said, tucking her hand over his arm. "I've been working on my French, but I regret to report that my quadrille is hopeless."

"I promised you a house party free of quadrilles." She let him escort her to the park and through the garden, but his words would not leave her. "You were truly captive in Crosspatch Corners?"

"Closer to a prisoner on parole. Within the confines of the neighborhood, I had unlimited freedom. I could venture into Reading or Windsor if I pleased to, but when I should have been learning to venture, I was instead learning birdcalls and how to beat Vicar at chess. London terrifies me, if you must know. The noise, the crowds, the incessant activity. Drives me barmy."

"As it did me, at first. Now Town is a familiar purgatory. You mustn't tell anybody I said that." They climbed the terrace steps, and with each one, Hecate felt more keenly the bow wave of fatigue she'd been pushing before her.

"Your secrets, Miss Brompton, will always be safe with me."

From him, those assurances were not simply a playful cliché. "We still should have discussed the weather." Hecate glanced up at Nunnsuch's façade, which even when viewed from the garden was imposing. "I do not want to go back into that house."

She hadn't meant to say that aloud. The look his lordship gave her said he knew as much.

"At supper, we will discuss the weather," Hecate muttered, preceding his lordship into the house. "You violate that dictum at peril of being sentenced to partner me in a Mayfair quadrille."

"I am a-tremble with dread, Miss Brompton." He bowed to her at the foot of the curved staircase. "May your dreams be of gentle showers, joyous rainbows, and breezes fragrant with honeysuckle."

She ascended the steps with as much dignity as she could muster, though somehow, even Lord Phillip's meteorological references tossed her off-balance. When she glanced behind her, he was still at the foot of the steps, looking dusty and devilish.

Hecate slept for three straight hours, and her dreams were of thunderstorms and talking horses.

CHAPTER FOUR

"Miss Brompton rattled off a lot of begats and resides-ats," Phillip said, "but I cannot put names to faces. For example, who is that woman impersonating a drunken ostrich?"

Phillip was again delaying the inevitable, lurking at the French doors of Gavin DeWitt's sitting room. On the terrace below, a loose crowd gathered, the noise increasing by the moment.

DeWitt held out a bony wrist. "Do me up, would you? The lady with the plumes is our hostess, Edna Brompton. A Houghton by birth, said to have been well dowered. Mother to the current heir. A previous contender for the succession died of consumption. Thanks."

DeWitt examined his reflection in the cheval mirror and fluffed his cravat, then began warbling random syllables like an Italian baritone preparing for a revival of *Don Giovanni*. A slight improvement over soliloquies from murderous princelings.

Hecate moved about below in a gown of medium brown trimmed with black, a cream lace shawl draped about her arms. The neckline was suitable for a Puritan governess. The governess's spinster auntie would have approved of the plain bun passing as a coiffeur. She was a wren among parakeets, kingfishers, and bullfinches.

"The tittering fellow is Charles Brompton?" Phillip asked.

DeWitt ceased his noise and rejoined Phillip at the French doors. "I see an embarrassment of tittering fellows. The one with the quizzing glass is Charles. Amaryllis ordered me to avoid him."

"So of course you will lurk in corners glowering until he wets himself."

"No, alas for my sense of family pride. Lissa says he has a wife and two children dependent upon him. I am to be a gracious exponent of wealthy bachelordom, overshadowed by your titled self, of course."

"Charles Brompton is stupid," Phillip translated, "and it's not worth the bother to chastise him for his dishonorable conduct. I remain unconvinced. If a lowly bullock can be taught not to kick at the traces, an English fribble can learn to keep his falls buttoned."

"Ah, but a bullock has been relieved of his testicles. Brompton doubtless treasures his. Should we go down?"

Phillip would rather have crawled back to Berkshire, but crawling was not his forte. Never had been.

Miss Brompton conferred with a footman for the third time in twelve minutes. This one handed her a glass of punch. She sipped and nodded, and the fellow looked relieved. Edna the Ostrich, meanwhile, barnacled herself onto the arm of some dashing blade who affected, of all things, a monocle. Another female, younger, mere pheasant feathers sticking up from her head, looked up like a startled hare when an old fellow strutted onto the terrace.

"Nunn," DeWitt said. "Earl of. He'll put in an appearance at any formal dinners, but we won't see much of him otherwise. Tory, of course, and conscientious toward his tenants. Family seems to be a matter of indifference to him. Charles is the heir, which ought to give all good souls a pang of worry for the British aristocracy."

Hecate greeted the earl with a respectful curtsey. He nodded to her without speaking, took a glass from the tray of a passing footman, and strolled off in the direction of his heir.

"Let's go down," Phillip said, stepping back as the gaiety below became noisier still.

Gavin touched his sleeve. "It's Miss Brompton's money that makes the whole charade possible. You can't expect an aging martinet to like her for that."

Liking was a matter of personal taste, but civility to a benefactress shouldn't have been too great an imposition. "How do you know the family's financial situation?"

"All of London knows. If a fellow marries into the Brompton horde, he negotiates more or less with Miss Hecate regarding settlements. If a daughter of the house becomes engaged, Miss Hecate's solicitors negotiate on her behalf, though I understand Miss Hecate has recently changed firms. She inherited from her mother's side of the family and has turned a nest egg into a thriving henhouse of investments. A whole poultry farm, to hear some tell it."

And for that, she was nearly offered the cut direct by the head of the family?

"You will show Miss Hecate Brompton marked attention," Phillip said. "Charm her, DeWitt, or I will tell the ostrich woman that you are in search of a wife from a titled family."

DeWitt flashed his signature charming-lad smile. "No call for dirty tactics. Amaryllis likes Miss Brompton. Says she has backbone and a fine sense of humor. I am looking forward to making the lady's acquaintance. Lay on, Macduff..."

"Not the tragedies, please. A farce or a comedy, but no fights to the death and no madness."

"When did you grow so dull, Heyward? I mean, my lord. One despairs of your prospects. You will have to introduce me to Miss Brompton. One hasn't had the pleasure."

What pleasure was to be had in surrounds such as these?

But then Phillip recalled the feel of Hecate Brompton's hand in his, her light rosy scent blending with the spicy tang of dense woods, her voice harmonizing with the trickle of the brook at the old stone bridge.

"On second thought," Phillip said, "a few lines from the Saint Crispin's Day speech might suit."

DeWitt put a theatrical hand over his heart. "'...Gentlemen in England now a-bed, shall think themselves accurs'd they were not here, and hold their manhoods cheap whiles any speaks that fought with us upon Saint Crispin's day! We few, we happy few—'"

"That will do, and you bungled the sequence. The we-happy-few part comes first."

Phillip descended to the terrace with a sense of crushing homesickness—Shakespeare could do that in a few lines—but also possessed of a determination Henry V, facing terrible odds with an exhausted, tattered army, would have understood.

Phillip's objective was not to acquire a fortnight's experience moving in polite company at close quarters, nor even to see DeWitt subjected to the same exercise. His purpose had become to ensure that Miss Hecate Brompton received the respect she was due.

A task best begun immediately.

~

How was it possible that every time Hecate beheld Lord Phillip Vincent, he appeared more impressive? More... *séduisant?* Not simply good-looking, but alluring. She resented him for distracting her, but she also simply enjoyed the sight of him. Tall, dark, and reserved rather than handsome.

He stood on the terrace steps beside Gavin DeWitt. His lordship's hesitation should have conveyed timidity, a lack of polish. Instead, he surveyed the gathering as one looked over a flock of sheep. His indifferent expression pronounced the herd mostly culls, a few worthy specimens, nothing impressive.

Beside him, DeWitt was a slightly overdressed ornament. Every other person present would have said DeWitt was the more desirable supper companion, including, probably, DeWitt himself.

Lord Phillip sauntered down the stairs and made straight for her.

"Miss Brompton." He bowed correctly over her hand. "May I have the pleasure of introducing to you Mr. Gavin DeWitt, late of Berkshire. DeWitt, Miss Hecate Brompton."

They moved through the little pattern of bowing and nodding as Cousin Eglantine let forth a trill of all-heads-shall-now-turn-and-admire-me laughter. DeWitt obliged.

Lord Phillip subtly winced. "Perhaps you'd be good enough to introduce us to our host and hostess, Miss Brompton?"

"Of course. This way. Mr. DeWitt, I trust your rooms are in order?" Cousin Edna would not bother to ask.

"My rooms are lovely, thank you. Nunnsuch is a most impressive venue."

A flatterer. Hecate had learned to appreciate them. They were easier to endure than the men who sneered or leered.

"I'll happily give you the tour tomorrow afternoon," she said. "Parts of the house date back to Norman times, and the earl has only recently had the oubliette filled in."

Hecate had insisted. If Charles and Eglantine expected to raise children in this house, an oubliette was out of the question, and to blazes with family history.

"Venerable and interesting." DeWitt twinkled at her. "I so enjoy that combination."

Oh, for pity's sake. He was a persistent flatterer. "Then you must see the gallery. We immortalize our rogues as all conscientious families do. Cousin Edna."

Edna left off simpering at Hallowell DeGrange. Hecate so rarely claimed a handsome gentleman on each arm, and the slight surprise in Edna's eyes was gratifying.

"Miss Brompton." DeGrange was a decent fellow, by Brompton standards, past thirty and no longer given to foolish wagers. The monocle was a recent affectation, but Hecate preferred it to Charles's quizzing glass. "How do you do? And who are these fine fellows? A brace of bachelors, no doubt?"

He laughed at his own observation, Edna joined in, and Mr.

DeWitt looked amused. Lord Phillip, by contrast, appeared to be mentally culling two more underperforming sheep from his herd.

"Cousin Edna, I have the pleasure to make known to you Lord Phillip Vincent and Mr. Gavin DeWitt. Gentlemen, your hostess and my cousin, Mrs. Edna Brompton."

Cousin Edna held out her hand, and more tedium ensued. DeWitt exerted himself to be adorable and succeeded in being annoying, while Lord Phillip's behavior was correct. Edna, who possessed good instincts for self-preservation, did not attempt to flirt with either man—she was nearly old enough to be Mr. DeWitt's mama—but neither did she offer to take up the hostess's duties and introduce her guests to the earl.

Nothing for it, then.

"Lord Nunn will want to make your acquaintance," Hecate said when Edna and her flirt du jour excused themselves. In truth, the earl didn't bother making anybody's acquaintance. He preferred instead to look down his nose, nod, and retreat into his study. To his credit, he didn't put up with toadying, which flummoxed most of his Brompton relations.

If Lord Nunn was in residence at Nunnsuch, Hecate bided in London rather than presume on his hospitality. In recent years, he'd kept increasingly to Nunnsuch rather than Town, where impecunious relations lurked behind every potted palm.

"My lord," Hecate murmured when Nunn's audience, Mrs. Rose Roberts, smiled at Hecate in greeting. "If you have a moment, I'd like to introduce two more guests to you."

Nunn brushed a glance over her, then arched an eyebrow at Mr. DeWitt and Lord Phillip. DeWitt smiled genially. Lord Phillip looked bored.

"Proceed," Nunn said. He had the looks to be a convivial old raconteur—snowy white hair, blue eyes, lean save for a bit of a paunch, but he instead attempted relentless majesty. Hecate used to contemplate dashing a serving of punch in his face, but punch cost money. Then too, by the time she was Nunn's age, the Bromptons might well have put her in a permanent ill humor too.

She stepped through the ritual, and Nunn bestirred himself to exhibit his manners. He was a peer, true, but in terms of family standing, a marquessate outranked an earldom. Mr. DeWitt ingratiated himself with Mrs. Roberts and inveigled her into showing him the wonders of the herbaceous borders, while Lord Phillip remained at Hecate's elbow.

"Hail from Berkshire, do you?" Nunn asked. "I thought the Tavistock marquessate had its seat in Surrey."

As opening salvos went, that one should have landed sizzling with menace at Lord Phillip's feet. Hecate doubted his lordship had clapped eyes on that family seat, his banishment to Berkshire a blatant indicator of paternal rejection.

"As it happens, I prefer Lark's Nest," Lord Phillip replied mildly. "My estate is not only profitable, but lovely. Tavistock deeded it to me outright, and I do so admire generosity, especially in those with many demands upon their resources. Don't you agree?"

His tone was pleasant, but heads had turned. Charles sent Hecate a do-something look. Edna's plumes were for once still, and over by the punchbowl, Cousin Portia was whispering furiously into Cousin Flavia's ear.

"Decent thing for the marquess to do," Nunn harrumphed. "One cannot fault his intentions."

"Tavistock is the best of brothers," Phillip replied. "When he learned that he had family in my humble person, he dropped the Town whirl flat and presented himself on my doorstep in Berkshire. He's been biding there more or less ever since, and we hope he and the marchioness will make a permanent home in the surrounds. Family is as family does, after all."

In the distance, an owl hooted, the sound dying away into the shadows of the home wood and leaving a vast silence in its wake. Then somebody commenced a coughing fit, while Portia snickered, and Flavia rapped her sister on the arm with a folded-up fan.

"Perhaps you'd like a glass of punch, my lord?" Hecate said, gesturing with her empty glass. "I could certainly use more. The earl has many other guests to greet, and I'd like to introduce you to more of my cousins."

Lord Phillip offered his arm. "A glass of punch would suit."

Hecate wrapped her fingers around his elbow and all but dragged him past the punchbowl and into the relative shadows of the conservatory.

"What on earth were you doing?" she hissed when she'd hauled him among the potted lemons.

"Greeting my host. I thought it went rather well. The old bore must be lonely, racketing about this enormous place with nothing to do but fill in his oubliette and wait for his next quarterly allowance. One pities him."

"Does one really?" Hecate felt a great lecture welling up, about decorum and civility and the duties of a guest and first impressions... and the list went on from there. A long, worthy, sanctimonious list, intended to prevent further disasters of the kind Lord Phillip had just visited upon himself.

"You are distressed," Phillip said. "I do apologize, but somebody had to remind the old fellow of a host's obligations. I don't mind that he was uppish with me, but he had no excuse for his rudeness to you."

Oh, that. "He's rude to everybody. Gruff, rather, by nature."

"Then the lesson was overdue. He has all this family—cousins and nephews and nieces—and he can't spare a drop of gratitude for that abundance, much less for the coin you part with to keep him in gardeners and embroidered dressing gowns. I'd half a mind to deliver him a true tongue-lashing."

Hecate's imagination was seized by the image of Lord Phillip, fist on hip, shaking an admonitory finger at Nunn as the earl stood, shame-faced, in one of his many richly adorned silk dressing gowns.

"Does my lord have earls thick on the ground in Crosspatch Corners that he feels qualified to comment on Nunn's deportment?"

"Oh, now I've done it. You are my-lording me. I will tell you this: In Crosspatch Corners, we have common decency by the hectare. The crop flourishes when all are dedicated to its care."

"Don't turn up Farmer Phillip on me when you've insulted your host. I will be blamed for your rudeness."

"I wasn't rude," Phillip said gently. "I was polite. If Nunn chose to hear insults, then he did the damage to himself. You cannot continue to cosset these buffoons, Hecate Brompton. They forget to whom they owe the punch they drink and the pretty frocks they wear."

He was lecturing her, and his reproach was all the more devasting for being brief and kindly.

"They are all I have." She'd not put that into words before, though what pathetic, inadequate words they were.

Phillip peered down at her. "In their present condition, they are not worth having. Besides, you have me. Please recall that I treasure my friends, even if they are a bit misguided on topics such as loyalty, generosity, and self-respect. Are you hungry? I'm famished. At what point is it permissible to plunder the buffet? And might I fetch you another glass of punch? Haranguing me is thirsty work, and I can see you're winding up for a grand peroration."

Hecate's grand peroration slipped from her grasp. "A glass of punch would be much appreciated. We're a quarter hour away from the buffet opening."

"No, we are not. Wait here. Help yourself to my drink."

He kissed her forehead and marched off, and Hecate wanted to call him back. He'd make a cake of himself, snitching from the buffet without permission, but then, he should have made a cake of himself arriving early, sauntering up the drive on foot, tucking his horse into his stall, and insulting his host.

But he hadn't.

Hecate tried to identify the emotions welling where her extensive lecture had been. She wanted to cry, but crying was an outward indulgence. Tears were nothing but bother. Not worth wrinkling a handkerchief over.

What had Phillip said...? Not the part about Nunn's rudeness, or the family's general selfishness, something meant to be casual and fleeting... mostly bluster, but not entirely.

I treasure my friends.

He'd said that before, but just now, he'd said it about Hecate. She brushed her thumb over her forehead, where the hopeless man had kissed her. The riot he caused inside her included consternation and gratitude, but also... admiration.

Lord Phillip was a social disaster on two sizable feet, but he'd meet his ruin on his own terms, honor bright. For that, she had to sincerely admire him, provided he didn't involve her in his downfall.

~

"She's taken you to the conservatory to give you a dressing down, hasn't she?"

The question was put to Phillip by one of two nearly identical young females who appeared to be joined at the hip. They were blond, afflicted with masses of ringlets, and attired in dressing gowns doubtless intended to hint of Grecian sophistication.

Phillip tried to leaven his consternation with a hint of Gavin DeWitt's friendliness. "Ladies, have we been introduced? Phillip Vincent at your service."

"You forgot the lord part," the one on the left said. "But we *know*. You are heir to the Tavistock marquessate, *for now*, and Hecate somehow got you onto the guest list."

"She does that," the second one said. "Manages *feats*, and we have no idea how. Charles claims Hecate communes with the dark arts, but he's only teasing. I'm Portia Brompton, and this is my sister, Flavia."

They bobbed a synchronized curtsey. Phillip remembered to bow. "A pleasure, ladies. Are you having punch?"

"We are supposed to limit ourselves to one glass before supper," Portia said.

"Hecate's orders," Flavia added. "Lest we get tipsy. Tipsy is bad, but ever so diverting. One feels clever when tipsy, and Hecate's punch recipe is delicious. One must concede the obvious."

"The raspberries," Portia said, nodding sagely. "They are in season, and Nunnsuch has pots of them. We'll have raspberry crepes and raspberry punch and raspberry pie. I love a good raspberry pie with a dollop of cream. I'm also very fond of syllabub with—"

"Not *now*, Portia. As for you, my lord. Don't let Hecate go at you for too long," Flavia said, lowering her voice. "She has a way with a scold. Makes one feel two inches tall and hopelessly stupid."

"Reduces you to bumbling gudgeon status in about thirty seconds," Portia said, requisitioning the glasses of punch Phillip had requested for himself and Hecate. "She's had plenty of practice. We Bromptons are *lively*."

She and Flavia touched glasses and sipped in unison.

"I was a bit less than mannerly with the earl," Phillip said. "Miss Brompton is concerned that I make a good first impression on polite society. The earl is my host and my social superior."

"Great-Uncle Nunn is superior to the archangel Gabriel," Portia observed, with a confirming nod from Flavia. "Even Hecate only takes him on behind a closed door. You mustn't blame her for being worried. Great-Uncle belongs to all the best clubs and sits in the Lords."

"You know what that is, the House of Lords?" Flavia inquired.

"My brother sits in the Lords. I have a vague sense the job requires speechifying, robbing the nation blind, and assisting the monarchy to rob the nation blind."

Portia's eyes went round, and Flavia agitated the air with her fan.

"You're a Whig!" she said, fluttering madly. "Is that why your papa hid you away?"

Phillip accepted two filled glasses from the footman. "I'm a farmer. You are both sworn to secrecy." He'd just ensured they'd repeat the conversation word for word to any willing ears, of course, which was fine with him.

"Hecate means well," Flavia said when Phillip would have made his escape. "Her heart was broken at a young age—younger than we are now—and she has never recovered."

"And she has unfortunate antecedents," Portia said. "We aren't clear on the particulars, but Eglantine says we must make allowances. My antecedents are quite in order." She batted her lashes at Phillip, and Flavia smacked her with the fan.

"Mine are too," Flavia said. "And I don't gossip half so much as Portia does."

Not for lack of trying. "Do we know who broke Miss Hecate's youthful heart?" The question was doubtless a breach of eight social commandments, but if Hecate had to watch the object of her first attachment turning down the room with every other woman in Mayfair, Phillip wanted to know who the dunderhead was.

"Cousin Johnny," the ladies said in unison. "He went for a soldier in his dashing regimentals. Off to Canada, and he refused to take Hecate with him."

"He took Cousin Emeril, though," Portia continued, circling the rim of her glass with her index finger. "There is that. Emeril was a bit much, even for a Brompton, though he's not as bad as Uncle

Frank. Uncle prefers life on the Continent, which Mama says is mercy. Both cousins took a fancy to the New World, which is not a mercy. We get occasional letters, but they all say the same thing: 'Canada is beautiful, give my love to everybody.'"

"I wouldn't like that very much," Flavia observed. "'Give my love to *everybody*,' when Hecate gave her *heart* to Johnny. Very romantic and tragical. It explains *a lot*."

"Do you waltz?" Portia asked, sending her sister a repressive look. "We do. We were given permission last year, and I've stood up with your brother."

Before Phillip could answer, Flavia was sticking her oar back in.

"That was only the once, Portia. Tavistock promenaded *with me*. That counts as standing up as well."

"Does not."

Both occasions likely counted as Hecate inspiring Tavistock into some charity work. "I do not waltz," Phillip said. "I haven't been given the nod."

Flavia, who looked to be on the point of sticking her tongue out at her sister, sent him a keen glance. "It doesn't work like that. If Hecate told you it did, then she's in error."

An occasion for gloating, clearly. "I have not been given the nod *by Miss Hecate*, and I account her a faultless arbiter of all matters social. If you ladies will excuse me, I am overdue for my first lecture of the evening."

"Apologize like you mean it," Portia advised. "Look sincere. Tearing up might be a bit much in your case, but Flavia and I have resorted to desperate measures from time to time. Hecate can be so..."

"So *Hecate*," Flavia said. "She can't help it, so don't try to reason with her. She means well, and she... she means well, and she's getting on. Spinsters are deserving of understanding."

On that magnanimous proclamation, both magpies fell silent.

"I will bid you ladies good evening," Phillip said. "Enjoy your punch, though you might want to consider limiting yourselves to two glasses each. One can think oneself quite clever when tipsy, though in fact, we often become gibbering fools when we overindulge. I speak from experience."

He nodded and beat a retreat. Portia looked puzzled, but Flavia was smacking her closed fan against her palm as if she might just possibly have comprehended an unappreciated reprimand.

The most recent of many, no doubt.

Phillip detoured to the buffet where he found a tray and filled a plate with this and that. He half expected Hecate to have deserted her post, but she yet occupied a bench among the potted lemons. In the waning evening light, she looked not quite so tired as she had earlier in the day, and not as if she'd been rehearsing any lectures either.

"Shall we eat here," Phillip asked, "or find a table?"

"Let's use the side terrace." Hecate rose unassisted and surveyed the laden tray. "You've been naughty."

"I've been hungry. I was also accosted by Pythia Minor and Pythia Major, who strike me as having left the schoolroom far too soon."

"Portia and Flavia. They are Edna's current projects, and you must avoid anything approaching privacy with either one."

Hecate wended between lemons, oranges, ferns, and camellias until she came to a door that opened onto a blessedly quiet terrace.

"Do Portia and Flavia ever separate long enough to be private with anyone?" Phillip asked. "I took them for twins."

"They are eleven months apart. Portia is the elder, and yes, for strategic purposes, they separate. They nearly succeeded in compromising a viscount's pride and joy last year. They didn't want to marry him. They wanted to blackmail him."

"I'm not wealthy," Phillip said. "You will please inform them of my poverty in no uncertain terms. Blackmail would be pointless. Then too, the appeal of becoming a social outcast is growing on me." He set the tray on a wrought-iron table near a balustrade that faced the wooded border of the park.

"You see those oaks?" Hecate said, gesturing to the line of trees thirty yards off.

"We walked through part of them earlier today."

"And you rejoiced to be in the out of doors. You can probably trail game down unseen paths, identify every bird by its call, and tell the savory mushrooms from those that can kill."

"I admit to being at home in the woods and fields. I hope every child has the good luck to spend a few summers exploring hedgerows, meadows, brooks, and good climbing trees."

"Portia and Flavia know polite society's underbrush, birdcalls, and wildflowers the same way you know the countryside. They are at home lurking near punchbowls. They pore over Debrett's as you'd read tracks on the muddy banks of the Twid. Underestimate them at your peril, my lord."

Hecate delivered not a lecture, but rather, a serious warning, and Phillip took it as such. "If compromising is on the list of acceptable wilderness tactics here at Nunnsuch, why are you permitted to be private with me?"

Hecate gestured to a cushioned seat.

"I beg your pardon." Phillip dutifully held her chair for her before taking the one next to it. "Sorry. They flustered me. One doesn't expect an interrogation from a pair of giggling ninnyhammers."

Hecate took up a table napkin and spread it on her lap, which reminded Phillip to do likewise.

"I am on the shelf," Hecate said. "Firmly, completely, irreversibly. You could spend the night under my bed, and my family would not take it amiss. Spinsterhood was the bargain I struck with my father. The family's first tactic was to try to marry me—and my fortune—off to a cousin or in-law. Keep the money *where it will do the most good.*"

Phillip held the plate of sandwiches out to her. "You don't blame them for this conniving?"

"My fortune is all the money they have, so no, I don't blame them, but no suitably obliging fellow over the age of sixteen stepped forward. Next, they tried to marry me to greater wealth, but again, no candidates volunteered. The last strategy was to put me on offer to gentlemen of exceedingly great age, with the understanding that I'd come into my widow's portion in short order, but again, candidates were few and a bit too vigorous."

She chose a single sandwich of butter and cress.

Phillip added two of roast beef and Stilton to her plate. The sandwiches were about the size of pocket watches, for pity's sake. "You warned all these bachelors off."

"After the first few, overt warnings weren't necessary, but I hadn't realized that my own solicitors—my former solicitors—were abetting my spinsterhood. I'll have a raspberry tart, please."

Phillip put three on her plate and bit into his own sandwich. "Thus you struck a bargain with your father. He agreed to stop leading you about Mayfair like a brindle heifer available to join a new herd, and you agreed to use your fortune for the family's greater good."

Hecate finished her first sandwich. "Your agrarian analogies want some polish, my lord." She picked up a second sandwich.

"How old were you when you negotiated this cease-fire?"

"One and twenty, and I'd come into control of the first portion of my wealth. The whole of it is under my direction now, and I cannot tell you what a relief that is."

"Probably about like gaining title to Lark's Nest is for me. That place is my home, not simply the property where I dwell and sweat and snore. *Mine.* If Tavistock goes down in history as the worst brother ever to bear the label, I will still love and revere him for that single instance of generosity."

Hecate took up her glass of punch, and Phillip considered she'd soon be off to avert various disasters on the terrace, in the kitchen, or in the garden shadows. He had a question or two yet to put to her.

"Tell me, Miss Brompton, did you love your cousin Johnny, or did you commend him to the Canadian wilderness with a sense of relief?"

She put her glass down slowly, the punch untasted. "Fast work, even for Flavia and Portia."

Phillip waited, because her answer mattered.

"To be honest," Hecate said. "A bit of both."

CHAPTER FIVE

What had Flavia and Portia been about, regaling Lord Phillip with ancient family history? Their schemes ranged from outlandish to devious and both at the same time, and they were *always* scheming.

Edna doted on them shamelessly, which helped not one bit.

"Johnny is the one Brompton of whom the family is justifiably proud," Hecate said, starting a second sandwich and surprised to find meat and cheese where she'd been expecting a dab of butter and some greens. "He talked the solicitors into allowing him a lieutenant's commission and managed to get posted to Canada as hostilities on the Peninsula heated up. He even took a wayward younger brother with him."

"For whom you were also expected to buy a commission?"

"I pay for everything. You needn't carp on the fact. In any case, off they sailed, and in Canada they have remained. Johnny loves the out of doors, while Emeril is good with figures. Emeril attached himself to quartermastering in the eastern provinces, while Johnny went west. He eventually sold his commission and took to trapping and guiding. He's apparently happy doing what he excels at. Emeril bides in the east, employed by some trading outfit, though I think they see each other every couple of years or so."

How must it feel to have the vast, wild, whole of Canada to wander freely?

"And you are proud of them," Lord Phillip said. "Do they write?"

"They write to Great-Uncle Nunn once or twice a year, and he deigns to share the letters. What of you? Any far-flung relations waiting for letters from you?"

Too late, Hecate realized her attempt to change the subject had been awkward.

"I have lady cousins throughout the home counties. I have met two of them thanks to Tavistock's kind offices. I will meet the rest in the autumn if I return to London."

Hecate sipped her punch. This was her second glass—and would be her last of the evening. "I'm sorry. I ought not to have asked after your family. You truly don't know them?"

"They did not know I existed, and neither did Tavistock, by the old man's design." Lord Phillip munched on a second or third sandwich with what appeared to be complete equanimity. "I knew of them, though. We get the London papers in Crosspatch, and the nieces of a marquess were launched with some fanfare. I knew less of Tavistock because he was on evasive maneuvers in France."

Soon, Hecate would have to wade into the affray on the main terrace, monitoring the punchbowl and keeping an eye on the buffet. If Eglantine and Edna or Portia and Flavia—or all four of them— became quarrelsome, Hecate would separate the combatants before the gentlemen started exchanging bets.

"What was it like," she said, "to know you had family you were forbidden to meet?"

Phillip rose and propped a hip on the balustrade. "Probably like having cousins in Canada. You wish them well, you wait for the occasional word of them, you go on with your life. Did you love him?"

"We really must work on your small talk, my lord."

"He abandoned you," Phillip said. "I could not blame my relatives for ignoring somebody whose existence was unknown to them, but in the case of your Johnny..."

"He was all of twenty. I give him credit for understanding that with a fortune comes responsibilities. He preferred adventure, and at his age, the choice was understandable. He said I'd get the family sorted if I could avoid matrimony until age twenty-one, and he was right."

"Your family is sorted, then?" Lord Phillip lounged, drink in hand, just out of smacking range.

"Keeping the Bromptons sorted is a near run thing from Season to Season, but they are all on allowances and have learned for the most part to live within their allotted means."

For the most part, sometimes, in a manner of speaking.

Lord Phillip resumed his seat, gaze on the darkening line of trees. "Are you proud of yourself?"

A third sandwich awaited, and Hecate told herself she really shouldn't, and she ought not to, and Lord Phillip had had no business putting so much food on the plate.

"Why would I be proud of myself? My every need is met not because of some effort I put forth, but because I had the good fortune to inherit wealth. I'm healthy through no fault of my own, of sound mind and reasonable appearance. None of it my doing. What do I have to be proud of?"

Phillip peered over at her, his expression hard to read in the gathering shadows. "You describe a pair of cousins who used your money to make their way to Canada, where everything from their boots to their biscuits was provided by the crown until other employment beckoned. Yet you are proud of them for following a path smoothed by your coin.

"Great-Uncle Nincompoop," Phillip went on, resuming his seat, "has no idea how to make his land profitable despite having decades to study on the matter. When the Corn Laws are repealed—and they will be—he will expect you to keep Nunnsuch going, if you aren't already. Edna the Ostrich expects you to dower those two hoydens, and it will take a small fortune apiece to find souls stout enough to meet those two at the altar. Cousin Charles would have gambled himself into exile but for your steadying hand, and that's the recitation I can offer on one day's acquaintance with your family. But you take no pride in these accomplishments."

Hecate finished her third sandwich, hearing criticism rather than praise. "What is money for, if not caring for loved ones and the less fortunate?"

"Who cares for you?" Phillip passed her two more raspberry tarts. Had they been peach or apple, she might have refused.

"I care for me."

He propped a boot on the balustrade and tipped his chair back on two legs. "I haven't your great self-sufficiency. I look after Lark's Nest, which might be loosely analogous to a rackety family. Just when I think the irrigation system has finally been set up to manage all the right acres in the right manner, we get a wet spring and I have flooding.

"I choose a fine stud for my broodmares, and only half of them catch. I decide to put a field in mangel-wurzels—remind me to tell Tavistock about mangel-wurzel beer, which is very good for breeding females—and turnips become more fashionable. Managing a patch of ground is like playing chess with fate, but at least I can compare notes with my neighbors."

He popped a raspberry tart into his mouth while Hecate cast around for yet another subject they might pursue besides her family. Did they truly think her so antediluvian that she could dine virtually in seclusion with an eligible bachelor?

"I have reinforcements, though," Phillip went on. "The Crosspatch Committee for Outwitting Unkind Fate meets regularly in the common of the Crosspatch Arms. Fortified with our pints, we trade insights, share the latest pamphlets, and offer each other encouragement and ideas. The same committee meets in the churchyard and on market day. Occasional executive sessions pop up over Vicar's chessboard. My neighbors aren't related to me, but they took me on as family all the same."

"And you took them on as family." Amaryllis DeWitt had passed along that much. Phillip never entertained formally, but he was always available to assist with a difficult foaling or calving and never begrudged a neighbor the loan of a team or a plow.

"I didn't know any better," he said, finishing off a second tart. "Does nobody truly care that we are private as darkness falls?"

"My family trusts me." To be able to say that should have satisfied some dictate of pride or loyalty. Hecate appropriated the last tart and wished Phillip had brought more.

"But on what basis," Phillip said, "do they trust *me?* I'm Lord Bumpkin, unacquainted with Society's finer manners. Why trust such a one with the family treasure?"

Because the treasure is my fortune, not me. To put matters that bluntly would offend those finer manners.

"Why did you kiss me?" Hecate asked, tapping her forehead. "Here."

"Not done? Does nobody in the beau monde express affection? Does nobody touch? Nobody hug? I begin to think a lordly title more of a curse than a blessing if that's the case."

"They don't touch *me.*" Heaven help her, she'd downed too much punch too quickly. Or she'd still been short of sleep after a three-hour nap. Some imbalance in the humors had to account for such an unseemly admission.

The owl hooted out another warning just as a burst of laughter drifted up from the main terrace. Hecate wanted more punch and more cakes and to be anywhere else.

No, on second thought, that was incorrect. She wanted *her family* to be anywhere else, but then she'd worry about the mischief they were getting up to.

"I was born with a deformity," Lord Phillip said in the same tones he might have offered to fetch more food. "My right shoulder and the muscles around it didn't work properly. Forceps were to blame, apparently, but the old marquess chose to see my weakness as more proof that I was not his get. I could not crawl properly, and the strength on my right side is still not the equal to my left."

"What has this to do with...?" Hecate fell silent as her mind's eye filled with the memory of couples whirling on the dance floor. Hands held high, hands forming an arch for other couples, ladies twirled with confident strength by their manly partners.

How could one dance without a stout right arm?

"My neighbors touch me," Lord Phillip said. "A pat on the back, a hug, a handshake, but until recently, I shook with my left hand. Nobody remarked it—they were being kind—until Tavistock brandished his right in a manner I could not ignore. Like putting up his fives, though with the best of intentions."

"I'm... sorry." Nothing in Phillip's bearing or appearance suggested any imperfection. What point was he making with this disclosure?

"I wanted to shake with my right, but what if somebody took a notion to squeeze my hand too hard? Would that affect my shoulder? What if, knowing of my malady, they found my right hand distasteful? The whole business put me off greeting anybody face-to-face. To shake with the right hand is normal and manly, and yet..."

"You were not normal," Hecate said, grasping a thread of significance. "You wanted to be, but fate decreed otherwise."

"I am not normal," Phillip said, "but who is? I do believe, though, that it's normal to long to kiss a lovely woman when she has become dear to me. When I esteem her and enjoy her company and hope she can—despite my many shortcomings—enjoy mine."

He was saying he was... attracted to her? The notion was equally outlandish and intriguing. Lord Phillip Vincent was woefully inadequate at dissembling, and he was still self-conscious about his shoulder apparently, and he wasn't at all impressed with the Brompton Horde.

Who were, after two cups of punch, more than a bit tiresome.

"Are you wishing I'd kiss you, my lord?"

"If we're venturing onto that fraught ground, might you call me Phillip?"

"Answer the question, Phillip."

He took her hand. "One doesn't wish to presume, et cetera and so forth, but one is also compelled by honor to deal with a lady honestly, and therefore, I do admit to harboring—"

"Hecate!" Eglantine's soprano warbled out from the conservatory. "Oh, Hec-a-teeeee! My dear, you simply must come. Charles is trying to get up a whist party, and whist was invented by the devil to steal my pin money."

Eglantine emerged from the house, a pale form against the increasing darkness. "That *is* you? Who is your friend? Oh, Lord Phillip. Doing your bit for the family spinster? Too bad for you, I have need of her. Hecate, you must talk sense to Charles. Mr. DeGrange knows his way around a deck of cards, and Edna is encouraging this nonsense. My trunks haven't been unpacked, and Charles is already imperiling his sons' inheritance. Do excuse us, your lordship. Needs must."

Phillip had dropped Hecate's hand the instant Eglantine had called out, not that he need have bothered.

He rose and bowed. "I understand. Duty calls. Don't spare the horses. The fate of England, we happy few, and so forth..."

Hecate rose and curtseyed, when she wanted to pitch Eglantine over the balustrade. "I'm coming, though whist for farthing points would pose no threat."

Eglantine snorted. "You must set the stakes, Hecate. Charles won't listen to me, and Edna will argue for pounds and pence, because she always hopes to win and seldom does."

Hecate let herself be dragooned into the conservatory, though she paused to look over her shoulder. Phillip was lounging against the railing again, his glass in his hand.

When Hecate would have turned to go, he blew her a kiss, then tapped his lips. She could not be sure—no torches had been lit yet—but she was fairly certain he'd also winked at her.

Not done. Unspeakably sweet of him, but *not done*.

"He's coming home?" Edna Brompton asked, ready to snatch the blasted letter from Uncle Nunn's grasp. "Our Johnny is coming home?"

"So he claims." Nunn took a leisurely sip of his morning coffee. "Will take ship shortly, if he hasn't already. Wants to be home before the autumn storms start up. One doesn't trifle with North Atlantic weather."

Spoken as if Nunn, whose sailing exploits were limited to yachting on the Thames or a packet to Calais, were some sort of maritime authority.

"When is the letter dated?"

Nunn peered at the epistle. "Can't make it out. Salt-sea air is the very devil on paper and ink. Looks like last month."

He sat at his pretty desk, earl of all he surveyed, and set the blasted letter beside his breakfast tray. Edna had found him taking his first meal of the day in his personal library, which was Nunn's term for an estate office. Never let it be said a peer of the realm toiled in an office.

And truly, the room was too handsomely kitted out to be an office. Louis Quinze desk, chairs, and love seat; handsome landscapes of Nunnsuch and its surrounds on the green-silk-hung walls; new curtains chosen to match a vivid Aubusson carpet in hues of red, gold, and green; fireplace faced in pink Carrara marble... A peer's private retreat, right down to roses the same shade of red as the curtains and carpets.

The windows were open, the scent of scythed grass wafting on the morning breeze, sunbeams glinting on the silver tea service.

Flavia and Portia longed to live in such elegant surrounds, and Edna wanted that for them too. They were pretty enough by Mayfair standards, and Hecate could see them well dowered, but their connection to the earl was attenuated, and they were... lively. Their brother was in line for the title, though old Nunn was in deplorably sound health.

"We will of course welcome Johnny home with open arms," Edna said. "Is this a visit, or has he made his fortune and decided to come home to stay?" She posed the question brightly. Another wealthy Brompton could only benefit the family as a whole.

Eglantine permitted Charles far too loose a rein. He would someday be the earl, after all, and he was no longer nineteen and in love with his pizzle. Not every waking moment, anyway.

And if Johnny were wealthy... Such a lovely notion. Hecate wasn't awful, but she was so... *Hecate*. Always nattering on about budgets, priorities, and self-restraint. No duller topic existed than *reasonable economies*, and yet, Hecate would maunder on for days on that very subject.

"The letter doesn't say if this is a visit or a permanent return," Nunn replied, taking a bite of buttered toast. "I expect Johnny will make that decision when he gets here, though he doesn't seem to have pined for Merry Olde. If you are thinking of unloading Portia or Flavia on him, you might consider that Johnny's wife could end up in Canada for all the rest of her days."

"Better to be a wealthy wife in Canada than a poor relation anywhere else."

Nunn munched his toast placidly. "From what Hecate tells me, Lord Phillip is not wealthy, but both Portia and Flavia were thrusting their bosoms at him by the punchbowl last evening. Those two will be the ruin of this family, Edna, and when that happens, I will hold you accountable and close the doors of Nunnsuch to your wayward offspring."

He would do it too. Hecate held the purse strings, but Nunn had all the consequence. Two towering injustices that defied Edna's considerable reasoning powers.

"Lord Phillip's brother is a marquess," Edna said. "Lord Phillip is the marquess's heir. Either Flavia or Portia would do for him quite well." And Johnny, if wealthy, could have the remaining sister, provided he hadn't caught any dreadful diseases in the wilds of Canada.

"Have you set your cap for DeGrange?" Nunn inquired, spreading yet more butter on a second slice of toast.

"He's too young for me." Also a bit serious, behind the relentless geniality. "What of you? Will you succumb to Mrs. Roberts' charms?" Edna had lost sleep worrying about that very possibility. The only thing worse than the family consequence resting in Nunn's hands would be that same consequence held by a young and shrewish new wife.

Last year, she'd set Charles to charming Mrs. Roberts in hopes that an affair would render the lady unacceptable in Nunn's eyes. Mrs. Roberts had tired of Charles's escort without sampling his wares, and apparently felt no inclination to renew ties.

Though Eglantine would probably be relieved if Charles were to stray—again.

"Mrs. Roberts," Nunn said, "is a neighbor who shares with me the experience of spousal bereavement. She condoles me as well on the nature of my extended family, and one appreciates a sympathetic ear. Enough prying, Edna. Your fluttering about will spoil my digestion, and I'm of a mind to look in on the haying this morning. I haven't time to waste on your scheming. Marry DeGrange with my blessing if that's what you're after, and I'm sure Hecate will add a token sum to reward DeGrange for his optimism."

Edna tried, under the guise of straightening the curtains and rearranging the roses, to get a peek at Johnny's letter. "I will not remarry unless and until my daughters are happily settled."

"Nobody will take you on with those two clinging to your skirts, no matter how generously Hecate dowers the lot of you. You hope to get Lord Phillip in harness before he's wise to Society's ways, and I wish you the joy of that undertaking."

"Lord Phillip could do much worse. My girls would show him how to go on. They are received everywhere and quite accomplished."

"Phillip Vincent is nobody's fool," Nunn said, patting his lips with a monogrammed napkin. "He's not a fribble, though one could wish he had a finer appreciation for the subtleties of social standing. His late father was a strutting, rutting exponent of aristocratic arrogance, but old Tavistock was also shrewd and determined."

"You like Lord Phillip?" Edna couldn't fault the man's appearance, though he was on the tall and slightly brutish side. Nonetheless, he'd *walked* his horse up the carriageway, helped himself to the buffet a quarter hour before the third bell should have been rung, and had apparently secreted himself on the side terrace with Hecate for nearly half an hour.

His social instincts, in other words, were sadly lacking.

"I respect his lordship," Nunn said. "Not a concept I can expect a Brompton to grasp. Now cease trying to spy on my correspondence and say nothing of that letter to your offspring. Ships sink even in summer, and I only told you of Johnny's approaching arrival because, by rights, he should have first crack at the town house you intend to occupy come autumn. Best line up someplace else to bide if you plan to be in Town."

"Johnny's mama would not have wanted to see the girls and me turned out!" Unless she'd been indulging in one of her periodic disagreeable spells.

"You aren't spending the autumn here, madam. Now leave me in peace and keep this development to yourself."

Edna could rifle the desk when Nunn went off on his morning hack. The strongbox had yet to yield to her hatpins, but with any luck, Nunn would shove the letter into a drawer and forget about it. He was absent-minded, despite his lamentable vigor.

"Did Johnny mention how Emeril is getting on?" Em had been the merrier of the two boys, though Johnny was no high stickler.

"He says Emeril enjoys good health and has bought a property in Toronto. Johnny opined that Emeril might visit next summer. Now, shoo."

A visit next summer was a platitude all sons sent home from the distant corners of the empire. For now, Johnny's visit was disruption enough, or opportunity enough.

Edna fired off a final salvo. "Charles says Mrs. Roberts hasn't exactly been a saint. He knows of what he speaks, my lord."

"Because he hasn't been a saint either, but Mrs. Roberts can at least plead the temporary derangement of grief. *Go away*, Edna."

Edna curtseyed and withdrew, while Uncle Nunn dabbed jam on his toast.

Portia and Flavia, who had doubtless been up playing whist nearly until cockcrow, would remain abed for some time. She loaded a tray from the sideboard in the breakfast parlor and took her repast to the family parlor, where she was guaranteed the privacy necessary for serious thinking.

Every marquess's heir required the guidance and companionship of a well-born spouse, and Lord Phillip wouldn't be too choosy about settlements, given his own modest circumstances.

Mr. Gavin DeWitt, who was a mere two generations removed from the shop and possessed of a respectable fortune, also needed a well-born helpmeet. Matchmaking was a delicate art, and for all Hecate's unseemly skill with investing, that art was lost upon her.

Considerable planning and thought were necessary if Portia and Flavia were each to snabble the best bachelor for their temperaments and interests. Edna took out a sheet of foolscap and wrote two names across the top: Vincent and DeWitt.

Down the side, she began labeling rows: wealth, connections, appearance, property, health, accomplishments... all the characteristics that truly mattered. And if either bachelor proved unreceptive to his good fortune, then the unappreciated daughter might perhaps console herself with a suit from Cousin Johnny.

Though Johnny had always been sweet on Hecate.

Ah well, young men were prone to foolish fancies, and Hecate had chosen years ago to take up a dim and dusty corner of the spinster's shelf.

CHAPTER SIX

Phillip had done quick justice to the offerings in the breakfast parlor shortly after dawn and taken himself for a ramble in the sprawling wood and out across the pastures. Herne deserved a day of rest, while Phillip needed to move.

The birdsong soothed his soul, as did the scent of greenery, the blooming columbine and foxglove, and the particular shimmer of morning sunlight on a stand of white birches.

Nunnsuch was a lovely property, but neglect was evident on every hand. The bridle paths were overgrown, the hedgerows sprawling, the drainage ditches clogged with bracken, the pastures either too lush or overgrazed.

Phillip emerged from a bridle path into an overgrown hayfield and spotted a farm wagon unloading a crew with scythes and forks thirty yards off. Damned late in the season for haying, but then, rain, windstorms, ailing draft teams... Any number of factors interfered with a farmer's best-laid plans.

"Greetings," Phillip called, approaching the wagon. "Fine morning to see to the scything."

A stocky older fellow doffed a battered cap. "'Tis that, sir. Lads and lasses, get cracking."

A dozen young people—men and women, a few gangly adolescents, and one lady far gone with child—descended from the wagon and took up the long-handled, curved scythes used to cut tall grasses for haying.

"I know what you're thinking, good sir," the older fellow said. "We've left it nigh too late, and I agree, but himself wanted the teams for repairing his ha-has, and what himself wants is what happens. Henry Wortham, give me your whetstone."

A strapping, tow-headed lad with the shoulders of a stevedore shuffled over and produced a stone from his pocket. "I sharpened the first batch," he said.

"Then I'll work on the second batch while ye cut yonder field. Sooner begun is sooner done."

"Aye, Mr. Travers." Henry rolled his eyes, nodded to Phillip, and strolled off, his scythe casually resting across his shoulders. The other workers were ranging themselves along one side of the field at intervals of about twelve feet.

"Who is the young mother?" Phillip asked.

"Mavis Riley. Lost her fella to the influenza over the winter. Himself hasn't turned her out, but she hasn't a farthing to her name."

Phillip unbuttoned his jacket and then his waistcoat. "I can swing a scythe. Put her to sharpening the next batch of blades. Before too long, that sun will be fierce, and her time isn't far off."

"But, sir, I cannot allow a gentleman, a guest of the manor—"

Phillip took off his top hat and shoved it at the foreman, along with his jacket and waistcoat. "Try to stop me." He added his cravat to the pile—gracious angels, did it feel good to get rid of that thing—and strode off in Mrs. Riley's direction.

The crew proceeded by halves, with every other worker stepping forth to swing a blade in a slow, sweeping rhythm. When the first cohort had gained a few yards of progress, the second half of the crew would start on the spaces between them. The pattern minimized the likelihood that a tuft of grass would be missed, or that a trouser, skirt, or ankle would be inadvertently sliced.

Phillip approached Mrs. Riley, who waited with the second half of the crew. "Good morning, ma'am. Mr. Travers has asked that you take on the blade sharpening."

Blue eyes looked Phillip up and down. She was pretty, blond, and clearly determined to earn her day's pay.

"I can keep up," she said. "Been scything since I was a girl. My granny and dam scythed, and I know what I'm about."

Most haying crews included women wielding blades. The heavier work—forking the hay into wagons and ricks once dried— usually fell to the men.

"You are doubtless an expert, while I am a dabbler," Phillip said. "Humor me. Please."

She took off her straw hat, plopped it on Phillip's head, and muttered something about daft gents out from Town. Her gait had acquired the seafaring roll of a woman burdened by approaching motherhood, and yet, she managed to stomp away.

"Let's have a song!" Phillip called, taking up the scythe. "Henry, give us a tune!"

Young Henry was blessed with a fine baritone, and he chose well. Scything was best done at a relaxed pace, letting the natural swing of the blade do the work. Not a skill learned quickly, and one acquired at the cost of many blisters and aching muscles.

And yet, Phillip had known two brothers in their eighties who could wield a scythe all day next to their great-grandsons and great-granddaughters.

The work felt good, as did the heat, the sense of accomplishment, the pause at the end of the row for a pull from a flask. Mrs. Riley brought him a canteen, and Phillip half drained it at one go.

"Don't fall behind," she said, snatching her canteen back. "Ye'll rush to catch up and make a hash of your patch."

"Aye, ma'am." Hecate would like Mrs. Riley. Phillip took up his scythe and joined in the next song.

By the time the field was half done, he'd removed his shirt, as had every other fellow on the crew, and a second wagon had pulled up, this one bearing the nooning and a small keg.

"Who be ye?" Mr. Travers asked when Phillip had downed his first tankard of fine summer ale. "Ye know what you're about with that blade, and the other lads are bound a gent from Town won't show them up."

"Phillip Vincent. I have a small property up in Berkshire. I'm a guest at Nunnsuch. You'll see that Mrs. Riley is given appropriate compensation?"

"If that's your pleasure." Travers sipped his ale. "Berkshire folk go scything for a lark, do they? Have a taste for blisters on your hands and chaff on your neck?"

"I'm a farmer. I have a taste for getting the crops in and ensuring my livestock have enough fodder for winter. How far behind is Nunnsuch with the haying generally?"

"We got about half done when himself says his ha-has must be tended to. That were over a week ago. Damned foolishness, and if we don't get rain before the end of this day, my name is not Hiram Hercules Travers."

"No rain today," Phillip said. "My shoulder tells me when a storm approaches. You'll get this field in."

"Nah," Travers said. "We'll get it cut and possibly raked, and then it'll be soaked through. Himself will tell us to gather it up anyway, and we'll spend the next six months waiting for the wet rick to catch fire. Happens about every third year. We place bets down at the Pig and Pony with half the proceeds going to the ladies' charitable fund. Steward tries to reason with Nunn, but there's no reasoning with one of the anointed. Henry, lad, go easy on that ale. It'll kick you in the head come sundown if you keep at it like that."

"I'm thirsty," Henry said with the mulish logic of the young and vigorous.

"Mrs. Riley!" Phillip called. "Might you offer Henry some water?"

She gave Henry a look that spoke volumes, about stubborn men, foolish displays of pride, and a fine pair of shoulders worthy of some grudging appreciation. She passed him a full dipper of water drawn from a pot on the wagon bed.

"That's from the spring. It'll be cold. Mind you don't gulp."

Henry grinned—and gulped. "Thanks, Mavie."

"Mrs. Riley to you, Henry Wortham." She stalked off with her dipper and waterpot, offering a drink first to the other women on the crew.

Travers watched this interaction with a faint smile. "We'll none of us have much starch by the end of the day, save for Mavis. You never met a more stubborn lass. Shame about her husband. He were a good lad and worshipped his missus. Didn't leave her much, though."

Travers's tone implied that stubbornness was a fine quality in a woman, and Phillip agreed.

"If the haying is behind," Phillip said, "what about planting and harvest? Does Lord Nunn interfere with them as well?"

"Planting usually sees him larking about in Town, thank God, and the steward does his best with harvest. Even an earl can see when fruit's ripe in the orchards. Himself isn't a bad sort—pays a fair wage, does his bit with the Christmas baskets—but he's a *lord*."

Meaning the tasks Hecate could reach—the Boxing Day baskets, the wage book—were in good order. "And the woods?"

Travers cast an eye over his shoulder. "I'm not a woodsman, but my cousin is the ranger for a family in Surrey. Says Nunn's woods are a mess. Hedgerows just as bad. Those oaks will take over a field in twenty years flat, but himself must have his shady bridle paths."

"Do you run the hogs down those bridle paths in autumn and winter to clean up the acorns?"

"You'd have to talk to Silas Grove about that. He manages the home farm. Have you had enough of playing farmer, Mr. Vincent?"

The form of address jarred. For all of his life, Phillip had been Master Phillip, Master Heyward, Mr. Heyward, Young Heyward... then, recently, Lord Phillip. The Vincent part, the part that bound him to Tavistock and the whole peerage... He'd be a long time adjusting to that.

Phillip had already had enough of playing lordling. This morning of honest work had proved that, if nothing else.

"If I leave, Mrs. Riley will take up her scythe, won't she?"

"She'll take it up tomorrow if she doesn't take it up today. She's good with a blade. Steady and even. Not like the lads who try to storm through a field."

But to wield that blade this late into pregnancy had to take a toll on a woman's back. "I'll return tomorrow morning," Phillip said. "I'd take it as a favor if you'd keep her sharpening blades for the first few passes after nooning."

"Aye, and we'll send her back to the spring to give the horses a drink and refill the waterpot. Mavie can handle the reins as competently as she does the scythe and the lads. A proper Hampshire lass, that one. If I were ten years younger..." Travers's gaze landed on something behind Phillip. "Here now, look sharp. We've company from the manor house."

Those men without their shirts were putting them on, and the ladies had risen from blankets spread in the shade.

Phillip turned to see Gavin DeWitt at the reins of a dog cart, Hecate Brompton seated beside him.

"I see we're late," Hecate said. "And I'd hoped last night's leftover tarts wouldn't go to waste. Mr. Travers, good day."

She looked so pretty perched beside DeWitt on the bench, a straw hat tied in a fetching lopsided bow beneath her chin. She had seen Phillip—he was sure of that—and recognized him and was for some reason avoiding—

Where the hell is my shirt? The thought erupted in his mind like flames exploding from a rotten hayrick.

Mavis Riley flapped a voluminous quantity of white linen several times, then folded it neatly over her arm and brought it to Phillip at the slowest walk she'd evidenced for the entire morning.

"Your shirt, Mr. Vincent."

DeWitt had stepped down from the gig and was assisting Hecate to alight while Phillip shrugged into his shirt. The buttons were beyond him. Coherent speech was behind him, while DeWitt was grinning hugely.

"You brought tarts, Miss Brompton?" Henry Wortham asked. "I do fancy a tart." One of the other young men chuckled at Henry's word choice, and Henry's ears turned red.

"So do I," Mavis Riley said, "and I'm sure Miss Brompton brought along a few sandwiches and possibly a cake or two. Ladies, if you'd bestir yourselves?"

The next few minutes were absorbed with serving a second luncheon and gave Phillip time to do up some buttons and get his waistcoat on.

"If you don that jacket in this heat," Mavis Riley muttered as she passed him a piece of lemon cake, "I'll know you're dicked in the nob. And don't think to put on the neckcloth either."

"But a gentleman doesn't appear before a lady in his underpinnings." Much less naked from the waist up, God help him.

"A gentleman should not be too quick to deprive a lady of a chance to appreciate God's handiwork. Bring her a glass of cider before that other strutting nitwit can think to do it."

"Yes, ma'am." Phillip took the glass Mavis shoved into his hand, thanked heaven for proper Hampshire lasses, and made his way to the back of the gig, where Hecate was handing the last tray of tarts to one of the women.

"You've been hiding all morning here in the hayfield," she said. "Is that for me?"

Phillip passed over the glass. "Go slowly. Might have a kick." He waited for a lecture on proper attire, on gentlemanly pastimes, on fraternizing with the locals... He'd truly erred and deserved a dressing down for indulging in a morning of hard work.

"Travers says you inspired his crew to get twice as much done in half a day."

That was the initial flattery intended to soften a series of blows.

A scold would follow, and Phillip would bear up like the gentleman he longed to be when Hecate Brompton was on hand.

"Mrs. Riley is nearing her time," he said. "She was prepared to do the same work as young Henry there, but probably for half the coin Henry will earn. She'll have my wages instead."

Hecate's gaze went to Mavis, who rested one hand on the small of her back and the other on Henry's arm. Henry seemed to stand a little taller with Mavis beside him.

"Kind of you," Hecate said. "You've eaten?"

Had he? Phillip fumbled for words because he'd only that moment noticed that Hecate Brompton had a pale sprinkling of freckles across her cheeks. Faint and few, but present all the same.

"A meat pie," he said. "I'm sure I had a meat pie."

Hecate sent him a quizzical look. "Will you bide here for the rest of the day?"

"Will you tell me that's *not done?* That a gentleman would never? That I'm a hopeless philistine because I'd rather scythe hay than gossip away a fine summer morning?" If so, perhaps he could be finished with this house party, but that prospect didn't hold as much relief as it ought to. Not when Hecate would be disappointed in him.

"I will tell you," Hecate replied, "that Great-Uncle Nunn's estate management has been driving me to bad language for years and that your insights would be much appreciated." She took a sip of her cider, then passed him the drink. "I will also tell you that a gentleman does not offer a lady—or anybody else—falsehoods."

Phillip was too hot and thirsty to refuse a drink, and the cider was ambrosial. "I avoid dishonesty generally, except in the interests of kindness."

"You told me a very great bouncer, my lord." She batted gently at his hair, then took back the drink. "You claimed your shoulder is defective, that you are deformed. I have firsthand evidence, the evidence of my own eyes, to refute your statement. Your manly figure has no flaws *whatsoever.* I will expect you at three of the clock to join me and Mr. DeWitt on a tour of the gallery and public rooms."

She flounced off on a whiff of roses and joined the ladies munching lemon cake on their blankets in the shade.

"You'll be wanting this," Gavin DeWitt said, thrusting Phillip's coat at him.

How much of that exchange had DeWitt overheard, and did Phillip care in the slightest? Upon consideration, no, he did not.

"You have crumbs on your cravat, De-Nitwit, and I do not want my jacket. In this heat, wearing a jacket makes no sense, and you should probably get rid of yours."

DeWitt brushed at the lace frothing beneath his chin. "Whyever would I commit such an unpardonable breach of manners?"

"Because we have work to do, and we aren't expected in the gallery until three of the clock. Travers!" Phillip called. "We'll need another scythe."

Phillip peeled out of his waistcoat and rolled up his sleeves, then picked up his blade and started on a song. He was the first one back to work, though Henry joined him in less than two minutes.

～

Hecate checked her appearance in the mirror one more time and noted that her annual summer crop of freckles was threatening to emerge, drat the luck.

On the heels of that thought came another: Lord Phillip would not care one whit about a few freckles. He would, by contrast, regard nightly facial scrubs with a raw potato, avoiding the out of doors, and wearing veils in the hottest weather as so much ridiculousness.

"No potato scrubs," Hecate informed her reflection. "Not this year."

She made her way to the gallery and found her quarry in earnest contemplation of a portrait of the present Lord Nunn as a young man.

"Miss Brompton, greetings." Lord Phillip bowed politely. "He wasn't always such a prig, was he?"

"My mother could make him laugh." The artist had captured a hint of humor in Nunn's blue eyes. He'd been lean, blond, and aristocratically splendid in the lavish finery of an earlier time. The younger Lord Nunn posed with one hand fisted on his hip, the other resting on the head of an adoring hound. A lady's portrait was hinted at in the background.

"This is the late countess," Hecate said, moving on to the next painting, which had been hung such that Lord and Lady Nunn seemed to perpetually gaze toward each other. "A love match, according to my mother, but no sons survived long enough to carry on the line."

"Hence Charles's good fortune. He's a rackety fribble, isn't he?"

Lord Phillip had bathed. His hair was neatly queued back, and his attire was free of dust, chaff, and even wrinkles. He was also no longer sporting a grin, airing a fine baritone, or wielding a scythe while half naked beneath the summer sun.

More's the pity.

The muscles of his back, chest, and arms would make the Apollo Belvedere moan with envy. Mavis Riley, a grieving widow who'd been devoted to her husband, had followed Lord Phillip's progress with a wistful hint of smile. Henry Wortham, the blacksmith's oldest son, was taller and brawnier, but not as mesmerizing to watch at his work.

"What became of your mother?" Lord Phillip asked, studying the late countess's rings.

"A wasting disease, and yet, she was a happy woman most of the time."

"Was she a happy wife?"

A voice in Hecate's head told her to chide Lord Phillip for such a forward question, but they were not at some duchess's ridotto, where a dozen ears would overhear. Then too, nobody ever mentioned Mama.

"She tried to be a happy wife. Papa is not warmhearted by nature, though he can be very charming when he wants something. He and

Uncle Nunn are opposite sides of an ill-humored coin. Uncle Nunn is bereaved and without children, so his discontent with life is understandable. Papa married Mama for her money and lost interest when she, too, was unable to produce sons."

"Is that why she took up with your true father?" Lord Phillip asked, moving on to the first Baron Nunnville.

Ancestors organized by date marched along the inside wall, and Hecate had seen them all hundreds of times. Men, mostly, with a nod to the occasional viscountess or countess. The baronesses hadn't signified.

"Where is Mr. DeWitt, my lord?"

"I bring you his regrets. He felt the need for some activity after being shut up in the coach all day yesterday. He took my place on the haying crew and asks that you reserve another day for his tour."

"Let's sit, then, shall we? You had a busy morning."

"And if the weather is obliging, I will indulge myself similarly tomorrow and the day after, until Travers waves me off. Nunnsuch is going ragged around the edges."

He was understating the matter. Uncle Nunn's steward had likely served an apprenticeship to Noah upon the landing of the ark and had long since given up on arguing with the earl. Mr. Jamison was a Bristol man by birth and spent as much time as possible with his family on the coast.

"One suspected the estate was in need of a steadying hand," Hecate said, "but that hand cannot be mine. I have hopes that Mrs. Roberts might sidle into a more active role—she is nobody's fool—but she's doubtless reluctant to take on Edna, Charles, and the rest of them."

"Then tell her to take on the hedgerows," Phillip said. "They've spread, as hedgerows will do, and up to a point, that's a fine thing for the birds and bunnies, but as the branches cast more and more shade, the adjoining arable land becomes less productive. The rain can't reach the soil as easily, and what does fall is snatched up by the thicker vegetation of the hedgerows.

"The tallest of the oaks should come down," he went on, "and something shorter planted, if Nunn must have his shady bridle paths. And as to that, the hogs can tidy up many an acorn and save the woodsman the bother of thinning saplings."

"Hogs?"

"Pigs, swine. They can't have a steady diet of acorns, and one doesn't feed acorns to the young stock, but the larger specimens can and should be permitted their autumn pannage through the hedges and forests. Spares the cows and horses from snacking on a treat they ought not to have."

Hecate did not want to discuss pigs or pannage, whatever that was. She wasn't all that keen on introducing Lord Phillip to the ancestors either, truth be known. She unlatched a set of French doors and stepped out onto the balcony that ran the width of the gallery.

"Pretty view," Phillip said, joining her. "One can say that for Nunn's lackadaisical husbandry. His overgrown woods and park make a pleasing vista. I am comforted by big, healthy trees. If the land can grow such as that, then my sheep and corn are likely well situated too."

"Your insights are appreciated, but I do not want to discuss the earl's trees at the moment."

"Do you want to lecture me?" The wretch sounded hopeful.

The breeze teased his dark locks, and the afternoon sun garnished it with dancing highlights. Hecate had touched that silky hair on the pretext of whisking the chaff from it, and no handy glass of punch had been available to blame for her forwardness.

Nor could she blame the punch for her current thoughts. She shaded her eyes against the sunshine and pretended to study the arched bridge in the distance.

"I want to kiss you."

Lord Phillip led her to a bench that faced out over the rolling treetops. To the left, the garden stretched in tidy parterres, but this wing of the house did not face the busier view. The park, the home wood, the stone bridge, the roof of the distant stable-cum-carriage house stretched beneath them.

"Is this urge to sample my charms distasteful to you, Miss Brompton?"

"Distasteful? Why would...?"

He gestured for Hecate to take a seat, but did not offer his hand and did not take the place beside her.

She looked up at him—he was quite tall—and tried to fathom his thoughts. "I tried frolicking," she said. "Years ago. When I'd made my bargain with Papa and realized that perpetual spinsterhood could be dull. Frolicking can be dull, too, a lowering discovery." *Why won't you sit beside me?*

"Mindless, you mean? Shallow and trivial? For some, that is part of its charm. A passing pleasure without weight or worry."

"For you?" She patted the place beside her, and he appeared to ignore the invitation.

"For me, a bit complicated. In Crosspatch Corners, I was known as Mr. Phillip Heyward, a shy, somewhat backward, bookish, squire-ish sort of fellow. I was good at foaling, lambing, and calving and up to date on the latest pamphlets, but too retiring to attend the local assemblies. Some of the older folk knew my specific antecedents, or guessed them accurately, but I was generally believed to be some nob's by-blow."

"Did you believe that of yourself?"

"I knew the truth. My nanny, my mother—who visited me occasionally—and the household staff made certain I knew my own patrimony. Explaining the details to a young lady upon whom I had matrimonial designs would have been awkward, and yet, a fellow gets... lonely."

She believed he meant that. Meant that he had been *lonely* for closeness and affection, for a cuddle and a romp, not merely for the romp itself.

"Spinsters get lonely, too, or some of us do. Why won't you sit beside me, Phillip?"

"Because if I sit beside you, I will take your hand. If I take your hand, I will want to stroke your fingers and kiss your palm and catch a whiff of the particular spot on your wrist where you casually dab a drop of scent when you are dressing for the day. If such liberties are permitted, I will want to kiss your mouth, Hecate Brompton, and then I will want to do more than kiss you."

He might have been discoursing on his preferred method of crop rotation as he stood at the railing, gaze on puffy summer clouds drifting across a blue sky.

Hecate rose and took his hand. "I have seen men unclothed, though my family would never believe me capable of such a lapse of propriety. If one is discreet, one can bend many rules. They were simply men without clothing, and pleased to be so. This morning..."

He brought her fingers to his lips. "Yes?"

"You were so joyous. You exuded such vitality and exuberance. To wield that scythe, to join in the songs, to sweat and toil and labor for a worthy goal... I was captivated by your jubilation. Exhilarated vicariously." She rested her head against his shoulder, as if the recitation had exhausted her as much as haying could exhaust a fit, grown man.

"I heard the dog cart clattering up from behind me," Phillip said, squeezing her fingers, "and I expected the vicar had come to bless the blades, or something equally innocuous. I turned, and there you were, but not as I'd seen you in London. You wore a straw hat with a ribbon that perfectly matches your eyes, and the bow was crooked, and the ends of the ribbons trailed so fetchingly. You eschewed your usual proper, mincing steps and marched about, skirts swinging, and that was fetching too. You have freckles. I noticed that you have freckles, and I adore your freckles. Somebody should kiss those freckles, and that somebody, I pray God, should be me."

His arms came around her gently, and Hecate stood for a moment, reveling in a wonder that felt as mutual as any kiss. *More* mutual for being unlooked for and unhoped for.

"My mother was trying to conceive a son," Hecate said. "She told me that, but she said instead she got the best possible gift in me, and in my father's love. He was a sea captain, handsome, generous, kind, and he knew exactly what she was about and loved her anyway. I've never met him, but I want you to know my provenance."

"Then your provenance is a loving, honest union, and nobody should ask for more than that." He kissed her forehead again, a request for assurances, and Hecate kissed his cheek. Her arms slipped around his waist, and she rested against him as the urge to cry and the need to laugh waltzed in her heart.

Phillip stroked her hair and her shoulders. His thumb brushed lazy circles over her nape, and Hecate felt like a cat who'd found a warm patch of sunlight in deepest midwinter. She held very still, every particle attuned to Phillip's touch. She breathed with him. She memorized the scent of him this close—lavender, a hint of starch, and meadow grass.

The rhythm of his heart matched the slow, graceful sweep of the curved blade that had so enthralled Hecate earlier, and when Phillip cupped her cheek and brushed his lips against hers, she fell into his kisses as gently as scythed grass came to rest upon the earth.

CHAPTER SEVEN

"If they aren't out riding, and they aren't in the library, and they aren't strolling the garden," Portia asked, "where could they have got off to?" She'd been worrying that question for the better part of an hour, and she was growing both hot and cross.

"This is so like a pair of eligible bachelors," Flavia groused, marching at her side. "To be invited to a lovely house party full of congenial and attractive company and then to simply disappear. I had thought better of Mr. DeWitt. Truly, I had."

"Lord Phillip is a marquess's brother and heir," Portia fumed as the arched bridge came into view. "He ought to be more *au fait* regarding such matters. I love you dearly, Flave, but a handsome, masculine escort on this little constitutional would have been ever so agreeable."

"One takes your point, sister dearest, and my slippers will be ruined for all this trekking through the wilds. I wore my favorite pair for everyday too."

Flavia's favorite pair bore a suspicious resemblance to Mama's favorite pair. Darling Flavia was prone to creatively borrowing whatever caught her eye, but she'd better not think to borrow Lord Phillip.

"Unconscionable rogues," Portia grumbled, "to force us to hike over hill and dale in pursuit. This is what comes from Mama allowing Hecate to make up the guest list. Poor Hecate's on the shelf, as is known to all, and she can hardly—ouch!"

Flavia had stopped halfway across the bridge and smacked Portia in the ribs. "Give me your field glasses, Portia."

"Why?" As soon as Portia posed the question, she caught sight of the figures on the distant gallery balcony. A man and a woman, both bare-headed. The fellow was tall, while the lady...

"Is that *Hecate*?" Portia whispered, using her field glasses to confirm the unthinkable. "That is Hecate, and she is in a most inappropriate embrace with a man."

Flavia snatched the field glasses. "With Lord Phillip Vincent. I don't know whether to be appalled at his poor taste or aghast at her lack of decorum."

"They don't appear to be kissing."

"They are kissing now."

Portia snatched back her field glasses and halfway wished she hadn't. Lord Phillip was a leisurely kisser, and before her very eyes, Hecate Brompton, pattern card of probity, pence, and quid, became a siren in his arms. She kissed him back with the same sumptuous languor, her hands trailing over his broad shoulders and long back.

"We ought not to be watching," Flavia said, gaze riveted on the balcony. "This is private."

"This is a disaster. Hecate is working her wiles on the unsuspecting, Flave. How dare she?"

"Hecate hasn't any wiles, and Lord Phillip knows what he's about."

Did he *ever*. His hand glossed gently down Hecate's back, inviting her closer without exerting a hint of force.

"Hecate knows what she's about too," Portia said, feeling a sense of bitter, bitter betrayal. "She's her mother's daughter. Mama says so at least once a week."

"Mama says a lot of things. Nobody has ever kissed me like that."

Me either. Portia remained silent rather than risk sounding as forlorn as Flavia had. The kissing went on, interspersed with long moments of quiet embracing. Lord Phillip kissed Hecate's fingers—drat him to the devil and back—and murmured something into her ear.

She nodded, and they passed into the gallery, arms around each other's waists.

"We were not supposed to see that," Flavia said. "Hecate must be top over tail for his lordship to so far forget herself."

"Hecate does not fall top over tail. Not for his lordship. Not for any man. She's been enthralled with her ledgers ever since Cousin Johnny broke her heart."

"According to Mama." A hint of disloyalty colored Flavia's observation as she left the bridge for the path through the park. "Mama is all but cooing at Mr. DeGrange. We have been out for two Seasons, Portia, and Mama has failed to secure so much as a request to court either one of us. I fear she's decided to pursue her own interests at our expense."

"Mama wouldn't." Portia trailed behind Flavia, still much preoccupied with that business on the balcony. "Hecate never forgets herself. She must be toying with Lord Phillip's affections. He's been ruralizing for ages and isn't accustomed to polite society's ways."

"But you said he's a marquess's brother and ought to—"

Portia caught up with her sister. "I know what I said, but since when has Hecate ever taken notice of a fellow? Lord Phillip must be richer than Mama knows, Flave. Hecate must be after his money." This theory made sense, given what Portia knew of Hecate and of Mama's imperfect intelligence-gathering abilities. Mama was losing her touch, alas, and Eglantine was no help whatsoever, while Charles was utterly useless.

Portia and Flavia were on their own, and Portia forgot that at her peril.

"Lord Phillip is certainly well turned out," Flavia allowed. "He doesn't cut nearly the dash Mr. DeWitt does, and Mr. DeWitt is *known* to be wealthy, but you might have a point about Hecate's motivations. Given her unfortunate antecedents, one must make allowances."

Flavia's signal virtue was her loyalty. As younger sisters went, she wasn't that clever, and she often said the first thing to pop into her head, but she was unswervingly loyal.

"We must do something, Flave. Lord Phillip is new to Society, a lamb to be shorn by the first scheming spinster to whip out her shears. Hecate could have had no other purpose for putting his lordship on the guest list besides getting her hooks into him before the matchmakers have a go."

"Unsporting of her, and there's his lordship with all that money."

"Thousands of acres of prime Berkshire land too," Portia observed, for surely a marquess's brother would have a largish estate. "And not bad-looking."

"Mr. DeWitt is the handsomer of the two."

"Where is Mr. DeWitt?"

Flavia stopped at the foot of the garden. "Where is Mrs. Roberts?"

Portia voiced a more intriguing possibility. "Where is Eglantine?"

"Porry, no!" Flavia sank onto the steps that led up to the formal parterres. "Eglantine is devoted to Charles. Dotes on him. Adores him for his Gallant Sacrifice."

Portia would not risk getting her skirts dirty by taking an undignified seat on the steps, but neither would she allow Flavia to deceive herself about a real possibility.

"Charles got his mitts on a considerable fortune when he married his Eggy, Flave. The fortune is gone in less than ten years. She might resent that, and she has presented Charles with an heir and spare, despite the heir's lineage being somewhat irregular."

"In true aristocratic fashion, though."

"In true aristocratic fashion. We also know Charles has a wandering eye."

"A wandering pizzle, you mean. He's a hound, Porry. If he wasn't in line for the earldom, hostesses wouldn't bother with him."

Portia began to pace as her theory acquired supporting principles and corollaries. "Yes, they would, because he is a witty and charming hound. All the male cousins know how to open doors, including bedroom doors. They dance well, and they are handsome."

"We dance well and are very pretty."

"Just so, but if Eglantine has grown tired of Charles's philandering, then she might embark on a little adventure of her own."

"To make him jealous?"

"And to pass the time, now that the heir and spare are in the nursery. And there's Mr. DeWitt, all handsome and friendly and immediately to hand. One could not blame her for indulging in a private moment or two."

Flavia rose and shook out her skirts. "Yes, one could. Let's find Eglantine if we can't find Mr. DeWitt. We need her expert opinion on dresses for tonight's supper."

"You find her," Portia said, opening the garden gate. "All this hiking about has left me with aching feet. I will search for Mama."

"Will you tell her that Hecate has accosted Lord Phillip in a most shocking manner?"

Portia considered strategy and options. "I think we'd best keep Lord Phillip's foolishness to ourselves, Flave, for the sake of his dignity. Then too, if Mama gets her oar in, she might inform Hecate that we are on to her scheme. I'd prefer to handle matters without Mama's flair for complications."

Flavia trailed a hand along the lavender border. "I don't think it's supposed to be this hard, Porry. I think we are supposed to make our curtsey at court, stand up with dozens of handsome eligibles who are charmed by our many accomplishments, and then we have three offers by the end of our first Season. Maybe we're doing something wrong."

Flavia was so sentimental. "Letting Lord Phillip and Mr. DeWitt out of our sight was wrong. Older ladies lose all sense of decorum, and Eglantine and Hecate are both getting on."

Flavia's gaze was on the balcony running along the back of the gallery wing. "I don't think that's the problem. Why can Mama disport with all the rogues she pleases, but Hecate's mother did likewise, and it was an endless family scandal? Doesn't seem fair, Porry."

"Mama had Charles, and that makes all the difference. Go find Eggy. I'll tell Mama we've enjoyed our constitutional very much."

"Tell her we won sixpence at whist."

They'd cheated, of course. An elaborate series of signals—a twist to a ring, a finger tapped on the table—made plain what cards were held by a partnering sister. Needs must, and even sixpence could bribe a maid or footman.

"I will make sure she knows. Away with you."

Flavia grabbed Portia in a hug, then scampered off, intent on thwarting Eglantine's wayward overtures.

Eggy would never cheat on Charles, of course, but Portia had a marquess's heir to accost, and for that delicate undertaking, she had no need of Flavia's assistance.

~

Hecate prattled on about whose dowery had brought how much acreage, or what architect had been hired by which earl. Phillip let the words course around him as a boulder in a stream was bathed and more firmly anchored by the flowing water.

He settled into the joy of her scent, her hand on his arm, the lush pleasure of her breast pressed momentarily to his biceps when she leaned over to rub her thumb over a dusty signature.

"You are clearly not of the same ilk as these Bromptons," Phillip said when they'd toured the lot. No portrait of Hecate or her mother had been included, though her Brompton father had been immortalized as a dashing young blade.

"Why do you say that? They aren't all blond. Some of them are a bit more generously rounded."

The defensive note was well hidden between proper elocution and feminine dignity, but Phillip heard it.

"That one,"—he gestured down the room—"married four times and inherited a fortune from each wife. The only way wives three and four could have been talked into accepting his proposal is if he'd been a charming bounder."

"He was."

"That one,"—Phillip nodded at a be-ruffed fellow across the room —"had thirteen bastards with twelve women. Was he trying to out-fornicate Charles II? This old rip,"—he indicated the present earl's grandfather—"played Jacobite skittles with the title, selling guns to all comers and somehow avoiding accusations of treason. You describe a true rogue's gallery. A regiment of selfish ne'er-do-wells dressed up as peers. Their fellow aristocrats might consider them shrewd, lucky, or colorful, but to you, they are more than a little embarrassing."

Hecate leaned closer, a sort of arm-hug. "Nary a gentleman in the lot, which raises the present earl in my estimation. He's a decent fellow, for all he's impressed with his own consequence."

"Consequence does not bring in the hay before the rain comes down."

"You know you cannot say such things in Mayfair?" Hecate peered up at him with real concern. "They will mimic your words, your walk, your mannerisms. The average formal ball can become nastier than any schoolyard."

Phillip wanted to take her into his arms, to whisper to her that she'd never have to endure the taunting and insults again, but at any moment, Gavin DeWitt, the earl, or one of the magpies might charge through the doors.

"You had nobody," he said. "You made your come out without a single ally. I'm sorry for that. Take us somewhere we can talk."

"I should be checking on the kitchen. We're having an informal supper tonight, and that's a bit more complicated than a buffet."

Even an informal supper would not be laid for another three hours. "Give me one hour, Hecate. I promise I will maunder on about marling and fall calves and all manner of riveting topics that you can use to your advantage with Nunn's stewards."

He simply wanted to be with her. To revel in the knowledge that she'd welcomed his kisses and—his elation touched the heavens—kissed him back. Held him, caressed and petted and damned near cuddled up to him.

Hecate dropped his arm. "I feel as if I've had too much punch," she said, "and I need time for the spirits to wear off before I can face the dance floor."

"Precisely. Inebriated, awash in bliss and hope. If I promise not to kiss you again, will you spare me a little more of your time?"

Hecate was incapable of rudeness, but she could make a point. She let her gaze rove boldly over Phillip's person, with a lingering focus on his mouth.

"I want to be very foolish with you, Phillip. Very foolish."

"I want to be brave with you," Phillip countered. "To lay my dreams and aspirations at your feet and hear what you think of them. I want to keep my hand in yours, to sit too close to you, to hear what longings you've never shared with another."

"The recitation would be brief and boring." She moved toward the door, and Phillip let her go.

The entire Brompton family crowded her, put demands on her, took her for granted, and relied on her. He would not add to her burdens.

"The recitation of your hopes and dreams would be precious and surprising," Phillip said. "You'd like to take Nunnsuch in hand, I'm guessing, but keeping your cousins out of debtors' prison and free of scandal is an ongoing battle that leaves you no time or energy for farming."

Hecate paused to straighten a portrait of the fourth countess. "The Brompton cousins and in-laws are legion, all pockets to let and all convinced of their own cleverness. I fear Eglantine will soon develop a wandering eye, and Charles could so easily be blackmailed over his numerous dalliances. It's a wonder I'm not blackmailing him, except I myself would have to pay any sum I attempted to extort from him."

"Charles's mother doesn't wander," Phillip said. "She mounts an armed charge into forbidden territory, and those daughters of hers..."

Hecate nodded. "Charles says the betting books mention Portia and Flavia: Which one will misstep first and with whom? Will it be somebody else's spouse? A known rake? A charming roué? Edna made an effort the year they came out and again this year, but Edna has a taste for slippers and parasols that would beggar the national exchequer."

Hecate closed the distance between them and looped her arms around him. "Those two think they are so sophisticated, so worldly, but they have no idea the havoc a man with indecent objectives can wreak on a young lady's plans."

Phillip's ideas were not indecent. They were tender and wonderful and erotic, but never indecent.

"You worry," he said, stroking her hair. How lovely simply to hold her. "You worry endlessly, and they resent you, and I promise you, Hecate Brompton, they do not deserve you."

She relaxed against him. "Tell them that. Please. They have it in their heads that because my mother's husband didn't set her and me aside, I am eternally in their debt."

"They would say that, when the boot is so clearly on the other foot, but you are not orphaned, sixteen, and ignorant of the world. They know that, too, and it drives them barmy."

Hecate pulled back far enough to consider him. "I won't leave my family penniless on the street corner."

You might have to, if they are ever to amount to anything. "I would rather not spend our time discussing the dodgy antics of your Brompton relations." Though, in truth, not a drop of Brompton blood ran in Hecate's veins. "I would rather be strolling the woods with you, riding the bridle paths, or reading you poetry on some shady stream bank."

She took his hand. "Tell me about the hogs and the acorns, about fall calves and marling."

Phillip's heart, usually a private and quiet place, felt as if it could encompass all of the Home Counties plus half the Channel.

"You will tell me about informal suppers in the country and proper topics for breakfast conversation."

They sat, arms around each other, among all the Brompton rakes and rapscallions, and talked and talked and talked. About cousins and calves, clearing ditches and escorting debutantes. Phillip had never strung together so many words in his life, nor listened half so intently.

To Hecate's words, to her pauses and silences, to her tone, to her delicate inferences.

And all the while, they sat close enough to breathe in unison, to become as one, contented, happy creatures on an afternoon touched with the particular stillness known only to high summer.

This is courtship. The truth landed in Phillip's mind and heart at the same time, a seed falling upon rich soil. Driving in Hyde Park, waltzing beneath the chandeliers, sipping punch at Almack's had nothing whatsoever to do with courting Hecate Brompton, but listening to her, confiding in her, sharing affection with her did.

They eventually fell silent, content simply to be together, and that was courtship too.

The dressing gong sounded, and Hecate started. "Oh dear heavens, the time. The kitchen will be in chaos, when I promised Cook I'd stop by. I haven't told my maid what ensemble to lay out, and I ought to catch up with Portia and Flavia. They were playing whist very late last night. A tactic to elude supervision because they know I am an early riser."

And yet, Hecate did not leave Phillip's side.

"Put me between them at supper," he said. "They can entertain themselves at my expense. DeWitt has social stamina—an apparent necessity for young strolling players—and he's up to their weight, so stick him in their vicinity as well."

"You wouldn't mind?"

For her, Phillip was prepared to bear up manfully under even Portia's and Flavia's torments. "I would be delighted." He rose and offered his hand.

"That was very convincing," she said, rising. "I have never been very fond of the gallery. Such a lot of space to devote to what amounts to vanity."

"But we had privacy here, and time, and now we have lovely memories too." He kissed her again, because he needed the fortification—he'd agreed to take his meal flanked by the magpies—and because words were inadequate for some sentiments. "I will walk out that door, doing my best imitation of the polite squire enjoying a social gathering, but my heart will remain with you, Hecate Brompton."

She looked puzzled and a bit dazed. "A farmer poet. Until supper, my lord."

Back to my-lording. Ah, well. "Thank you for an enlightening tour of the gallery, Miss Brompton."

Hecate let go of his hand, he bowed, and by gathering every jot and tittle of his dignity, he managed to chart a straight path for the door.

"Phillip?"

He was back by her side in an instant. "Yes?"

"Tonight..." She, who could face down Wellington at his most charming and likely reduced Prinny to a blancmange, looked uncertain. "The others will resume their whist. Portia and Flavia have a system of signals, and they augment their pin money by cheating at the card table."

"While you retire early?" Was he hearing aright?

She nodded. "I thought we might talk a bit more... Take a final stroll in the garden?"

Phillip did not know precisely what her invitation entailed, but he knew what it cost her to make the offer. In what she'd said, implied, and muttered, he'd learned exactly how lonely and difficult her early years in Society had been.

"I would adore a constitutional with you beneath the summer moon. When the ladies retire to the parlor, I will excuse myself and await you on the bridge."

"I'll have to deal with the teapot."

"Pass that duty to Edna. Tell the lot of them the truth, Hecate: You will be tired and want some peace and quiet at the end of your very long day. They can manage scandal broth and tippling without you."

"You're sure?"

He took her in his arms, where she fit so well. "If you do not join me on the arched bridge, then come morning, I will still be there. As the leaves change and the harvest is brought in, I will yet bide where I've promised you I'll be. The first snowfall, the first crocus, will yet find me awaiting my love's arrival."

She sighed, kissed him soundly upon the lips, and left him concocting more farmer's poetry in the rogues' gallery.

~

The food was always better when Hecate was on hand, and Portia resented her for that bitterly. Hecate had never had her own household, and yet, she knew how to run Nunnsuch in the midst of a house party.

What spinster put herself forward like that?

Though, of course, relying on Mama to direct matters was pointless. Portia took a sip of a decent Rhenish vintage—Hecate even dealt with the wine pairings—and knew she was neglecting Mr. DeGrange, her dining companion on the left.

Difficult to listen to what Lord Phillip—on her right—was saying to Flavia and to Mr. DeWitt's conversation with Eglantine across the table if one also had to chatter to an aging bachelor. Mr. DeGrange was four-and-thirty if he was a day.

"More wine, Miss Brompton?" Lord Phillip asked.

Even though the meal was growing more informal by the moment, he really ought not to pour for her himself.

She gave the standard answer. "Just a drop. It's quite good." The idea that he was being gallant rather than flirtatious made her bilious.

"I could use a drop too," Flavia said.

Across the table, Mr. DeWitt, who was a bit too pretty for Portia's tastes, smiled at Lord Phillip in that smug way men had. That smile said, *Sweet young things ought to imbibe slowly, but what do they know?*

Because Flavia had for the moment run out of flattery to pour into Lord Phillip's ear, Portia launched the expected salvo.

"Does my lord have a favorite dance?" she inquired, batting her lashes at him over her wineglass.

"I do not, as it happens." He set the wine bottle in the middle of the table. "I have little skill on the dance floor, but I suspect the choice of partners makes a greater difference than the pattern of the steps."

Lord Phillip had apparently not encountered the waltz, though he had a point. The wrong partner turned even that romantic fancy into a tribulation.

"Cousin Johnny once said something very like that," Flavia said, nearly gulping her wine. "He was so gallant. I do miss him."

"He bides in Canada?" Lord Phillip asked, taking no more wine for himself.

"Very successfully," Flavia said. "Goes adventuring into the wilderness and is making a killing in the fur trade, but you mustn't tell anybody I was discussing commerce in polite surrounds. Truly, I was discussing dear Cousin Johnny. We miss him so."

Heaven help her, Flavia was getting tipsy—again.

"I am at a loss to understand why commerce is considered an impolite topic," Lord Phillip observed. "Commerce affects our situation every bit as much as the weather. What's a drought, but a celestial boycott from the rain clouds? What's a deluge, if not a market literally flooded? Please give us your opinion on the suitability of trade as a topic for supper discussion, Miss Portia."

Mrs. Roberts, whom Portia alternately admired and loathed, laughed at something Charles had said, and that inspired Eglantine into patting Mr. DeWitt's arm.

"So many worthy topics call for our attention in polite surrounds," Portia said. "If fashion decrees one or the other is less acceptable, why not choose from those remaining and reduce the possibility of boring or offending one's companions in conversation?"

That homily had come off splendidly, if she did say so herself. Worthy of Hecate, who was seated next to Vicar and some companion or other.

"Portia is being deep," Flavia said. "She'll bore us all to tears before the fruit and cheeses arrive."

"Miss Portia is being wise," Lord Phillip said. "Why antagonize the less tolerant when doing so will only annoy them?"

At a signal from Hecate—Mama was in earnest flirtation with some baronet—the footmen stepped forward to remove plates. Dessert came next, raspberry something or other, no doubt, and Portia nearly dashed her wine in Lord Phillip's face.

She'd waited years for him in the corridor outside the gallery, and still he'd bided with Hecate among the ancestors. Portia hadn't lurked close enough to actually eavesdrop—what could be more boring than a recitation of the House of Nunn's past?—but she'd caught the tone.

Conversational, personal, *intimate*.

Hecate's presumption, being private for eternities with the ranking male guest, the same eligible fellow she'd allowed unspeakable liberties, was not to be borne. Even now, while Lord Phillip bleated on about deluges and boycotts, he and Hecate shared the occasional glance.

Hecate didn't smile, but her gaze warmed, then shied off, and then wandered back to Lord Phillip's end of the table.

Such nonsense. Utter rot. The vilest insult, when Hecate was on the shelf and Lord Phillip needed a lively young wife to accompany him into the highest reaches of polite society—reaches Hecate, given her unfortunate antecedents—ought not to frequent.

"You've grown quiet, Miss Portia," Lord Phillip said. "Is the company less than scintillating?"

"Johnny was scintillating," Flavia all but brayed. "He could make even Hecate laugh, and that is some feat, my lord. Hecate hasn't yielded to unladylike merriment since Johnny took ship."

Lord Phillip's air of gracious courtesy acquired a hint of patience. "I'm sure you all miss him."

"Hecate misses him," Flavia said, nodding vigorously. That made her ringlets bounce, which poor Flave believed gave her a saucy, vivacious air. "She never says, but Johnny left for Canada in summer, and Hecate always goes into a decline in summer."

Hecate usually bided in Town for the summer, which was not exactly sociable of her, but neither was it a decline.

An individual serving of *crème brûlée* was placed before Portia, with the inevitable garnish of raspberries. In one of her many pedantic moods, Hecate had explained that the recipe called for a mere four ingredients and was thus exceedingly simple for the kitchen.

Portia longed to pitch her sweet at dear Hecate and pelt Lord Phillip with a few raspberries. He was supposed to flirt, not be so hopelessly correct, and he was not supposed to canoodle with Hecate in the gallery.

He probably felt sorry for her.

"I do miss Johnny," Flavia said, "and Cousin Em, too, though he was a scamp. I adore a rich *crème brûlée*, and these are so pretty. What's your favorite dessert, my lord?"

"I'm fond of cranachan, or raspberry fool made with a dash of raspberry liqueur."

He would be. "I like apple tarts," Portia said. "Or pear tarts, or anything but raspberries. I cannot abide raspberries." She set her dessert dish aside and wanted to kick his lordship.

Flavia reached around Lord Phillip and appropriated Portia's untouched sweet. Lord Phillip looked amused, and that was... That exceeded all bounds.

Hecate was not to have him. Hecate was on the shelf, and Portia would soon join her unless Lord Phillip saw the good fortune sitting right beside him, which he was apparently too dull-witted to do.

Desperate times called for desperate measures. Vicar burst out laughing, Mrs. Roberts joined in, and Portia came to the only logical conclusion: She'd have to get herself compromised with Lord Phillip, the sooner the better.

CHAPTER EIGHT

Supper had passed in a lovely blur for Hecate. The food had been excellent, the conversation entertaining, and the occasional glance shared with Phillip magical.

I feel as giddy as a girl making her come out should feel. The notion pleased her, though she was positively ecstatic when Nunn indicated by a nod at the clock that the time had come for the ladies to withdraw.

Hecate relayed that command to Cousin Edna by virtue of a murmured word—Edna was absorbed with patting Hallowell DeGrange's sleeve, his wrist, and probably his thigh—and the women rose on the arms of their escorts.

"Miss Brompton." DeGrange bowed to her and winged his elbow. "Might I say you are in particularly fine looks this evening?"

"You may, though you needn't. How is your dear mother?"

"Mama despairs of me. Longs to see me settled, but what's the rush? It's not as if I have a title, and that affords one a certain freedom to choose, wouldn't you say?"

He smiled at her, and without his monocle, he was handsome

enough in a blond, blue-eyed way. He'd served honorably on the Peninsula and didn't feel compelled to remind everybody of that twice in every conversation. Hecate had invited DeGrange because he had a good sense of humor, he wasn't overly prone to gossip, and he'd be a good influence on Charles.

A reliable bachelor, just as Hecate was a reliable spinster, but DeGrange's smile this evening looked a bit conspiratorial. They waited for the crowd at the dining room door to thin, Cousin Eglantine clinging to Phillip's arm, while Portia and Flavia had to content themselves with the brothers Corviser.

"Shoes and Boots seem to be getting on well with your lady cousins," DeGrange observed, referring to the siblings Schumann and Boothby Corviser. As Portia and Flavia trundled down the corridor, they giggled and fawned and comported themselves like young women who'd done too much justice to the dinner wines.

"Did you just give them those nicknames?" If so, DeGrange had hidden depths of cleverness. A corviser in days of old had been a shoemaker.

"Schoolyard wits get the credit, as usual. We arrive too soon to the withdrawing room, and I must bid you a temporary farewell. Say you'll think of me."

He bowed over her hand and came up smiling, and Hecate was faced with the extraordinary conclusion that he was flirting with her.

"I will think of retiring early, I'm afraid. I still haven't made up the teams for tomorrow's scavenger hunt." Hecate had devised those teams days ago and, during the journey from London, had made six copies of the list of items to be searched for. She was on no team, being relegated to the role of organizer, of course.

"I'd like to go searching with you on a fine summer day," DeGrange said. "One has the sense victory would be assured."

"Of course it would be, because I decided what must be sought, and thus putting myself on a team would be cheating."

The crush at the parlor door was thinning, and Phillip passed her on his way back to the dining room. Even the meadowy scent of his shaving soap left her wanting to smile, sigh, and make a fatuous study of his retreating form.

"Don't you ever cheat, Miss Brompton?" DeGrange asked. "Just a little? Risk a discreet compromise with the unrelenting dictates of decorum? Does your soul never long for a little diversion and mischief?"

If he only knew. "The Bromptons indulge in mischief and diversions aplenty, I'm afraid. Somebody must remain firmly in possession of her common sense in this family, and that somebody is me."

"And for that,"—he tossed off a bow—"you remain in firm possession of my admiration. If you were on a scavenger team, I'd insist on being assigned to it. Perhaps you'll look with favor on my humble person when it's time to form squares for tomorrow's picnic."

He sauntered off, and Hecate felt as if he'd mistaken her for another woman who'd brought charm, beauty, and some accomplishments among her luggage. Hecate had always been wealthy, but DeGrange had no reputation as a fortune hunter.

His mild flirtation had been enjoyable and harmless, but also... odd.

Very odd.

Hecate made her excuses to Edna, who was perfectly happy for Hecate to spend the rest of her evening on organizational chores while Edna collected gossip over the tea tray.

"DeGrange is very sweet, isn't he?" Edna said as the ladies arranged themselves on sofas and hassocks. "He comes from a good family too."

"Are you thinking of remarrying, Edna?"

Edna gave her a puzzled look. "Whyever would I do that? You of all people know how marriage impinges on a lady's freedom. My late husband, God rest his soul, was a prince among men, but he was still *a husband.*"

As Hecate made her way abovestairs, she reflected that until recently, she would have echoed Edna's sentiments, but there was Edna, compromising her dignity in an attempt to catch the eye of a baronet.

Edna, scheming endlessly to see her daughters launched.

Edna, trying to make a quarterly allowance do the work of a small fortune.

Edna, hoping to turn an evening of whist into a windfall.

A husband—the right husband—would have rendered all that effort and indignity unnecessary.

Hecate went straight to her room, took out a dark blue merino wool shawl, and traded house slippers for sturdier footwear.

Phillip would likely be half an hour over the port and cheroots. A more conscientious lady would review tomorrow's menus, look in on the housekeeper, have a word with the butler...

Hecate changed into a morning dress of aubergine silk that was years out of fashion and completely unacceptable for evening wear. She undid the pair of braids coiled into her chignon and pinned the lot into a loose bun.

She removed her jewelry and dabbed a drop of scent on the inside of each wrist.

While one part of her mind watched these activities with growing consternation, another part—perhaps the part connected to her heart—wildly applauded. She used her toothpowder, blew out the bedroom candles, and slipped down the maids' stairs.

A quick exit through the conservatory, and she was free in the luscious air of a summer night and preparing for her first assignation in years.

~

Phillip did not smoke.

He did not believe that after hours of sitting before a lavish feast and sipping a different wine with each course, a man also needed to imbibe several glasses of port. He was none too keen on the blatant and public use of the chamber pots when the ladies withdrew either. Several of the tipsier fellows had bad aim, and ye gods, what a thankless task the footman would have cleaning up in the morning.

The drinking and smoking he could have tolerated, but the next part—the snide innuendos aimed at the ladies—he found frankly disturbing. He waited out his indenture to masculinity by a pair of French doors that brought in a blessedly fresh breeze.

"I had no idea you favored ladies of a certain age, DeGrange," a sandy-haired fellow remarked. His evening coat sported overly padded shoulders, and his cravat was the equivalent of a puzzle box wrought in linen. "Our hostess is a bit long in the tooth for frolicking. Perhaps you'd best trade in your monocle for a fine set of spectacles."

DeGrange considered his port. "A lady is never too old to enjoy a mild flirtation, Winover, or to merit a little harmless flattery."

"Were you flattering the Brompton antidote with all that bowing and bobbing at the parlor door?" Winover shot back. "Nobody has placed a bet in that direction in years. Wouldn't want you to waste your firepower on a forlorn hope, as you soldierly fellows would say."

The Earl of Nunn had declined to remain on hand for the port and piss pots, which meant the assemblage bore an unfortunate resemblance to a pack of spoiled boys sorting out their schoolyard politics. Phillip hadn't been to public school, and he was glad of it.

DeWitt lounged in elegant splendor against the mantel. "I like Miss Hecate Brompton," he said. "She has a wealth of good sense, is loyal to her family, and doesn't suffer fools."

"That lets you out, Winover," somebody quipped.

"Why waste my time tilting at that windmill when the younger Misses Brompton are ever so much more amenable to a fellow's overtures?" Winover drawled. "They are so nearly twins they conjure all manner of interesting fantasies."

Phillip longed to pitch Winover into the roses, but alas, the dining room was on the first floor, and the drop would have been insufficient to see justice done.

"You only have the one prick," the same wag observed, "and anybody can see that Portia and Flavia aren't twins."

"Right," a third fellow said. "Portia is scheming, and Flavia hasn't a brain in her head. Easy to tell them apart."

Phillip sent DeWitt a hard stare, but DeWitt was looking bored and handsome at the hearth.

"Better scheming," Phillip said, "which some might call shrewd, and stupid, which could more kindly be termed innocent, than insolent, arrogant, and a disgrace to one's upbringing. The ladies deserve our respect, and I find this company beyond tedious. Excuse me."

Somebody guffawed as Phillip headed for the door, and Winover offered a languid salute with his cigar, but the conversation had been halted, as well it should have been.

What a pack of fat-headed, yowling, tomcats. They even pissed indiscriminately like tomcats, and these were the fellows Hecate had invited after much thought. Phillip shuddered to consider the bachelors and baronets who had not made the list.

He stalked along the corridor, wishing he could spend an hour stacking hay, mucking stalls, or clearing some weed-choked drainage ditch.

"They will talk about me now," he muttered, letting himself into his room. "Concoct witty insults, dub me Lord Finicky, or worse." He kept going straight out to his balcony. Hecate would not expect him quite yet—port and cigars amid a miasma of flatulence and urine was a man's reward for enduring good food and pleasant conversation.

A fashionable fellow did not hasten through his reward, even when it bore a very close resemblance to purgatory. *Not done.*

Phillip shrugged out of his jacket, which would need a thorough airing, and stripped down to the skin. He did the best he could with soap and cold water, then changed into breeches, a plain shirt, and an unembroidered waistcoat.

The old boots he'd worn for the journey down from Berkshire completed his ensemble, and trading his formal evening kit for a farmer's attire helped settle his temper.

How dare those imbeciles publicly insult women, first for being unattainable, as Hecate had been, and then for being too willing to tolerate a fellow's overtures, as Portia and Flavia might be? Hardly rational to criticize both responses.

Phillip dragged a brush through damp hair, used his toothpowder, and escaped down the footmen's stairs into the blessedly dark night. Hecate was waiting for him on the bridge, and in all his years of appreciating nature's splendors, he had never seen a sight half so breathtaking.

"You're early," she said, remaining where she was.

"Is that bad? Shall I lurk in the bushes admiring your profile until the appointed hour?" Did he take her hands, perhaps bow? Was there protocol for such encounters? If so, he'd already bungled his opening lines.

"I have no doubt that you excel at lurking in bushes," Hecate said, rearranging her shawl. "Was dinner awful?"

Oh, lovely. Now he'd thrown her off stride too. Phillip closed the distance between them and perched on the wide stone wall that formed the bridge railing.

"Dinner was delightful. I had only to look up, and I could behold the loveliest lady in the room, and sometimes she was even glancing my direction." He patted the place beside him and hoped he hadn't committed four violations of good manners by failing to offer Hecate his hand.

"I had only to look up," Hecate said, settling right next to him, "to behold the most impressive gentleman of the gathering, and sometimes he was even smiling in my direction."

This was supposed to be an assignation, an exploration of further steps toward intimate congress, but Phillip wasn't feeling amorous. Relieved to be once again in the fresh air and delighted to share the stars with Hecate, but not... swainly.

"I made a cake of myself over the port and cigars. Insulted the company."

"They aren't a very impressive lot," Hecate replied. "I had to content myself with who was available on short notice for a gathering that would offer no deep play, no orgies, no obliging housemaids. I can't speak for Nunn's footmen when it comes to frolicking, but I trust them around Portia and Flavia."

Phillip looped an arm around Hecate's waist, and she rested her head on his shoulder. "I can see why this house-party business exhausts you. Without scheduled entertainment, that lot in the dining room turns to prurience and strutting. I left in high dudgeon when they started on Portia and Flavia."

"That would be... Winover's doing?"

"He led the pack. I wanted to kick him in the cods, Hecate. I can see why Nunn begs off at his own house party."

"Uncle is getting on, though he enjoys good health, much to Charles's frustration. I've warned Edna that she needs to keep a closer eye on Portia especially, but my warnings are brushed off as the anxious imaginings of a sheltered spinster."

Perhaps Hecate did not expect amorous advances, or perhaps she, too, needed to air the day's burdens. Phillip gathered her closer and kissed her temple.

"I wish we could slip away to Lark's Nest," he said. "High summer is lovely in Berkshire. Not lazy—farm life admits of no laziness—but satisfying. I make a list over the winter of summer projects —repair this fence, clear that acre, reroute another irrigation scheme —and seeing to my list gratifies me inordinately."

"I plan in winter too," Hecate said, taking his hand and lacing her fingers through his. "The year's expenditures and income get a thorough review, and then I contemplate what ought to be changed going forward. Should I move some investments? Is my sailors' charity performing adequately? Is the local house of worship in good trim? Nunn holds the living, but he can't see rising damp in the vestry, and Vicar won't show it to him."

They were quiet for a time, while Phillip let the peace of a luscious moment sink into his mind and body. The stream burbled along, one of the most tranquil sounds known to humankind, and a song thrush serenaded the moon. A robin answered occasionally, and some horse enjoying his night at grass whinnied to his fellows.

Hecate might be giving him time to marshal his courage, but he suspected she was also appreciative of a chance to put the evening's busyness behind her.

"What do the ladies discuss over the teapot?" he asked.

"The gentlemen, mostly, and sometimes the latest news from Town." She cuddled closer and sighed. "I was supposed to kiss you witless and part you from your reason. I had planned to, in a general sort of way."

"And I promise to dazzle you with my charm, just as soon as I've settled my nerves." He kissed her fingers. "Those people exhaust you, and they rattle me. I was happy cutting hay this morning, Hecate. That's who I am. A farmer who has enjoyed more good luck than most, nothing more. I was miserable trussed up like the Christmas goose in evening finery, listening to a lot of peacocks deride the ladies. Portia is frustrated with her situation, and I think you are right to be worried about her, even in the company you've recruited for this gathering."

"And if Portia steps past the line of good behavior, she'll take Flavia with her by association. I tell myself they are doing the best they can, though they are headstrong. I was headstrong, too, but not like those two."

Phillip kissed Hecate's ear and considered her words. "Portia and Flavia are what you could have become, but you resisted both Portia's bitterness and Flavia's surrender of her intelligence. I admire you for that. Society would probably call you headstrong, but I call you brave and determined."

Hecate kissed his cheek, which he probably should have taken the time to shave again. "Society calls me unnatural, on the shelf, managing. I like your words better."

She kissed him again, not a ravishing charge into an erotic affray, but rather, a gentle invitation. Phillip obliged, and by soft, sweet degrees, the evening's frustrations and bewilderments fell from his grasp. He shifted so he straddled the stone wall, and Hecate was nestled against his chest.

"I could spend the night like this," she said, "cuddling, talking, kissing. I loved seeing you with your shirt off."

I love you. He caught the words before they would have become audible, but the rightness of them was beyond debate. To hold Hecate on a soft summer night, to hold her trust and her confidences while desire hummed quietly to life was precious. Soil that rich could grow a family, a happy and long old age, a thriving estate.

"I loved sitting in the gallery with you," Phillip said, "time flying past while we talked about anything and everything."

"And we kissed," she said, hiking her legs over his thigh. "I would like to see Lark's Nest. Tell me about it."

Hecate became a warm weight on his heart while Phillip prosed on about his broodmares, his favorite bridle paths, his neighbors, and his ideas for building a small conservatory and propagation house, until Hecate's breathing was regular, and her eyes closed.

"I've farmer-ed you to sleep," he said, which doubtless went squarely under the heading of Not Done when a man was bent on courtship.

"No, you have not. I like the feel of your speaking voice here." She patted his chest. "You are passionate about your acres, not merely a good steward of them. I am the same way about my investments."

"Tell me."

She did, her recitation gathering momentum and wandering from a sailors' home—her favorite charity—to the cent-per-cents, to her father's complete lack of interest in anything other than the total of her wealth.

"Papa is a pragmatist," she said, yawning. "We understand each other."

Phillip heard in that statement both acceptance and longing.

Would it have been too much to ask for Isaac Brompton to have shown her some fondness? Some appreciation? Some loyalty?

"I'd like to meet him." The notion of asking Brompton for permission to court his daughter struck Phillip as ridiculous, but Hecate deserved that courtesy.

"I'd rather we slip away to Lark's Nest." Hecate sat up. "Papa can be charming, but I'm a penance to him."

"You are a reproach. He's a grown man without inherited wealth or title, and he's spent his life sitting on his arse resenting your capabilities."

Hecate brushed her thumb over Phillip's lips. "And my patrimony, let's not forget that." She stretched luxuriously, which strained the fabric of her bodice most intriguingly. "I am no sort of siren, Phillip. I apologize for that, but supper did tax me somewhat."

Now that the time had apparently come to part, Phillip wished it hadn't. He wanted to take down Hecate's hair, to slide that fetching frock from her shoulders, to feel her hands on his bare flesh.

"Sirens are flighty creatures bent on luring a fellow to his doom," Phillip said. "Perhaps we both need some time to adjust to this... attraction."

Hecate swung her legs down and stood. "You are like no fellow I could have imagined. I don't need time to adjust, and neither do I regard the past hour as anything but delightful. I have..." She waved a hand. "Romped. I can romp again this very night if I please to. With you, I'm not romping, and I don't want to romp."

Phillip rose and dusted off his backside. "What do you want of me, then?" A gentleman had to ask, and worse than that, he had to accept the lady's answer with good grace.

She hugged him fiercely. "That you would inquire into my wishes... I want to wallow, Phillip. To luxuriate in the wonder of you, to have all afternoon to talk and touch and meander along. I want to see you with your shirt off and smile at you down the table while everybody else looks on. I want to have you to myself and show you off to the world. I'm not making sense."

"I want," Phillip said, looping his arms around her shoulders, "to go carefully and to gallop. To toss caution to the wind and exercise the greatest prudence. To offer you flowers, poetry, and all my dreams, and to sit with you in silence while we watch the sun rise on a new and wonderful day."

I am smitten and inebriated and terrified and determined.

Hecate kissed him, and this kiss had an edge. "Even your words," she muttered against his mouth. "Your ditches and hedges and silences..."

He had no idea what she referred to, but he was very aware of her person pressed to him from chest to thighs. In some purely male corner of his mind, he realized that Hecate Brompton had eschewed stays, and his dreams trotted off in the direction of a soft bed of clover and a blanket of night stars.

Hecate glossed a hand over his falls. "You too," she murmured. "I was supposed to ravish you, and then I lost my nerve, and now..."

She swooped back in, anchored a hand in Phillip's hair, and twined a leg around his hips. He shifted them, hiking Hecate onto the stone balustrade, and the fit was *sublime.*

He'd found two of the pins securing her bun when an odd sound checked his explorations.

"What?" Hecate rested her forehead against his chest, her breathing labored. "Is somebody coming? I am not inclined to care."

Phillip shoved the pins back into her bun. "Either somebody is already here, or the owl nesting in your home wood has taken to tippling. Let's get back to the house, shall we?"

Hecate gave him a peevish expression that would have been adorable but for the circumstances, and even then...

Phillip was certain that a gentleman suffering the frustrated pangs of inchoate passion did not tug at his falls, so he offered his arm and tried to steady his breathing. They were off the bridge and halfway to the garden before a whiff of fancy shaving soap alerted him to the identity of the spy.

He bowed his good night to Hecate on the back terrace, resisted with the fortitude of Saint George himself the temptation to kiss her one more time, and returned to the shadows of the garden.

"Show yourself," he said over the trickling of the fountain and the chirping of crickets, "and be prepared to give a very good account with your fives, because right about now, I would cheerfully put out your lights."

CHAPTER NINE

Gavin DeWitt paced beneath the torches on the terrace while Phillip watched Hecate slip into the house. Another fifteen minutes on the bridge, and he'd have been offering the lady a proper tryst rather than lovely preliminaries.

Or perhaps not. Perhaps he'd once again fall under the spell of intimacy of the heart and spirit as well as of the body. Thank heavens Hecate seemed equally enthralled with closeness that encompassed more than a mere romp.

"Are you even listening to me?" DeWitt asked, fetching up against a statue of some half-bird, half-woman creature whose bodice had slipped to a significant degree.

How could one ignore the third-act soliloquy DeWitt had been offering? "You report that the gentlemen—using the term in its ironic sense—left off maligning the ladies long enough to malign me as well. Had it not been imperative for them to join those same ladies over the teapot, they might well have moved on to casting aspersion on their host, our gracious king—after they toasted him, of course—and the apostles in alphabetical order. You are the experienced fribble, DeWitt. Why didn't you throw them off the scent?"

"Because the decoy then becomes the prey. Watch Winover especially. He's devious by nature, and the Winover family hires only old, plain housemaids. The Corvisers are competitively reckless. If Boots puts a frog in your jewelry box, Shoes will put half a dozen in your bed."

"That pair couldn't catch a frog stone-cold sober in broad daylight. Toads are much calmer by nature and make easier quarry, not that the Corvisers could tell one from the other."

DeWitt kicked a pebble that skittered across the terrace and bounced down the steps. "They will put the stable boys up to the actual catching. They will turn your horse loose, put manure in your best boots, and affix notes to the back of your evening coat under the guise of delivering a friendly whack to your shoulder."

Phillip wanted solitude to ponder the wonders of privacy with Hecate, because all the talking and cuddling and quiet had been profoundly intimate. A type of closeness new to him and apparently to her as well. A sharing and trusting that went so far beyond what he'd imagined courtship offered that...

"We should leave," DeWitt said. "You are off on the wrong foot with the wrong people. They will bear tales in Town about you."

"They are fribbles, DeWitt, and you might mean well by suggesting we decamp, but that won't stop them from jeopardizing on my good name."

"A strategic retreat would allow your lecturing to fade over the course of the next two weeks while some other diversion caught their attention."

Phillip wanted to say that DeWitt was overreacting, but DeWitt had seen polite society as one of its number and, then again, as a lowly player offered a pittance to entertain his supposed betters.

"If a mild reproof to some half-sozzled brats in breeches earns me Society's contempt, then I won't have to learn the rubbishing quadrille after all," Phillip said. "I will be dropped from guest lists, I will be spared all the starch and lace, and I can resume tending my acres in peace."

And that had, until very recently, been the sum of his ambitions.

"What of Miss Brompton?" DeWitt said. "What of Tavistock, for whose sake you have taken up this apprenticeship in manners and deportment? Will you content yourself to be Squire Bumpkin for all the rest of your days?"

No, Phillip would not—another recent development—not unless Hecate was willing to become Lady Bumpkin, and she deserved much more than that.

"I refuse to admit defeat after one skirmish," Phillip said, struck by the notion that DeWitt wanted to leave for reasons of his own. "How do you suggest I thwart my detractors?"

"You don't. You prepare to be pranked and made the butt of practical jokes, and you bear up with good grace. Your penance is to look like a fool and seek no redress. Acknowledge that you overstepped, and they will consider the score even."

"I did not overstep. They forgot the basic manners any boy learns by age seven."

DeWitt pushed away from the winged creature. "The truth doesn't matter here, my lord. Society turns on appearances, innuendo, whispers, and wagers."

How had Hecate learned to navigate such waters with her dignity intact? "And stupidity."

"Pride. You insulted fellows who were jabbering simply to hear themselves talk. Bachelors who have failed to earn the reward of a woman's trust and loyalty."

Men who'd been exiled, at least for the nonce. That perspective gave Phillip a bit of purchase on his temper.

"I am tired." Phillip was abruptly aware that he'd been up early and put in hours of hard work before he'd joined Hecate in the gallery. He wanted to wallow—Hecate's word—in the memories he'd made with her this day and to let his imagination roam freely over memories yet to be made. "I promised Travers I'd be back at the scything in the morning."

"Don't let the other guests catch you at it."

"Right. Or they will make a jest of that, too, though without fodder in winter, their handsome cattle will starve. Such hilarity. Do me a favor, DeWitt."

"Another favor." The tone was so aggrieved that Phillip realized DeWitt was even more uncomfortable at this house party than Phillip himself.

"Keep an eye on Portia and Flavia," Phillip said. "A discreet eye. DeGrange might assist with the task, and Mrs. Roberts strikes me as sensible too. Portia is working up to a tantrum of some sort."

"How can you know that?"

"Broodmares," Phillip said, starting for the house. "I watch them by the hour, and pay particular attention to the eyes. Portia has the look of a junior mare contemplating the unthinkable folly of challenging the herd's reigning duchess. Portia cannot abide life at the bottom of the pecking order, and despair will make her foolish."

DeWitt fell in step beside him. "And encouraging Hecate Brompton to twine about you as if you're her personal maypole is wise?"

"If I'm her personal maypole, then I will enjoy the privilege. Miss Brompton twines herself where and how she pleases."

DeWitt stopped on the threshold. "Be careful, Phillip. You might enjoy the lady's attentions, but she is not well liked, and you could too easily give the gossips enough ammunition to ruin her. If I saw you two on the bridge, somebody else might have as well."

Every sensible particle of Phillip's being wanted to argue: Hecate Brompton was of age and of sound mind. If she found pleasure in Phillip's company, that was nobody's business but hers. Her generosity had made the whole gathering possible, and surely her guests owed her discretion and respect?

Except that DeWitt was right, and Phillip had best mind his step. "I appreciate the warning. We aren't leaving, but I will be careful in future."

"And accept the pranking with good grace. Smile, laugh it off, be a good sport who takes a birching in stride."

A good sport in the stupidest of games. "I understand. If I'm to be up early, I'd best seek my bed."

"To have Tavistock summon you back to Berkshire wouldn't be difficult. I can get a message to him in a few hours."

DeWitt had run from his responsibilities two years ago, and increasingly, Phillip understood why, if those responsibilities consisted largely of fribbling.

"Thank you for the offer, but I'm here to learn precisely the curriculum in which you now instruct me," Phillip said. "I will prepare to show all toads and frogs my best good humor. Good night."

~

Hecate spent three days in a fog of wonderment. On two of those days, she'd gone riding directly after an early breakfast and lurked on the bridle path adjoining the hayfield. Phillip without his shirt was too great a temptation to resist, though by the end of the second afternoon, the field was cut.

She and Phillip finished their days with a placid round of cribbage in the library, though what that man could do with a passing glance or a brush of hands defied decent description. They talked about everything—Hecate's investments, Phillip's inventions, the first time he'd seen Tavistock as an adult. He'd lurked among the birches and simply stared at his brother for nearly an hour, torn between curiosity, fear, and amazement.

That much honesty emboldened Hecate to talk about her mother, whom she never mentioned to anybody. The conversation and fleeting touches were delightful, also... maddening.

Phillip had promised to come to Hecate's room that night, and thus minutes had turned to eons and hours to eternities.

"Haying has wrapped up?" Mrs. Roberts asked, taking the seat next to Hecate on the back terrace.

"The hay is cut. The raking can proceed with less urgency, apparently."

Mrs. Roberts, like Hecate, had eschewed a bonnet. She turned a pretty profile to the late afternoon sun and closed her eyes.

"I had to have it all explained to me," she said. "The haying. The cut, rake, rake again if the crop isn't dry, and then stack. I had a vague idea that horses eat dried grasses through winter, but there's art to it, and I knew nothing of the art despite owning thousands of acres."

They had wealth in common, which might have been part of the reason Hecate liked Rose Roberts. Yes, the widow had spared Charles more than a passing glance, but not much more. A lady was entitled to her discreet pleasures, and if Charles had one talent...

"I have tried inquiring of the steward," Hecate said, "but I fear he'll tattle to Uncle Nunn that I'd been prying, and Uncle has his pride."

Mrs. Roberts peered over at her, while out in the park, the loud crack of a mallet whacking a ball split the afternoon's quiet. A few shouts followed, along with some laughter.

"Your uncle is half the reason I survived second mourning. He is at heart an exceedingly decent fellow."

Uncle Nunn was nearly twice Mrs. Roberts's age, and while Hecate would agree—Uncle was a decent fellow—that's not precisely what Mrs. Roberts had meant.

"He is a gentleman," Hecate said, "and thus he would not like me prying into how he manages his land."

"Have Lord Phillip do the prying. That one clearly knows his way around farm equipment."

An idea worth considering. "Lord Phillip has already told me the estate is suffering for want of competent management. I'll suggest he broach agricultural topics with Uncle Nunn, but Uncle isn't exactly a congenial host."

"Nunn is proud, you're right, but not arrogant. He lost his wife, whom he truly adored, and thus when I was bereaved, Nunn knew exactly what I sought."

"And that would be?"

"A polite escort who didn't chatter, who didn't burden me with expectations of gaiety and flirtation. A companion who came between me and isolation, but who also knew—he did not have to be told—that grief would accompany me everywhere. He assured me that time was the best tonic, and he was right."

Hecate could see Uncle Nunn rising to such a challenge and making no fuss about it whatsoever. "There was talk, about you and the earl. There still is."

"Nunn was willing to risk that result when he saw how poorly I was coping. I'd sit in divine services, barely moving my lips to the hymns, my heart filled with hatred for a God who'd inflict such suffering for no possible gain. I hoped second mourning would yield some relief, but having to go about in Society and entertain callers only added to my bitterness."

"You don't seem miserable now."

"Nunn was right," Mrs. Roberts said, her smile sad. "Time is the best tonic, though I will admit I sampled other elixirs occasionally, with varying degrees of success."

Her gaze went to Gavin DeWitt, who made a handsome picture with a croquet mallet balanced across his shoulders, his form displayed without benefit of a jacket. The day was warm, after all, and smacking a ball around qualified as exertion to some.

To others... the image of Phillip singing in rhythm with the sweep of his blade came to mind. Naked from the waist up, hair curling damply at his forehead, muscles bunching and rippling...

"Your Lord Phillip isn't playing croquet," Mrs. Roberts said. "Have Portia and Flavia kidnapped him?"

"I suspect they want to, but his lordship won't kidnap easily." Phillip had attached himself to the crew clearing the main drainage artery running through the Nunnsuch estate proper. He'd informed Hecate of his plans when he'd stopped by her room before breakfast. They'd conferred at her door—all very proper—and she'd explained to him the rudiments of her schedule.

Such a mundane conversation, and yet, that he'd bother to

consult with her at the start of the day was more delicious than a box of French chocolates and sweeter than a violin serenade.

"Portia worries me," Mrs. Roberts said. "A widow's frolics are tolerated, provided she's discreet, but Portia nurses a sense of injury out of all proportion to her circumstances. She reminds me of those Italian volcanoes... They smolder, the smoke creating striking sunrises and sunsets, but real destruction can result without much notice."

"She's a Brompton," Hecate said. "She was born for dramatics and a sense of entitlement. I've warned Edna to keep a closer eye on her daughters, but Edna regards me as a meddler without portfolio."

"Why do you do it?" Mrs. Roberts asked. "Why keep the whole Brompton ship afloat? Why not put at least your male dependents on notice that the well will go dry twelve months hence?"

"You'd have me cut off Uncle Nunn?"

Another rousing cry came from the croquet court.

"Nunn isn't impossible," Mrs. Roberts said. "He's excessively dignified, but he can be human. He needs to retire his steward and doesn't know how to go about it."

"He told you that?" That Uncle had a confidante both pleased Hecate and made her sad. Why wasn't *she* that confidante? Any member of the family? Why hadn't Papa ever troubled to ingratiate himself with the family earl?

But then, a confidante had to be trustworthy, and that excused all family members from the duty.

"Perhaps the issue is a pension," Hecate said slowly. "Uncle cannot afford to pension his steward and older retainers, and ending their tenure might be awkward even with adequate funds."

Phillip would have seen that. He had an instinctive grasp of every detail of running an estate.

A final hard whack was followed by a round of applause. "I ought to look over the buffet," Hecate said, though she'd rather linger here with Mrs. Roberts, pondering possibilities and not quite gossiping.

"That plague of locusts would devour dry bread without

complaint as long as you provided enough summer ale to wash it down."

"They'd complain." Hecate ought not to have said that.

Mrs. Roberts rose. "They will whine and carp over a full spread with all the trimmings, so why bother yourself about what's on offer? You wrote the menus, the kitchen is competent, and the Bromptons will eat what's put before them, even as they criticize good food. Honestly, Miss Brompton, they do not deserve you, and Lord Nunn would agree with me."

Hecate had no reply to that blunt observation. A tallish gentleman in a top hat and riding attire was making a slow progress along the path from the stable. She knew his walk, knew the way he slapped his riding crop against his boots as he...

"What is my father doing here?" she murmured, coming to her feet. "He never attends these gatherings, and he will expect the Hawthorne Suite, which Edna will never give up."

Several of the croquet spectators and players detoured to welcome the newcomer, and Mrs. Roberts slanted a wry look at Hecate.

"You haven't seen your father in how long, he arrives unannounced, and all you can think is: He will provoke a squabble with Edna. And yet, you lay your fortune at the feet of such as these?" She patted Hecate's shoulder and made for the buffet.

Hecate was not especially glad to see Papa, true, but then, he wasn't her papa, and that always lay between them. And he would most assuredly provoke a squabble with Edna, while casting subtle aspersions on Charles, Eglantine, their children, the weather, and every arrangement Hecate made for the comfort of Nunnsuch's guests.

"But he's the only papa I have," she muttered, not as satisfied with that defense as she should have been.

~

"What do we know of Isaac Brompton?" Phillip asked from the depths of a luscious, tepid bath. Haying meant chaff got everywhere, but clearing a ditch was usually dusty work. The resulting blisters were different, too, if a fellow hadn't done either job in some time.

"I don't know much," Gavin DeWitt replied, opening Phillip's wardrobe. "A noted Corinthian in his younger days, occupied the fringes of the Carlton House set, the fringes of the Devonshire House set. Charming, particularly with the wives of his dearest friends, though he drew the line at daughters and housemaids. Parlayed his connection to the Brompton titled branch into an advantageous match to an heiress. Nothing unusual in that tale, save that he had no sons and only the one daughter, but then, his missus lasted a mere ten years or so."

Phillip had brought the soap with him, a fine recipe with a meadowy, lavender grassy fragrance. "How do you recall such trivia?"

"The same way I recalled my lines onstage, I suppose. The details stick when I tell them to. Have you given any more thought to leaving?"

DeWitt was rehearsing that sentiment a bit too frequently. "I have lasted for the first week more or less and only blotted my copybook once with no apparent evil consequences."

To get clean after a hard day's work had to be one of the greatest pleasures known to man—though not the greatest. Not if that man had earned Hecate Brompton's esteem. Phillip soaped his hair, dunked, and came up.

"Rinse, please."

DeWitt obliged, then set aside the empty ewer. "Why hasn't Winover sought his revenge yet? His pride demands that he make you publicly crawl."

"I gave him the blue feather that secured his victory in the scavenger hunt. I'm fairly certain he now thinks I'm so backward that to punish me would amount to kicking the dog." Phillip rose. "Towel."

DeWitt threw a wadded-up cloth at his chest. "What has a blue feather to do with anything?"

"Portia was preparing a tantrum worthy of Mrs. Siddons over the fact that their team was short only the blue feather, which is, admittedly, not an item found in great abundance. But nesting season is behind us, and Hecate—Miss Brompton—considered the grounds when she made up the scavenger list."

"And?"

"House martins have blue feathers, and they nest on dwellings, barns, sheds... usually several nests on one building. Those searching need not comb the whole park, they had only to look as far as the stable, the laundry, the drying shed, the springhouse, the summer kitchen... Miss Brompton's list was meant to be challenging but fair. I gave Winover several blue feathers, knowing those to be the object most difficult to find on the whole list."

Phillip stepped from the tub, feeling refreshed, relaxed, and in charity with the world. Tonight's supper was another buffet—he much preferred those to any other sort of company meal—and he and Hecate had plans for the end of the evening.

"Have you ever considered pugilism?" DeWitt said, eyeing Phillip's naked frame. "You'd put the fear of a hard right into many of Jackson's acolytes."

"You try wrestling with a contrary draft mare when she's not inclined to tolerate a manicure. You'd sprout a few muscles too. I do not understand why a manly physique is fashionable if the fellow got his strength through idle pursuits, but not if he earned his power in honest labor." Phillip finished toweling off and embarked on the dressing nonsense.

Sleeve buttons, cravat pin, and watch must all match. Embroidery could be lavish, but lace had to be tastefully restrained, despite neither embroidery nor lace adding one whit to a garment's serviceability. Footwear must be polished to a high shine, though ostentatious shoe buckles were inadvisable.

"I still think we should leave," DeWitt said, apropos of nothing. "You might have convinced Winover that you're dicked in the nob, but Portia and Flavia are another matter."

Phillip began the careful process of tying a starched cravat just so. What the starch added, besides some work for the laundry and itchiness for the wearer, he did not know, but Hecate liked to see him all tidied up almost as much as she enjoyed seeing him half naked.

If the day ended as planned, she'd see even more of him than that.

"Don't smile at Portia like that," DeWitt said, neatly folding the towel Phillip had draped over the back of the vanity stool. "She's already casting dark looks your direction."

"Portia is frustrated. She considers herself to be prettier than Hecate Brompton, smarter, more socially astute, younger, in every way the more estimable creature, and yet, she lacks coin, and thus she hasn't one-tenth the consequence her cousin has. That is unfair, and from a certain perspective, Portia is correct."

"Portia is a scheming, devious minx who has designs on your future."

Phillip dragged a comb through his hair and tied his locks back with a black ribbon. "Will I do?"

"Damnably well."

"You and Mrs. Roberts have been exchanging veiled glances for the past week," Phillip said. "Either cease being so obvious, or invite the lady to admire the roses by moonlight and clear the air."

DeWitt shook his head. "There is no clearing the air, and we are not being obvious. You will be on your best behavior with Isaac Brompton."

Phillip regarded his reflection and beheld a somewhat largish, though well-turned-out fellow who'd clearly spent too much time in the sun to be truly fashionable. The embroidery, gold, lace, and starch bothered him, but they were precisely the appointments he needed to become comfortable with as a marquess's heir.

A stubborn voice in his head brayed the inevitable counterargument: Why be fashionable when a man could instead be happy, comfortable, and useful?

"You plan to offer for Hecate Brompton, don't you?" DeWitt said. "Fast work, but then, you don't have to compete for her hand."

"Because the assembled dimwits and their Mayfair brethren have been too stupid to give me any competition. Should I bring gloves?"

"Not for an informal supper buffet, but you should wear your signet ring." DeWitt held up his right hand, the smallest finger of which sported what looked like an emerald ring.

Phillip did not hold with men wearing rings. Too fussy by half, and dangerous if the fellow was working with livestock. He slipped the signet ring on his finger anyway. The other guests might be ornery and contrary, but they were not barnyard beasts.

"Will you request permission to court Miss Hecate first?" DeWitt asked. "Do the pretty and all that other whatnot?"

Phillip left his room and made for the footmen's stairs, DeWitt in tow. "I will go down on bended knee in the middle of the Hyde Park carriage parade if she'll allow it, but I thought a word with Mr. Brompton might also be in order."

They rounded the first landing. "Do you know what to say?"

"To Mr. Brompton? What I have to say is hardly polite, but I won't pummel him."

DeWitt trotted along for two more floors. "You can't lecture him, Phillip. You cannot scold and sermonize. Hecate Brompton is his daughter, all but his chattel in the eyes of the law, or she was until she reached her majority. You must tread lightly with him, be respectful."

"No," Phillip said, hauling open the door to the main floor. "When a fractious colt is testing his handler, treading lightly and being respectful is a certain path to creating a difficult horse. The situation wants firmness and clarity, within the bounds of decorum. Isaac Brompton has made a poor showing as Hecate's father, but he can and will do better going forward."

"Don't do this," DeWitt muttered, nodding genially at one of the Corvisers. "Please just play the game, Phillip. Be respectful and humble. Don't treat Brompton as if he's unruly livestock."

Brompton certainly qualified as an ass. "Is this when you tell me, once again, that we should leave? Would you like to leave, DeWitt?"

Mrs. Roberts sashayed past on the Earl of Nunn's arm, and Nunn was for once smiling. Faintly, mostly about the eyes, but the old fellow appeared downright charming when he beheld Mrs. Roberts. DeWitt, by contrast, looked as if he wanted to hide behind the nearest potted palm.

"Yes," DeWitt said quietly. "I would like to leave and never come back. Let's go to dinner, shall we? I'm sure Portia and Flavia are eager to share their meal with their favorite courtesy lord."

Bollocks to you. Phillip knew better than to say that. "And I will once again delight in their company, gentleman that I am."

"For the love of God, be careful," DeWitt muttered, donning a smile as Eglantine Brompton swanned closer, looking intent on seizing DeWitt by the arm. "I bid you good evening, my lord. Please take my words to heart."

DeWitt went graciously to his fate, while Phillip considered that a house party that had loomed before him as a distasteful ordeal was now to be the scene of immense, shared happiness. He was not the awkward yokel newly initiated to Society's boring and silly ranks.

Or not only that. He was also a man in love with the most estimable and dear of ladies, and that made all the difference.

CHAPTER TEN

"And this is my father," Hecate said, feeling, as always when she used those words, like a trespasser on Isaac Brompton's tolerance. "Lord Phillip, may I make known to you Mr. Isaac Brompton. Papa, Lord Phillip Vincent."

Papa, as the man of lesser rank, bowed first, but it was a shallow, grudging effort. What else had Hecate expected?

"My lord, I am too delighted to meet you. Simply too delighted. I understand you are down from Berkshire. Does Hampshire agree with you?"

Phillip smiled. "Hampshire has fewer trees than we do up in Berkshire, but I believe the sheep here tend to be larger."

Papa blinked, then reciprocated with an alarmingly genuine smile of his own. "Always a plus, when the sheep are fat." He imbued the words with a double meaning that likely went over Phillip's head, an inference about lordly dupes and easy marks. "If you'd excuse us, I'd like a word with my daughter."

Another slight hesitation before the word *daughter*, and Hecate steeled herself to be lectured about the gross inappropriateness of allowing Edna to remain in the Hawthorne Suite. In the alternative,

Papa's shaving water hadn't been hot enough, or too hot, or the punch
—Mama's best recipe—had been too tart or too sweet.

Papa had a need to play the lecturing father even if he resented
every other aspect of the role.

Phillip bowed over Hecate's hand, then let her go with the
subtlest brush of his thumb over her knuckles. If Hecate could have
flown to the heavens, shoved the sun beneath the horizon, and
hastened the end of the day, she would have.

She contented herself with a curtsey instead.

"Not here," Papa said, striding off into the garden and leaving
Hecate to trundle after. Phillip had lingered close enough to watch
that rudeness, but he said nothing as Boots Corviser came up on his
left and clapped him on the shoulder.

Papa kept marching until he was well past the center of the
garden, then wheeled on Hecate. "I hope you know you are making
your usual hash of this gathering. I spent a fortune on finishing
governesses and deportment instructors, and you still can't manage
to house guests in a manner consistent with their stations. The
kitchen isn't doing half justice to the occasion, and Nunn is no sort of
host."

I've missed you too. Hecate had been biting back such retorts
since before she'd put up her hair. With Mama's death, Papa had
become meaner, more impatient... but that's when he'd realized that
he'd never get his hands on Mama's money.

"I will leave it to you to brace Nunn on his failings," Hecate said.
"If you'd like to look over the menus and suggest alterations, I will
relay them to Cook."

"While you expect me to content myself in a room under the
eaves. Good God, Hecate, it's only to be expected that no man would
have you for a wife."

Many men would have had Hecate for a wife, provided they'd
had her fortune to waste on their idle pleasures. As a footman came
by to light the nearest torch, Hecate realized she'd never once worried
that Phillip would try to touch her money.

And she was very much looking forward to the next time he touched *her*.

"I have subjected myself to this farce of a gathering for one reason," Papa said. "Nunn has received word that your cousin Johnny is on his way back from Canada. Johnny will in all likelihood begin his visit here at the family seat, greeting the earl before he makes the usual round in Town and at Horse Guards. You will welcome your cousin with open arms."

Cousin Johnny was returning from Canada.

Hecate mentally rummaged around for a reaction, and all she came up with was: *The best rooms are taken, but Phillip will happily give up his quarters and sleep in the summer cottage if I ask it of him. Then Papa will pout about Johnny getting a better apartment than I can offer Papa. Perhaps Phillip and Mr. DeWitt won't mind removing to the summer cottage together.*

"I will be very pleased to see Cousin Johnny," Hecate said. "He's doubtless bringing all manner of tales home with him from Canada, and we've all missed him."

Hecate had stopped missing Johnny within a year of his departure. She'd been too busy fending off the family's attempts to pillage her fortune, and by then, she'd realized not to expect any letters from the gallant soldier.

Even Uncle Frank wrote to her occasionally, cheerful travelogues always postscripted by a request for money.

"Edna might be thinking of pairing Johnny with one of her girls," Papa said. "I'll not have it. He'd be a first cousin to either of them, and I do not approve of first cousins marrying."

And Papa's myriad disapprovals should carry the weight of royal decrees.

"I truly appreciate your warning me of Johnny's possible arrival. That gives me an excuse to rearrange rooms and guests and to put you in more commodious quarters. Did Nunn give you any idea when Johnny might appear?"

"I gather, given the vagaries of ocean travel and the Canadian mail service, he might grace us with his presence any day. You will see to the practicalities with all possible haste, Hecate. I won't have one of our own made to loiter in the parlor while the maids dust off the governess's old bedroom."

The nursery suite was actually spacious and comfortable, if one didn't mind two screaming little boys thundering about.

"I will alert the staff first thing tomorrow, Papa. Was there anything else?"

"Which of Edna's little harpies has set her cap for the courtesy lout? The sheep are fatter here in Hampshire. Did you know that, Hecate?"

"I believe Portia is making an effort in Lord Phillip's direction, when she isn't flirting with the Corviser brothers or trying to distract Mr. DeWitt from admiring Flavia's charms."

Papa shot his lacy cuffs. "DeWitt's the good-looking devil with all the money?"

"He is wealthy and charming, and he's here at Lord Phillip's request."

"A bear leader by any other name. I suppose Edna put together this gathering because her girls once again failed to inspire any proposals. Always a pity, when a young lady has no suitors."

Years ago, Papa's barb would have landed close to Hecate's heart, or to her dignity. Now, she found it easier to ignore him—mostly.

"I put together this gathering at Edna's request," Hecate said. "In years past, Cousin Charles dealt very shabbily with the current Marquess of Tavistock's new marchioness. Charles sought to mend fences by extending hospitality to Lord Phillip, who is heir presumptive to the marquessate."

"And Lord Phillip could probably advise Charlie on the specifics of mending fences right down to the placement of the posts and rails. The aristocracy never ceases to appall. You will situate Johnny handsomely and do all in your power to make him welcome."

"Of course."

"Then I'm off to content myself with the meager fare on offer at yonder buffet. If you can get Edna's girls matched up with DeWitt and Lord Lout, I might count myself amazed."

He sauntered off, an aging roué in better trim than most of his ilk. Hecate sank onto the nearest bench and tried counting to ten in German. She made it to one hundred before she'd gained a measure of calm.

Papa was nothing if not predictable. After criticizing Hecate's best efforts and setting monumental challenges before her—move the highest-ranking guest to the most humble accommodations, while finding another spacious apartment for Papa himself—he'd dangled the possibility of a moment's approval: Get Edna's daughters engaged to the two most impressive eligibles at the gathering, neither of whom would be caught dead offering advances to Portia or Flavia, and Papa *might* count himself amazed.

Not pleased or impressed, but amazed. Maybe.

Not for the first time, Hecate permitted herself a silent, traitorous thought: *I am glad you are not my father.* On the heels of that notion came the usual disclaimers. Papa had not had an easy life, by his standards, and he'd been bitterly disappointed in his marriage and in the financial arrangements resulting therefrom.

He was pathetic, viewed in a certain light, and Hecate struggled to respect him.

"I heard most of that," Phillip said, emerging from the shadows at the bottom of the garden. "Speaking as one who appreciates thriving flocks, a mere lout dressed up as a lord, I will beat him to flinders if you allow it. We louts take exception to any who treat a lady ill, and that man... My dear, how do you stand him?"

The usual defenses were beyond Hecate. *He's not that bad. His bark is worse than his bite,* which was a way of acknowledging that all of Papa's blows were verbal rather than physical. Lord Nunn, Mrs. Roberts, Phillip, any number of people had weathered bitter disappointments in life and not turned to cruelty as their consolation.

Phillip settled on the bench beside her, his arm coming around her shoulders. Hecate leaned into his warmth and wished the whole blazing house party to perdition.

"Papa wants to be on hand to welcome Cousin Johnny home. He probably hopes Johnny has become wealthy in Canada—many do—and to ingratiate himself with our dear cousin if that's the case. A gentleman doesn't eavesdrop."

"And thus I once again fail to make the ranks, because as your devoted admirer, I won't leave you to do solo combat with a bitter, aging fribble. Have you ever met your real father?"

Hecate shook her head. "What if he's worse than the one I have?"

"The imagination trembles to conceive of such a notion."

Phillip rested his cheek against her temple, and though the conversation with Papa hadn't been terrible, it had still left Hecate off-balance. She'd come right soon enough—she'd been on the receiving end of enough paternal criticism to know that—but still, that he'd insult Phillip...

Phillip brushed her hair back from her shoulder and stroked her earlobe. The caress was oddly soothing, just as Phillip's simple, quiet presence, his lavender scent, and the rhythm of his breathing were soothing.

Hecate's spirit calmed, her mind quieted, and her heart seized upon a truth: She struggled to respect her Papa, and someday she might lose that struggle altogether, but she loved Phillip Vincent, and she always would.

~

"Well, well, well," Portia murmured as she and Flavia followed Isaac Brompton into the house at a discreet distance. "Cousin Johnny's coming home. This is perfect."

Flavia stopped to shake out her slipper, which Portia suspected was a tad loose because Sister Dear had been foraging in Mama's wardrobe again.

"I always felt," Flavia said, "that Johnny was being agreeable for show, while considering the lot of us rather silly."

"You were still in the nursery when he left. Of course he thought you were silly." He would still think her silly, because darling Flave was no great intellect and never would be. "Johnny's arrival creates possibilities."

Flavia got her slipper back on by virtue of undignified hopping. "I was in the schoolroom by the time he left. I don't like how Cousin Isaac spoke to Hecate. Hecate does *try*. He declined his invitation, and now here he is, expecting the staterooms. He didn't have to be so unkind."

"Nunnsuch doesn't have staterooms." Portia paused at the bottom of the terrace steps, mind whirling with plans only possible because dear, dear Cousin Johnny was on his way home. He'd always been up for a lark, as best she recalled, and he'd certainly been handsome enough—though not quite as handsome as Cousin Emeril or as charming as Charlie.

Nor was Johnny as dashing as Uncle Frank, who was gorgeous, adorable, and wicked. He was Portia's favorite uncle, and Hecate had all but banished him.

Hecate would be much better off as the wife of a handsome fur trader in Canada.

"Porry, what are you thinking? The last time you got that look on your face, I ended up locked in a linen closet with a viscount's heir whose breath would have knocked a regiment flat."

"And his purse would have financed the regimental wardrobe, but Hecate had to ruin that too." Hecate had come upon the couple before Portia and Eglantine could be properly horrified to find the gentleman in a compromising—blackmail-able—position.

Hecate was always wrecking everything, but surely married to Cousin Johnny and whisked away to Canada...

"We've failed to get me compromised with Lord Phillip," Portia said, "though there's another week to accomplish that goal."

"Mr. DeWitt sticks to him like a barnacle," Flavia said, shaking out the other slipper. "And Hecate plays cribbage with him in plain view of other guests. It's most vexing."

"He is smitten with Hecate, but Cousin Johnny can retire her from the lists, as it were." Portia had been considering Mr. DeWitt for that role—*sorry, Flave*—but Mr. DeWitt was protected by Lord Phillip and conversely.

Rubbishing bachelors and their male loyalties.

"I think Boots Corviser likes you." Flavia got her slipper back on and smoothed down her skirts. "He's merry and not bad-looking."

"Merry and not bad-looking doesn't go far when a man has only two thousand a year and the one property. His brother is in the same lamentable posture. Once their papa dies, their situations might improve, but they are younger sons."

Besides, if Portia married the one brother, Flavia would likely wed the other, and as dear as Flavia was, Portia didn't want her underfoot in perpetuity. A woman sought to preside over her own household and not have to listen to a younger sibling's vapid chatter for the rest of her life.

"You have plans for Cousin Johnny?" Flavia asked.

"Plans that will remove Hecate from Lord Phillip's consideration and leave him free to appreciate my own vast charms." Or at least buy some time to get locked into a linen closet with his lordship.

Portia was honest with herself. Lord Phillip wasn't in love with her and never would be. Before his first real Season, he'd realize that polite society made strategic alliances rather than sentimental matches. Tavistock's own marchioness had considered a connection with the Bromptons desirable, or she had back when she'd been plain Miss Amaryllis DeWitt of Greater Bog Trot, Berkshire.

"My plans will not directly involve you," Portia said, "though your support will be invaluable, as usual. I'm hungry. Let's have at the buffet before the bachelors eat all the desserts." She slipped her arm through Flavia's and donned her most agreeable smile.

"I'm glad you have a use for me," Flavia said. "I'm not sure anybody else does."

"Nonsense." Portia patted her sister's hand. "I'd be lost without you, dearest, and you know it."

~

Phillip could see no light shining from beneath Hecate's bedroom door, and his heart sank. Her benighted family had exhausted her, and the house party wasn't half over. He didn't risk even a soft tap, but rather, let himself into her bedroom, because she'd denied herself one of the apartments that included a sitting room.

"You came." She rose from the wing chair before the hearth—no fire—and crossed to him in shadows. "I was afraid you'd fall asleep."

"Not likely." He enfolded her in a hug, taking a moment to revel in something as simple as an embrace. Simple and precious. "DeWitt deliberately drew out our chess game. He's a good player too."

Hecate bussed Phillip's cheek and stepped back. "But you contrived to lose with good grace and not too much haste. You're wearing boots. Good. Come along."

Phillip normally eschewed even a nightshirt and would have felt ridiculous wafting along the corridors in dressing gown and slippers. He was thus attired in his farmer's garb.

"Where are we going?" The conservatory called to him, a contrived replication of the out of doors and, in the middle of the night, reliably deserted.

"It's a surprise. I hope you like it." Hecate took up a dark blue merino shawl and swirled it about her shoulders.

Phillip offered his hand. "Lead on. I am your willing accomplice in all adventures." Nonsense, though he meant every word.

Hecate led him down the maids' stairs, through the conservatory, and onto the terrace where they'd first shared a meal. From there, she skirted the garden, crossed the arched bridge, and five minutes later, Phillip realized their destination was the newly scythed hayfield.

He realized a few other things too: Hecate had worn a pale blue ensemble at supper, but she'd changed into darker attire. Not so much as a golden earbob glinted in the light of the three-quarter moon. She was surefooted in the darkness, and though she wasn't hurrying, she was covering ground.

Eager, then. Or nervous.

He was both. "I love that the robins sing even at night," Phillip said, slipping his signet ring into his empty watch pocket. "Even in winter. They are tireless in their song, and I find that comforting."

"A pretty song too." Hecate struck out across the newly scythed grass. "Confident and clear. I will miss you when this house party is over."

"I've no intention of becoming a stranger. Will you return to London?"

They topped a slight rise, and in the shallow depression below, Phillip could just make out the shapes of a dark blanket, a pair of pillows, and a wicker hamper.

"I thought I might break my journey in Berkshire," Hecate said. "Pay a call on my good friend, the new Marchioness of Tavistock, and see how married life agrees with her."

A bit of moonglow seeped into Phillip's heart, silvery, soft, and wonderful. He enfolded Hecate in another hug. "You did, did you? Have you any other friends in the vicinity of Crosspatch Corners you'd like to call on?"

"I do, as it happens. What of you? Any acquaintances in Town you'd look in on as you prepare for the Little Season?"

She tucked close, Phillip rested his cheek against her temple, and life became a sweet progression of possibilities that could turn into sweeter memories.

"I want to court you properly," he said, "to out-gentleman the fanciest gentlemen in Town so all of polite society knows that Miss Hecate Brompton has a very dedicated suitor." For her, he'd make that effort and enjoy it.

"You needn't."

She was wrong. Mayfair's dandies and matchmakers had lessons to learn when it came to their treatment of her, but Phillip would make that point some other time.

"Are we to enjoy a picnic by moonlight?"

Hecate kissed him lingeringly on the mouth. "The food is to keep up our strength."

How he loved her practical nature. "Is that a threat?"

She kissed him again, adding a sinuous female undulation when she pressed close. "I want you, Phillip. Passionately. Kisses and conversation, as lovely as they are, will not do this time."

Thank heavens for a lady who knew her own mind. "You shall have me." He handed her onto the blanket, and Hecate set to removing her footwear with endearing dispatch. She knew all the etiquette and protocol in the world, but for the next few hours, she would jettison that nonsense and devote herself purely to being Phillip's lover.

And he would devote himself to being hers. *Hours.* Ye heavenly angels. He took the place beside her and pulled off his boots and stockings.

"I love the smell of cut grass," he said. "To me, that's the fragrance of a winter safely passed, of the good earth giving forth what we need to thrive. Of a conscientious farmer keeping after his acres."

"Your shaving soap has a hint of the same scent," Hecate said, starting on a garter below her knee. "Along with the lavender, I can detect—"

Phillip shifted to face her on the blanket. "Allow me."

She regarded him in the moonlight, her expression nearly solemn. She leaned back, bracing on her hands, and extended a silk-clad foot toward him. He grasped her arch, pressing gently against the bottom of her foot, and her eyes closed.

That subtle willingness to experience physical pleasure fortified him, and thus he made the simple exercise of removing her stockings into a prelude to passion. Hecate had lovely feet, delicate ankles, sturdy calves.

Phillip limited his explorations to that territory, rolling down her stockings, drawing the silk slowly over her flesh, and familiarizing himself by caresses and kisses with her particulars.

"A scar?" He traced a thin white line that trailed across her anklebone.

"I jumped into the creek when I was eight. My foot slipped on a rock, and that's the result. No more jumping into creeks. I learned my lesson. When you touch me like that, my thoughts turn the consistency of honey."

Phillip gently kneaded her calf a few more times for good measure. At some point, Hecate had lain flat on her back, and the picture she made, feet bare, skirts frothed above her knees, sent Phillip's thoughts in a very sweet direction.

Before he became utterly witless, he sat back and unbuttoned his breeches.

Hecate watched and then made an impatient gesture with her hand.

"DeWitt says I have the dimensions of a pugilist."

"I don't care that,"—Hecate snapped her fingers, a crisp report in the darkness—"for what Mr. DeWitt says. I'm not sylphlike. One of my myriad failings. If my modiste mutters even one more time that we do as best we can with what heaven gives us, I shall smite her."

"Sack her at least." Phillip untied his cravat, shed his jacket, peeled out of his waistcoat, and pulled his shirt over his head in less than a minute. He'd been naked beneath the moonlight any number of times. Ending a summer day with a dip in the pond behind Lark's Nest's stable was a delightful pleasure and saved the household the bother of preparing a bath.

But those occasions behind the stable had never had his heart thumping a slow tattoo of desire, or hoping that the lady liked what she saw.

"My proportions are not gentlemanly," he said, remaining seated two feet from where Hecate lay, "but the muscles are honestly come by."

Hecate sat up and arranged herself tailor-fashion. "Phillip, gentlemen come in all shapes and sizes. It's what's in here,"—she smoothed a hand over his chest—"that makes the difference. A lady doesn't plan moonlit seductions in a hayfield, but I could think of no better place to embark on this adventure with you. I saw you with your shirt off, swinging that blade, and I thought, 'He pitched in without being asked. He did not stand on pride or appearances. He is precisely who he appears to be, and I *adore* him.'"

"And I adore you." Phillip knelt up and kissed Hecate onto her back, then situated himself over her.

The kissing took on a different, more deliberate rhythm. By degrees, he got her skirts up around her waist, but at that point, Hecate patted his bum and gave him a little push.

Up you go. He was loath to allow even that much distance between them. They'd begun to move together, only the thin layers of her dress between them. To be skin to skin might well be too much, but Phillip had been entranced by the growing intimacy, part frustration, part pleasure.

Another little push, more insistent. He yielded to Hecate's direction and levered up on all fours.

"I want my dress off. I want to be as naked as a pagan and twice as wanton."

Wanton and Hecate Brompton were a lovely combination. She whisked off her clothing with the sort of determination Phillip had long associated with her and then sat, regally naked, and gave him her profile.

"Will I do?"

"Beyond my most passionate imaginings." He gently tackled her, and she lashed her legs around his flanks. Phillip commanded himself to go slowly and cherishingly, even as he longed to ransack Hecate's wits and reave her control.

The lady wasn't having any of that go-slowly nonsense. She wiggled lower, shifting the fit between them, and on the next glide of her hips, she nearly took Phillip into her body.

"For God's sake, woman." He stilled and held himself away from her. "A moment."

She stroked his hair back from his brow. "For God's sake, man, another moment's delay will wreck me."

As Phillip commenced a slow nuzzle from her throat to her shoulder, he identified the source of the last increment of his hesitation. He was not concerned that he'd fall short as a gentleman. The situation had passed the point where any sort of propriety applied.

He was concerned that he'd fail her as a man. That she'd try his gaits, consider a lifetime in harness with him, and then let the pull of family obligations serve as her excuse for waving him on. His own father had found him wanting, his Crosspatch Corners neighbors considered him eccentric, and he'd left a trail of faux pas in Mayfair wider than the Thames.

"I want to get this right," he said, lips pressed to Hecate's brow.

"You already have. Please, Phillip."

Never, ever did he want to hear Hecate begging. He gave himself up to the intoxicating pleasure of joining his body to hers, and the whole world came right.

Here, on the good earth, under the summer stars, the robins serenading the darkness, everything came right, and Phillip was home at last.

CHAPTER ELEVEN

The pleasure Phillip wrought with Hecate was beyond her wildest, most private imaginings. He was inexorable in his loving, relentless, like the approach of nightfall or a gathering storm.

Nothing distracted him, and to be the sole object of his adoring focus brought an intensity to his loving that scoured Hecate's defenses. She fought for control even as she moved with him, fought for reason even as she grabbed with her entire body for bliss.

She lost those battles in a glorious cascade of sensation blended with emotion, a bonfire of oneness in pleasure, that by degrees became oneness in peace and no less wondrous. She was sweating —*sweating*—and naked beneath the stars and beneath Phillip, who had wrapped her close and cradled her gently against his chest.

Hecate kissed the nearest available part of him—his throat—and opened her eyes to behold the heavens over his shoulder.

"I'm crushing you." His voice had acquired a lovely rasp.

"Don't you dare move."

He sighed and pressed his cheek to hers. That he'd await her pleasure even now, even in this, made Hecate tear up. Nobody took orders from her, nobody awaited her pleasure.

"If you farm half as well as you make love, then Lark's Nest is the premier rural estate in all the world," Hecate said, stroking his bum.

He kissed her cheek. "So well I've moved you to tears?"

She was warm and safe in his embrace, and yet, if he moved, if he got all brisk and satisfied, or rolled over and had himself a restorative nap, she'd dry her tears and be brisk right along with him.

Which her heart could not allow. This softness of spirit, the glow in her heart, was too precious to part with.

"I open my eyes after enduring the madness you visited upon me, Phillip, and I behold the stars. The entire heavens are awash in nocturnal splendor, and that is how I feel inside right now. It's too much."

Too much for a woman who'd devoted herself to ledgers, investments, allowances, and pensions because those had been the only means she'd had of mattering to her family. How little, how small she'd become, trying to fit into the narrow box they'd allotted her.

How exhausted and lonely. *Spent.*

I love you. The words welled with greater conviction than any Hecate had ever uttered, but she hesitated. *Please don't leave me* crowded close behind them, and she would not spoil the moment with pleading.

"What if," Phillip murmured near her ear, "I go only far enough to allow us to tidy up, and then we can admire the stars together, until my strength is restored? You have loved me to flinders, Hecate Brompton. I am a man at his last prayers, and they are prayers of gratitude."

"If I had the strength to pray, mine would be as well." Blasphemous, no doubt, to offer thanks for a tryst that was so much more than a stolen moment, but Hecate felt no remorse. In fact, she predicted more blasphemy in her immediate future and contemplated the prospect with relish.

Phillip produced a plain linen handkerchief from a jacket pocket, a white flag amid the night shadows, and dealt with practicalities. He rummaged in the wicker hamper, found the flask of lemonade, and passed it to Hecate.

"This was the right place," he said as Hecate sat up to enjoy a drink. "The right hour, the right everything. I am so drunk with wonderment right now, you will have to lead me back to the manor house by slow, small steps."

She passed him the flask, wishing Nunnsuch in all its grandeur far, far out along the Cornish coast, or perhaps over the cliffs and into the sea.

"You should find some sandwiches in the hamper."

"I am more interested in holding you," Phillip said, draping her shawl around her shoulders. "I need to, in fact, or I will waft away on the night breeze like so much thistledown. I am that inebriated on joy."

The things he said. "Can't have you wafting away."

They arranged themselves like a pair of spoons, Hecate's shawl over them both. The robin had gone silent, and the quiet was profound. Hecate pillowed her head on Phillip's biceps, his arm about her waist.

"Sleep if you want to," he said. "I'll be here when you waken."

Until the snowdrops bloomed. The marvel was not that he'd offer her such sentiments, but that she trusted what lay behind them. Phillip wouldn't return to Lark's Nest and consign her to the category of pleasant memory. He was in her life to stay and in her heart to stay.

"I love you," Hecate said, just as a star dropped from the zenith of the firmament. A brief, surprising trail of light that blazed more brightly as it fell, then winked into darkness.

Phillip shifted over her, and Hecate rolled to her back.

"Again, please," he said. "I want to see your eyes when all my dreams come true."

"I love you," she said. "I esteem, adore, desire, and respect you, et cetera and so forth, but the truth of my heart is that I love you."

He brushed his thumb over her brow. "How you honor me. How you honor and decimate me." He kissed her forehead, then her cheeks, then her mouth, a romantic benediction. "I love you, too, and I always will."

Desire rose again, just as sweet and fierce, but less frantic, less anxious. Hecate gave up any pretense of control and bobbed along on a tide of pleasure, letting Phillip work out for them both the path to satisfaction. He took his time. He meandered and moseyed until Hecate was flailing against him, and then the heavens once more revealed their magnificence, and Hecate became a temple to shared, incandescent joy.

She dozed off, to her mild chagrin, while Phillip held her and stroked her hair. When she awoke, they needed those sandwiches she'd packed, and the robin was once again in good voice. Nights were so short in summer.

And so lovely.

"Do we return the hamper and blanket to the kitchen?" Phillip asked when he'd assisted Hecate to dress and shrugged into his own clothing.

"We do not. I haven't the strength, and there's no need." Hecate brushed her fingers through his hair and contemplated the monumental effort involved in getting to her feet. She was leaving the blanket a different woman from the person who'd lain down upon it just a few hours previously.

A happier woman, a more loving woman.

Phillip rose, stretched, and offered her a hand. He had her on her feet as easily as if he were plucking daisies, and then he hugged her.

"Never, ever will I forget the miracle of this night. You are a marvel, Hecate, and that you'd look with favor upon me to this extent... I am agog."

"The marvel is mutual." She hugged him back and knew they should be returning to the house. "Will I see you at breakfast?"

He brushed his fingers over her knuckles. "If only we could return here for breakfast or, better yet, never leave this place. You will think me a coward, but I do not want to face the people you call family."

"I haven't wanted to face them for years, but you have fortified me. I'm moving you to the summer cottage."

Phillip began their progress across the field, hand in hand. "Does this summer cottage enjoy privacy?"

Hecate halted. "As a matter of fact, it does. A great deal of privacy. It sits across the park from the stream, shaded by tall maples and out of sight of the garden."

They shared a smile, and Hecate's steps were lighter as she resumed walking.

"Why am I to have the great boon of private quarters?"

"Papa's arrival has thrown the arrangements into disarray, and you might recall that there's some possibility another cousin will show up in the near term. I don't have a specific date."

"Cousin Johnny, late of the Canadian wilderness. I overheard your father's announcement. Will you move DeWitt into the summer cottage with me?"

The discussion was mundane—who should be housed where?—but also novel. Guest accommodations were Hecate's problem to solve, and yet, here she was, talking the situation over with Phillip.

"What is the benefit of moving DeWitt to the summer cottage?" She could see the inconvenience of assigning Phillip a cottage mate all too easily.

"I do not trust your lady cousins. Portia is trailing after me like a hound after a bitch in season and watching me from windows and stairways. She is a woman bent on mischief. DeWitt, as my chaperone, has foiled her plans already, I'm sure."

"I am sorry. Portia has grown worse lately, as her mother has been distracted by other matters."

"DeGrange? He has to be ten years her junior."

"He's also the great-nephew of a marquess and quite solvent. What matters age compared to those consideration?"

"When is your birthday?" Phillip asked as they reached the path through the woods.

"The week after next, as it happens. Yours?"

"October, the fourteenth or fifteenth. I'm never sure. I have to look it up each year in the parish registry and count the years to make sure I know my own age."

Because he'd had nobody with whom to celebrate his natal day. Hecate stopped and hugged him again. "We'll remark the occasion this year. Give you some memories to anchor the date on your mental calendar."

He held her loosely, his arms around her shoulders. "And the week after next, perhaps you'll be in Crosspatch Corners that I might do the same for you."

The exchange should have been heartwarming, acknowledging a mutual desire for a shared future, but Hecate was also unsettled by it. To admit of that desire without speaking of matrimony was to admit of a vulnerability, a potential loss. A dream dashed.

Phillip had withdrawn both times when they'd made love. Had that been an insurance policy guaranteeing his freedom, or a courteous attempt to guarantee Hecate's?

Falling in love with Phillip Vincent is not an investment to be assessed in terms of risk and reward. The warning in Hecate's head was delivered in her mother's voice. But then, Mama hadn't been an expert on marital or romantic success.

"I'll move DeWitt to the summer cottage with you," Hecate said when they were strolling over the arched bridge. "Like you, I do not trust Portia, though for all I know, she'll set her cap for Cousin Johnny, if he deigns to join us."

"The conquering Canadian is to become Portia's loyal swain? I will comfort myself with the hope that he and Portia become enamored."

On the side terrace outside the conservatory, Phillip kissed Hecate farewell, a tantalizing reminder of pleasures shared and pleasure still to come.

"Into the house with you," Hecate said, stepping back. Far to the east, the sky was acquiring a hint of gray. "I'll see you at breakfast."

"My darling lady, do not, for the love of spring lambs, come down to breakfast. Have a damned lie-in. Rest. Linger at your bath. Let the world for once spin forth on its own inertia. You have earned a respite."

"While you will clear ditches and fell trees and work yourself to exhaustion."

"The estate isn't beyond salvaging," Phillip said. "I'll do what I can while I'm here, but I will also hope you have a spare key to the summer cottage."

Hecate did not dare touch him again. "I do. Away with you. I will take a tray for breakfast, but rearranging guest quarters will take some managing."

Phillip kissed her cheek, bowed, and slipped into the house. Hecate sank onto the wrought-iron chair near the balustrade and contemplated the past few hours.

She was changed—in love, hoping for a future with Phillip, confiding her worries and dreams in him—and she was the same. A glorified house steward expected to keep an entire horde of Bromptons from the River Tick and other sources of scandal.

The old Hecate could obliterate the new Hecate all too easily, and the Bromptons would aid in her destruction. Phillip would fight for her, but he could take the battle only so far. Hecate sought her bed on that thought, her mind awhirl even as fatigue dragged at her.

She was drifting into the nearer reaches of slumber, thoughts washing about in a fog of hope, worry, longing, and pride—she had a lover, and *such* a lover—when it occurred to her that Phillip was different.

The pleasure they'd shared had been amazing, a revelation in itself, but Hecate also realized that Phillip had never once alluded to her money as anything other than a means for her family to plague her. Not obliquely, not overtly, not in jest.

He did not *see* her money as a marital inducement, and that left her naked in a sense, without camouflage or a protective costume, but also *free*.

Wonderfully free.

Wonderfully, terribly free.

~

The summer cottage was a bit of heaven, at least to Phillip. He could not answer for DeWitt's impressions, because that good fellow had taken to collecting a fishing pole and disappearing after breakfast, returning only when the dressing bell rang for supper.

Staff came and went discreetly, leaving a breakfast tray and tidying up. The house party moved into its second week, with Portia glaring daggers from behind potted lemons, the Corvisers losing more than a few pence at whist, and Isaac Brompton maintaining a bored distance from the other guests.

No great loss, though Brompton continued to treat Hecate with drawling condescension, while Lord Nunn had barely bestirred himself to preside over Sunday dinner. As long as Phillip spent much of his days in hard, useful labor, he could survive his first house party without running afoul of Society's myriad unwritten regulations.

Though as to that, hard, useful labor was apparently an infraction in and of itself. "Oh, the Quality," Phillip muttered, passing his scythe to Henry Wortham.

"You are the Quality." Henry added the blade to the collection in the wagon bed. "Never seen a toff willing to toil in such earnest."

"I wasn't always a toff, and wearing a toff's clothes doesn't mean a man deserves the insult. How is Mrs. Riley?"

Henry became focused on organizing a pile of sickles and scythes that needed no organizing.

"Had a healthy girl baby just this morning. Named her Willa, after William, her late da. Midwife says everything went well."

"Leave Mrs. Riley some flowers." Phillip dusted his fingers through his hair and wiped his face with a handkerchief. "Two bouquets, one for the mama, one for the baby. Pick them yourself." Phillip had picked flowers for Hecate that morning and left them in her bedroom. She'd been fast asleep, done in by a visit to the summer cottage.

Making love under the stars was wonderful. Making love in a big, soft bed while the night breezes stirred the curtains was another kind of magic entirely.

"Flowers?" Henry appeared to be working out a complicated math problem. "Two bouquets?"

A Crosspatch Corners tradition shared from father to son and uncle to nephew. "Two. When Mavis is recovered enough to receive callers, ask to hold the baby. Admire the child, who is doubtless beautiful, as all babies are beautiful. Bathe before you call and bring Mavis some smoked beef or a quarter ham. She needs to regain her strength."

Henry perched a hip on the wagon bed. "I'm the oldest of eight. I know all about babies. They are little and troublesome and loud, when they aren't little, troublesome, and smelly."

Ah, youth. "That tiny girl is all Mavis has of the man who loved her enough to spend the rest of his life with her. When you admire the baby, you respect Mavis's memories."

Henry made a face. "I respect Mavis, but William was the better man. Smarter than me. Not such a brute. I stink of the forge when I'm not stinking of worse. Pa won't give up smithing, and yet, I'm supposed to take over for him if he doesn't outlive me."

"Are you thinking of looking for work in London?" Phillip took out his flask and offered it to Henry. This was a discussion he'd had with many a young fellow in Crosspatch. "That's lemonade. Leave some for me."

Henry sipped and passed it back. "Wages are higher in London, and I'm a hard worker."

"You're the one directing the crews, aren't you? Travers barks the orders, but you're telling him what work needs to be done."

"Travers is a tenant. He knows his patch and does right by it, but I've rambled the whole estate since I was old enough to toddle, and I like to be busy. I'm also bringing in a bit of coin when the forge is slow."

Phillip drained what remained in the flask—his spare—and knew he ought to be getting back to the summer cottage. The sun was still far above the horizon, but the house party was observing country hours, and all that aside, he missed Hecate.

"London wages are higher, but everybody and his cross-eyed dog are in Town looking for work. All the soldiers who've mustered out, the domestics whose rural households can't pay them, the weavers who can't make a living because of the factory looms, the sawyers replaced by steam power, *everybody*. I'd advise against a foray into Town."

"I know," Henry said. "We get the London papers. People starving in the streets, turning to gin, perishing of disease. I don't want to leave, but..."

"I'll put in a word with Tavistock," Phillip said. "He recently bought a property in Berkshire, and every estate can use workers who know what they're doing."

Henry's smile was wan. "Can't court Mavis if I'm in Berkshire."

"You can write to her."

Henry looked intrigued, as if the concept of using the royal mail to further the interests of true love had never occurred to him.

Phillip put away his flask and bid Henry and the rest of the crew farewell. The walk across the park was pleasant, and the long hours of work passed the time between sightings of Hecate. Across the terrace, at supper, over a chessboard ... She was always lovely, always poised and correct, but to Phillip's eye, she had also acquired a quiet sparkle.

Maybe he was sparkling a bit, too, if such a thing—

"My lord." The Earl of Nunn, attired for riding, emerged from the bend in the path that led to the arched bridge. "Out impersonating a peasant again, I see."

The old besom was very much on his dignity, while Phillip could not be bothered to be offended. In less than six hours, he'd once again be abed, listening for Hecate's key turning the latch on his French doors.

"I impersonate a peasant every chance I get," Phillip said, wondering if he should have bowed. "The land thrives when those charged with tending it take a direct hand in matters. You have a beautiful estate, my lord."

Nunn sent a glance in the direction of the stable. "I have a large estate. When the Corn Laws are repealed, which will happen the instant suffrage is expanded, I won't be able to afford jam for my toast, much less wine with supper or fair wages for the domestics."

"Suffrage won't expand that much," Phillip said. "Not at first. The geniuses in the Lords will give voting rights to just enough more men to quiet the grumbling, not enough to beggar the landed class. As an island nation, Britain needs to maintain food production more than most, though you must agree, rotten boroughs serve no proper governmental purpose."

"I will grant you that." To Phillip's surprise, Nunn fell in step beside him. "I've seen you, with the haying crew, in the ditches, mending wall. You must truly like the exertion."

To Nunn, that explanation probably made sense. "I like the stewardship," Phillip said. "An estate requires care, just as children, shops, and households do. I was raised without family, and the land became my passion."

"I knew your father." Nunn used his riding crop to whack the heads off a stand of blooming nettles. He'd just helped propagate the patch, did he but know it. "You have his height, and you bear a resemblance about the eyes, but he was a self-important, braying ass. I cannot credit that you are his get."

"Neither could he."

"Ah. One did wonder, and yet, you look like him."

As they ambled along, it occurred to Phillip that Nunn had yet to get to the point, and for all his hauteur and posturing, the earl had one. He was not a fellow to indulge in random conversations, an attribute in his favor.

"I should thank you," Nunn said, "for..." He waved a hand in the direction of the home farm. "For lending a hand. I was a younger son, off to subdue the Americans, and thus I wasn't raised to manage Nunnsuch. We have manuals for deportment and books that tell us how to cook a roast, but farming..."

"An art learned over a lifetime," Phillip said. "Henry Wortham has a talent for it. Promote him to assistant steward, and he'll soon know as much as your steward does. Henry was born on the estate and considers it his home, not merely a place to work."

Nunn ambled in silence for twenty yards, and the summer cottage came into view. "Loyalty is a fine quality. I'll consider your suggestion."

In for a penny... "Or you could simply tell Hecate that the estate is beyond you, and she'd have it in hand within five years." Particularly if Phillip assisted with the task.

Nunn decapitated a stand of wild carrots this time. "Do you know how incessantly this family expects Hecate to solve their problems? The woman gets no peace, and her thanks is to be maligned and resented, all because she has a good head on her shoulders and does not suffer fools. I'd trade her for the lot of them, and she's not even a true Brompton."

That Hecate had a supporter in the earl came as a surprise. "Then why not treat her with a little more respect, a little warmth?"

"I'd make her my damned heir if I could, but the instant I show her any favor at all, her lot will only worsen. She is loyal to the rogues and flirts I call my family, and if I so much as complimented her bonnet, they'd make her pay. Hecate has burden enough as it is. I rely on her to manage what investments I can afford, and she has extended Nunnsuch any number of unsecured loans, some of which I've even managed to repay. I draw the line at making her a target for the family's bile."

"You might tell her that," Phillip said, mounting the cottage steps and feeling every joint and tendon protest the effort. "Find a quiet moment to let her know how much you appreciate her."

"Mrs. Roberts agrees with you, but exactly when does one find a quiet moment amid the rioting of the Brompton throng? If Edna isn't making a ballyhoo over a lost hair ribbon, then Charlie is placing stupid wagers with men who can buy and sell him twice over, and Eglantine is weeping because her husband—*my heir*—has once again gambled away her pin money. Society refers to them as the Bedlam Bromptons for good reason."

And yet, for all Nunn's exasperation, there remained a thread of affection beneath his words.

"What of Hecate's father? Was he a rackety sort?"

Nunn paced the length of the porch, and Phillip thought he might ignore the question.

"I introduced Marianne to her dashing sea captain right here at Nunnsuch, if you must know. Hecate's parents were rounding out the numbers at a gathering much like this one, and Isaac was being the perfect ass that is apparently his birthright. Marianne got it into her head that if she could present Isaac with a son, he'd settle down."

"And instead," Phillip murmured, "she presented him with an excuse to hold her in contempt for the rest of her days." The late marquess was apparently not the only man to ride that weary horse.

"Certainly to disdain her. Isaac needed Marianne's money, and still does, though Hecate now controls the wealth. Drives Isaac barmy, which is exactly what he deserves. Marianne was a lamb to slaughter when her family agreed to Isaac's suit. He ought never to have treated her as he did, but try telling a Brompton what to do when they are set on stupidity."

Or when they were set on providing for an entire family of wastrels and wantons. "Is Hecate's father still alive?"

Nunn paused at the top of the steps. "Very much so. He bides in Bristol, though his mother's people are American. He's quite well-to-do. I suspect a substantial portion of Hecate's wealth comes from him, though she probably doesn't know that herself. Marianne learned to keep herself to herself. I write to the man regularly, in part so he has occasional word of his daughter's situation."

"She deserves to know him."

Nunn looked away, to where the roofline of Nunnsuch gleamed above the trees in the westering sun. "She doesn't ask about him, and he doesn't want to create awkwardness. She looks very much like him and has his talent with investments."

Phillip surmised, in what was not said, that Nunn feared to lose access to that talent and to Hecate's money. Married to a Berkshire courtesy lord, she could continue to supervise, support, and subsidize her Brompton family. With a doting papa to fly to—and American cousins—she might well cut her Brompton ties once and for all.

Not likely, but possible.

"I intend to offer for her," Phillip said, though he'd yet to work out the details. Another blanket under the stars suggested itself, though he wanted to exceed even the glory of that memory. The only ring he could offer her had belonged to his mother, and what if the size wasn't right? "I know I ought to ask Isaac's permission to court her, but he's not worthy of such a courtesy."

Nunn snorted. "He cannot refuse you permission. You are heir to a marquessate, of sound mind, and in obnoxiously good health."

"He can refuse me his blessing," Phillip said, "and all the etiquette manuals say I'm to then slink away and nurse my broken heart in solitude, like the gentleman I never aspired to be."

Nunn smiled, and the charm he'd possessed as a younger man glimmered past the dignity he wore like armor. "Fortunately for Hecate, you are not much given to elevating etiquette over a worthy objective, are you?"

"One ought to be able to pursue such objectives without losing sight of his manners." Phillip would have parted from Nunn then—a bath was imperative before changing for supper—but Nunn lingered at the top of the steps.

"I wish you the best of luck with your courtship. Hecate is long overdue for a worthy suitor, but I thought you should know that Johnny Brompton cantered up the drive today shortly after noon. At one time, he and Hecate were fond of each other."

One time, ten years ago, before Johnny had left a schoolgirl to defend herself from a mob of jackals. Though, of course the fellow would have sense enough to *ride* up the driveway, and probably on a white horse too.

"I hope Hecate and her cousin are still fond of each other," Phillip said. "Hecate will no doubt be pleased to see him, and I will be delighted to make his acquaintance."

Phillip told the lie as convincingly as any London swell had ever offered a false compliment to his Mayfair hostess, and that bothered him all the way to supper.

CHAPTER TWELVE

From the place at Edna's right hand, Johnny held forth like the returning hero he was, and Hecate was relieved to allow him the floor. A house party in its second week should offer more in the way of entertainment than the scavenger hunts, pall-mall matches, and whist parties of the first week.

She'd thought up nothing more interesting than tomorrow's horse race, along with the grand ball at week's end. Johnny bid fair to be the main attraction at that event, and for good reason.

"He's magnificent," Flavia murmured. "Canadian air must be very healthful."

Johnny had become what Charlie should have been: tall, robust, golden, and charming. He had the gift of laughing at himself, recounting stories of falling into rivers, felling an enormous tree only to have it land across his logging trail, and losing his fishing pole through a hole cut in the frozen surface of a lake.

"He has apparently prospered," Hecate replied quietly. Such was Johnny's gift with a story that even Portia appeared to have temporarily misplaced her sulks. His attire was exquisite without being ostentatious, his hair queued back in the old-fashioned manner that nonetheless looked dashing on him.

Hecate would not have known him, so kind had ten years in the wilderness been to the gangling young fellow who'd gone off with his regiment a decade past. The older Johnny had poise, self-possession, and muscles that the youth could only have dreamed of.

The differences time had wrought were subtle and pervasive. Johnny's hair had darkened from flaxen to gold and had more curl. His laugh was heartier. He wore only the gold jewelry suitable for evening, though like any gracious Englishman, he flirted equally with Eglantine and Edna.

He flirted with the entire female half of the table, truth be told, another skill apparently learned in Canada.

"Johnny *has* prospered," Flavia muttered from her place at Hecate's side. "But can you never see past the money? Johnny has grown beautiful. He has bloomed in the wilderness. He was never this much fun before."

"You were a child when he was last home." So, technically, had Hecate been a child. Children noticed far more than adults gave them credit for.

"I had eyes. I had ears. Johnny was more serious before he went for a soldier, more..." Flavia speared a section of orange from the compote before her. "More subdued. I like this Johnny better."

Because he'd made good his escape. He'd returned as a sort of anti-Brompton. Self-made, hardworking, adventurous, good-humored, unpretentious, solvent, friendly... His list of apparent virtues was dizzying, and Flavia was right: Johnny Brompton was also easy on the eyes.

Hecate slanted a glance down the table in Phillip's direction. He was easy on the eyes, too, in an entirely different sense. No flash or dash, just bone-deep honor and quiet competence in any number of pursuits a gentleman never turned his hand to.

Phillip saluted subtly with his wineglass, and Hecate nodded.

When she looked up, Johnny was smiling at her, and the glint in his eyes said he'd noted the exchange.

"Maybe Johnny hopes you've waited for him," Flavia said. "Maybe he's come home to court you, Hecate. Wouldn't that be wonderful?"

"More like absurd. Did he expect me to wait ten years for him without so much as a letter sending his kind regards?" She sipped her wine and began counting in German, though, in part, fatigue—not Johnny, not Portia, not feuding housemaids, or Edna's daily dramas—was making her testy.

"Ten years is a long time," Flavia said, collecting a spoonful of cream and fruit juice. "Maybe he was waiting for Porry to grow up. She was always quite fond of Johnny."

Rather than comment on Portia's talent for revisionist recollections—she'd been fond of playing duchess-and-lady's-maid when Johnny had decamped—Hecate finished her compote.

Nunn had deigned to join supper in honor of Johnny's arrival—and thus thrown the seating arrangements into disarray at the last minute. He gave Hecate a nod, and she contrived to brush Edna's arm when refilling her wineglass.

"Off we go," Hecate murmured.

"When Johnny has finished his tale," Edna retorted. "Really, Hecate. Have you no sense of timing?"

Hecate had the beginnings of a headache, a pinching around the temples. She counted it a small price to pay for spending hours each night in Phillip's arms, but the toll was mounting. Waiting for the household to batten down for the night, slipping across the park, then returning before dawn ran contrary to her usual well-ordered routine.

Racketing about in the dark made her feel like a Brompton in the harum-scarum sense, but then, by next week, the opportunities to be private with Phillip would be at an end.

"And that," Johnny said with a self-deprecating smile, "is how I came to be driving a donkey cart when I was dispatched to pick up my new commanding officer's lady wife. Let it be said, however, that they were matched donkeys, each one as malodorous and contrary as the other."

"How marvelous!" Flavia sighed as the rest of the audience laughed and tapped spoons against glasses. "Now I want to be driven in Hyde Park behind a matched pair of donkeys with Johnny at the ribbons."

"Matched asses in Hyde Park," Mrs. Roberts murmured across the table. "Intriguing concept. On that note, shall we ladies withdraw to the blandishments of the teapot?" Bless her, she directed her question to Edna, who had no choice but to rise.

Hecate waited for the guests to sort themselves out and found Johnny winging his arm at her.

"My dear, dear girl, grace me with your company, won't you please?"

Hecate wrapped her fingers around his arm while Phillip did the pretty for Mrs. Roberts. They passed close enough that Hecate could catch a whiff of Phillip's shaving soap, though he wasn't wearing his usual lavender meadow scent. Something heavier and sweeter, perhaps from the stores stocked in the summer cottage.

She didn't care for it. "I am not a girl," she said, offering Johnny a bland smile. "Haven't been for years."

"One notices the transformation." He imbued his words with a hint of flirtation. "Notices and appreciates. You're in charge of this gathering, aren't you?"

"I have assisted Edna with some details." That he'd see Hecate's hand on the reins pleased her, which was ridiculous.

Johnny laughed softly. "You were always excessively capable. I knew if I took you to Canada—as badly as I longed to—the whole lot of 'em would come to a scandalous end. Admit it, I made the right decision leaving you at your post while I made my fortune in the New World."

Hecate was torn between resentment—when had Johnny

Brompton acquired the right to assign her the duty of rescuing his family?—and confusion. He spoke to her as if they'd been on parallel missions on separate shores, all for the greater good.

"Your strategy proved successful," Hecate said as they approached the parlor door.

"My strategy? When have I ever had occasion to discuss strategy with you? So lovely a pair of ears ought not to be burdened with the details of maneuvers and means."

He'd always discussed his plans and dreams in terms of tactics, at least when conversing with Hecate in private. Johnny was shrewd, though perhaps he'd learned to hide the shrewdness behind blather.

"You advised me to fend off all offers of marriage until I was one-and-twenty, at which time, I'd begin acquiring control of my money. That was sound thinking, and I thank you for it. I manage my entire fortune now, and that would never have happened if I'd married."

"You manage the whole yourself?" Johnny patted her hand. "Good for you. I'm proud of you, Hecate. The entire family is in your debt, and I will be the one to acknowledge what we owe you. Well done."

The effect of his words was like expecting skimmed milk in her tea and finding somebody had stirred in heavy cream instead. The lavish praise felt heavy and sticky rather than rich.

"Thank you. I hope your rooms are in order?"

"Lovely. The staff says you kicked Lord Phillip out to make room for me. I will have to express my appreciation to him for accepting lesser quarters, but you need not have displaced the ranking guest on my behalf. In Canada, I spent many a night beside a campfire. A trapper goes for months without sleeping in a proper bed. It's a hard life, and I am well pleased to have it behind me."

He'd be back to Canada on a fast ship once the Bromptons started relieving him of his fortune.

"Then we must ensure your comfort while you're here," Hecate said as the gentlemen began filing back toward the dining room. "It's good to see you."

"Wonderful to see you." He held her hand and gazed at her with a seriousness that belied the raconteur's good spirits. "A dream come true." He bowed over her hand and departed, leaving Hecate alone in the corridor and wondering what on earth he'd intended with that excessive flummery.

∽

"The evening put me in mind of my attitude toward Crosspatch's churchyard gossips," Phillip said as he and DeWitt wandered toward the summer cottage. "Not a word of the proceedings ever involved me. I lack any aptitude for intemperance, flirtation, adultery, wagering, rage, or crime, and thus I was of no interest to them, nor they to me."

"You also," DeWitt said, "never ran off to join the traveling players, leaving your womenfolk to make shift. The Crosspatch neighbors must have made a great deal of hay over that."

"We worried about you," Phillip said, and to his consternation, he was still in some regard worried for DeWitt. The fellow was unsettled, and fishing generally lost its charm by the third hour. As far as Phillip knew, DeWitt had yet to catch anything save a few naps.

"I don't get the sense anybody worried about Cousin Johnny," DeWitt said. "His years in Canada were apparently one long, uninterrupted lark."

"A lucrative lark, based on his turnout." Two golden rings on his left hand, a third on his right. A tasteful cascade of lace beneath his chin, the fragrance of gardenias wafting about his person. Three gold watch chains across his flat middle and a dragon twisted onto the gold of his cravat pin.

Gardenias. The sooner Phillip washed away the stink of the fancy *parfum* his valet had insisted on packing, the sooner he'd breathe freely.

"You laughed at Johnny's jokes," DeWitt said. "I did, too, and the ladies positively swooned over him."

Hecate had not swooned, though Phillip was looking forward to hearing her reaction to her cousin's arrival. That assumed she didn't fall asleep at her vanity and skip their usual assignation altogether. She was getting as little rest as Phillip, and while the nights were lovely, they were also deucedly short.

"One is supposed to be polite," Phillip said. "As best I recall, commandeering the attention of the whole company for better than an hour is not polite."

"He's been gone ten years. Let him make his entrance."

DeWitt had been off in the provinces for two years. Had anybody greeted him with one-fifth the enthusiasm Cousin Johnny merited?

"I *watch* the gossip," Phillip said. "I don't participate in it, and my question is always: What is the motive here? Is an exchange driven by malice, concern, curiosity, or—Crosspatch Corners is a rural English village, after all—simple boredom?"

"I vote boredom," DeWitt said. "Polite society is frequently as bored as it is boring, much like village society. I will be glad to leave this place."

And get back to what? Ignoring his sister the marchioness making sheep's eyes at her new husband? Memorizing plays he'd never perform? Standing up with the village beauties at the next assembly? A farmer was never at a loss for six different pressing tasks to choose from, while a gentleman was to take pride in idleness.

The concept still baffled Phillip, though he'd had better than a week to watch the likes of Charlie Brompton and the Corvisers do just that.

"I am fortunate," Phillip said as the dark outline of the summer cottage came into view. "I am fascinated by such mysteries as why a speckled hen does not always lay speckled eggs, but a red hen can lay eggs that are both russet and speckled. Breeding comes into it, but it doesn't explain the whole puzzle."

"A mystery for the ages," DeWitt said. "All I know is, I don't like Cousin Johnny. Behind all that bonhomie, he's gauging the audience's reaction, keeping an eye on the till, and upstaging the rest of the troupe."

"If he inspires Portia to cease her histrionics," Phillip said around a yawn, "then he's welcome to teach the lot of us all the latest Canadian drinking songs."

They climbed the steps and let themselves into the darkened dwelling. No fires were lit in the grates, no lamps left burning, and Phillip liked it that way. Too much artificial light, and a man got out of step with the rhythm of the sun, moon, and stars.

"Portia was whispering with Flavia in the library when I arrived for supper," DeWitt said, tossing his key into a porcelain bowl on the sideboard. "I went in there to return a volume of poetry Miss Hecate found for me, and those two were stirring some cauldron of mischief known only to them."

"Probably what they do best. Setting their caps for their handsome cousin, no doubt. God in heaven, I am tired."

"Come fishing with me." DeWitt's voice sounded wistful in the darkness. "Let those mend wall who will be paid for it."

"My wages go to Mrs. Riley, newly delivered of a healthy girl child. Besides, Henry hasn't the knack of mending wall, and if you do it wrong, you just have to make the same repair after the next hard winter. He's learning from me, and his education is far from complete. Will you go fishing in the morning?"

"The horse race is tomorrow. I had Roland sent down from Twidboro Hall at the beginning of the week for the express purpose of upholding the honor of the Berkshire gentry."

"I noticed your colt napping in the shade today. Has he had enough time to recover from the journey?"

"Knackered and winded, Roland can beat anything on the Nunnsuch estate. Care for a brandy?"

"I'd fall asleep before the third sip. I bid you good night."

A horse race would liven up the day. Herne was fast—not as fast as Roland—but Herne also had bottom. The horse was tireless, well rested, and had a genius for gauging the distance to an obstacle.

Doubtless, Cousin Johnny's charger was faster, smarter, and more athletic.

Phillip washed thoroughly and still caught a lingering whiff of that damned cologne he never should have purchased. Foul stuff. Made him smell like a dowager trying to hide a tendency to tipple.

He peeled out of his clothing, lay down on the bed, and gave himself up to waiting for Hecate's arrival. Perhaps tonight they'd talk and nap and catch up on their rest. He really ought to be going to her, but that way lay... complications.

Portia lurking on the stairway, the Corvisers laying lewd wagers... Phillip dozed off to the image of Cousin Johnny Roman-riding up the drive, manly feet on the backs of a pair of donkeys. The scrape of a key in the lock of his French doors roused him.

He waited, more than ready to enjoy the pleasure of simply holding Hecate. He longed to feel her weight asleep on his chest, to hear her voice in the darkness...

Footsteps trailed away from the door, and he realized that she'd likely found him asleep and decided to leave him to his slumbers.

Bollocks to that. He rose and pulled on shirt, stockings, and breeches, then shoved his feet into his oldest pair of boots. A dark jacket completed his ensemble and off he went in pursuit of his beloved.

Only to stop at the foot of the garden steps as Cousin Johnny's voice cut across the darkness.

"Dearest Cousin Hecate. Dare I hope you came out here knowing I'd follow?"

"You dare not. One simply wants a breath of fresh air before bed."

Phillip silently applauded that sentiment.

Cousin Johnny's footsteps crunched closer. "Is that all one wants? I've missed you, Hecate. Missed you far, far more than you can possibly know."

A gentleman would not eavesdrop. A gentleman would slip away before another word was said.

Phillip longed to be a gentleman in the eyes of the world, to have the panache and presence of a Cousin Johnny. Instead, he had a good pair of ears and the burning conviction that the fellow was up to no good.

Phillip found a comfortable rock amid the ferns and bracken and settled down to do more than eavesdrop if necessary to safeguard Hecate's wellbeing.

～

"If you'll excuse me," Hecate said, frustration flaring, "I will seek my bed."

"Bide with me a moment," Johnny replied. "Only a moment."

Hecate weighed the price of delaying her slumbers another quarter hour against Johnny apparently feeling entitled to subject her to some sort of cousinly *moment*. Phillip had been fast asleep when Hecate had let herself into his bedroom, and she hadn't had the heart to wake him.

Had Johnny followed her to the summer cottage? He was an accomplished woodsman, after all, and familiar with Nunnsuch's grounds.

She settled on a bench and arranged her skirts. "If you have something to say, you'd best say it. The horse race tomorrow necessitates organizing a picnic buffet sufficient to feed half the shire. The whole neighborhood has been invited, and they will rejoice to learn of your return."

"I rejoice to be returned," Johnny said, taking the place directly beside her.

Hecate barely restrained herself from moving away. The Johnny who'd left had still had the lanky vestiges of youthful awkwardness. He'd known enough to regard his Canadian posting with both enthusiasm and caution. He'd been charming, but not like the Johnny who'd returned.

This fellow was confident and calculating. Hecate did not trust him and wasn't sure she even liked him.

"Do you know why I went to Canada?" Johnny asked, stretching out his legs and crossing his feet at the ankles. "The wilderness is endless, the frontier far from civilized, and the winters... You cannot imagine the winters, Hecate. Snow in June and September isn't unheard of out west, and yet, they claim to have a summer."

If Canada was so beastly inhospitable, then perhaps Britain ought to leave it in peace. "I'm told it's also beautiful beyond imagining."

"It is, when it's not trying to kill you. I bought my colors because I did not want to be yet another Brompton preying on your generous nature. I took Emeril with me because he was already hatching schemes to relieve you of your fortune."

"To compromise me? Miss Blanchard would have foiled those plans. My companion was skeptical of bachelors generally and of Brompton bachelors most of all."

"The truth is, I wanted to be worthy of your esteem."

Oh no. Not this and not now, when Hecate was exhausted, and wishing herself in Phillip's arms, and ready to be done with house parties forever more.

"You have my esteem," she said, scooting forward. "Anybody who escapes the pull of the Brompton tendency to mischief and insolvency deserves endless esteem, but right now, I deserve to find my bed."

When she would have risen, Johnny seized her wrist. His grip didn't hurt, but Hecate's urge to leave edged closer to anger.

"We're engaged, you know," Johnny said quietly. "You and I. Isaac hatched up the notion when he learned I was thinking of joining up. I was losing hope that the solicitors would approve the funds for my commission, so I signed the settlement agreements at Isaac's urging. A contingency plan, he said, but I signed them in good faith."

Engaged? Hecate nearly laughed with relief, except Johnny was for once serious. "Isaac excels at hatching schemes that come to nothing. We are not engaged."

"He says you signed the papers too." Johnny's grip shifted so his fingers were laced with Hecate's. "Said he slipped them in among all the documents and whatnot the solicitors were always having you sign. Managing a fortune apparently necessitates mountains of correspondence, bank drafts, and so forth."

"It doesn't matter what I signed," Hecate said, trying to keep her tone civil. "I was not yet of age. Having long since reached my legal majority, I can repudiate any contract I made when I was a minor." The rule had exceptions. Her new solicitors would know them, but the concept held true in the general case.

"You'd do that to me?" Gone was the swaggering prodigal. In his place was a good man humbled by looming and undeserved defeat. The transition was a little too smooth for credibility, but Hecate couldn't ignore the real bewilderment in Johnny's tone.

She marshaled her patience and kept her voice down. "You expect me to marry a man I haven't seen in ten years? A man who never once wrote to me or asked to be remembered to me—*in ten years?*"

"A bachelor doesn't correspond with an unattached young lady."

Utter balderdash. "We are cousins of some sort, which makes us family—family enough that *I* provided the funds to purchase the commission you hoped for so desperately. You could have sent regards to me by name in any of your rare general dispatches, but you did not. Not regards, not fond regards, not the kind of letters any man is allowed to exchange with his prospective bride."

"But my dearest—"

Hecate held up a hand. "We would not suit. I will not marry you, and you'd best be careful lest Portia get herself locked into a pantry with you."

"Portia was a scheming little girl ten years ago, and she's only grown into her potential. I'll not be locked into any pantries with her. I will be too busy courting you."

"Your suit is doomed, and you undertake it against my wishes." Exhaustion was making Hecate daft, because the idea that Johnny insisted on courting her struck her as laughable. This handsome, charming, golden adventurer would have at one time been her dream come true.

He was annoying when a lady was short of sleep and missing her true love.

"I am exceedingly tired," she said, shaking her hand free of Johnny's grasp and pushing to her feet. "You are correct that the house party has been my chore to organize, subsidize, and manage, and I am nearly asleep on my feet. I bid you good night and will expect you to jettison any notions of courting me. Court Flavia. She's sweet and overshadowed by Portia, though Flavie has a kind heart and better instincts than she knows." *I was like her once upon a time, long ago.*

Johnny rose and once again possessed himself of Hecate's hand.

Stop touching me. She bit back the words lest Johnny provoke some sort of scene that could be heard from the house—or the summer cottage.

"We are legally engaged," Johnny said. "That hasn't changed, and I intend to court you with every ounce of my considerable determination. All those years, Hecate, all those winters, I promised myself that someday I'd return to England and to you. I survived hardships and dangers you cannot imagine, and all the while, the thought of coming home to you kept me going."

Rank, febrile nonsense, but such was the quiet conviction in Johnny's words that Hecate hadn't the heart to name it as such.

"Listen to me. Isaac had us sign those papers—if any I did sign—because he planned to see us married, and then he would have insisted I remain in England while you risked your life in the wilderness. With your consent as my husband, he'd doubtless have had himself appointed trustee of my fortune, and you would have returned to find yourself married to a pauper. Isaac might well have been betting that you would not return at all. Be grateful that we are not married and that we were never truly engaged."

Isaac had hatched any number of such schemes, but Hecate's solicitors at the time had had their own agenda for abetting her continued independence, and thank heavens for that.

Johnny seized her other hand. "Tearing myself away from you was the hardest thing I ever did, Hecate, and that is saying a great deal, given the difficulty of life in the wilds of Canada. We shall be married. I will not renounce the agreement, and you must at least give me a chance to win your heart."

No, I must not. Ten years ago, a promise to return to her, a few letters, a lock of his hair... the slightest indication of loyalty or affection from him would have been enough to convince her of his esteem.

Instead, he'd given her some parting advice and a pat on the shoulder. Now he rivaled Portia in his ability to create false history to suit his present agenda.

"I am unwilling for you to court me," Hecate said, "much less marry me. The Church of England takes a dim view of a woman being forced to the altar against her will. A very dim view." Marriage could be nullified in the absence of true consent, though that was a scandalous road to travel.

"Marriage to me will be consistent with your wishes, Hecate. I assure you of that."

Her only warning was a tightening of his grip on her hands, then he swooped in, got an arm around her shoulders, and was mashing his lips against her cheek.

"John Brompton, what the rubbishing blazes do you think—?"

His mouth landed on hers, and Hecate's weariness and disbelief were joined by a spike of fear. The torches had been extinguished, the house was abed, and Johnny was much, much stronger than he'd been as a skinny youth in his loose-fitting uniform.

Hecate twisted, trying to aim a knee at the bounder's cods, but she succeeded only in getting a halfhearted heel stomp to his boot.

Then Johnny was gone.

Hecate braced herself against the bench, dragging in air and preparing to pelt straight for the house, but there was Phillip...

He had one hand in Johnny's golden locks, the other held one of Johnny's hands against his back. The pugilists doubtless had a name for that maneuver, while Hecate called it well timed.

"Is this what passes for courting in Canada?" Phillip asked pleasantly. "Brompton, you owe the lady an apology. Your fumbling attentions were clearly unwanted."

Even in the darkness, Hecate could see the calculation pass through Johnny's eyes. Phillip had let go of Johnny's hair, but still had a hand hiked behind him.

"Miss Brompton, I do apologize. I am to blame for misreading the situation, and it won't happen again."

Hecate's fear acquired a leavening of rage. How dare he, and what if Phillip hadn't come along, and what sort of thanks was this for spending a small fortune and working herself to exhaustion...?

And yet, a Brompton-style tantrum would not do. "Keep your distance from me," she said. "Lay a hand on me again, and you will long for those wilderness hardships."

She did her best to flounce off, but hadn't the energy for a grand exit. By the time she reached her room, she was shaking with a combination of fatigue, anger, shock, and horror. The whole scene had been outlandish, and yet, Johnny had spoken confidently of signed documents. Then too, matrimonial schemes had been Isaac's dearest preoccupation for several years.

She was nearly too tired to undress and certainly too far gone to do more than take down her hair and fashion it into a single braid. No hundred strokes with the brush or entering the day's tasks or tomorrow's challenges in her journal.

What if Phillip hadn't taken the situation in hand?

Rape wasn't necessary to compromise a lady. If she screamed for help and was caught in a private situation with a man who looked guilty, tongues would start wagging.

And Johnny had known that.

Hecate climbed into bed, furious in her bones, but grateful too. Phillip *had* come along. Phillip had sorted Johnny out. Johnny's stupid, wretched, miserable plan had been foiled, and Hecate was no more compromised than she was engaged to be married.

Johnny Brompton could take his handsome, scheming self straight back to the coldest depths of the worst winter Canada had to offer, and Hecate would wish him Godspeed.

CHAPTER THIRTEEN

"You can let go of me, my lord," Johnny Brompton said. "I'm sure dear Hecate will lock her door against thieves, brigands, and cousins overcome by passion."

Phillip let loose of Brompton reluctantly. The problem wasn't that Brompton required further restraint, but rather, that while keeping hold of him, Phillip could resist the temptation to beat the rotter bloody.

"Does the English language work differently in Canada?" Phillip asked. "Does 'I am unwilling for you to court me' suggest the lady was inviting your advances? Did her struggles to free herself somehow translate into welcoming your assault?"

Brompton tossed himself onto the bench and scrubbed a hand over his face. "I rushed my fences. I don't deny it. Badly done of me."

He'd not rushed his fences. He'd crashed straight through them, destroying all in his path.

"You have to admit," Brompton went on, "a woman sometimes protests too much." He tried for a smile of manly self-deprecation.

Phillip, instead of calming down, was growing angrier. What if he'd not heard Hecate relocking his door? What if he'd tarried a few minutes more to don waistcoat and neckcloth? What if Brompton had trailed Hecate and accosted her in her very bedroom?

"Miss Brompton was not protesting," Phillip said. "She was making it absolutely clear that your advances were unwelcome. You are not to touch her, not to be alone with her, not to impose on her in any manner whatsoever."

"That will be a bit difficult, given that we are engaged."

"She told you she has no intention of being coerced to the altar."

Brompton looked up at Phillip. "What are you doing wandering about the garden, half undressed, at such an hour? Were you eaves-dropping? Waiting for your own opportunity to persuade Hecate to the altar?"

"I was stopping a rapist from committing a hanging felony."

Brompton made a face. "You're gentry, aren't you? Despite the courtesy title. Gentry can be so uppish. I would not have raped her. Rape can get loud. A man has to be furious to make a proper job of rape. I'm not furious, I'm besotted. There's a difference."

Phillip would have said the Bromptons generally were lazy, scheming, venal, and shallow, but their nastiness was petty. They were too lazy for true evil.

Johnny's casual assessment of the conditions conducive to rape, his reference to making *a proper job* of violating another person, put him in a different league. He was not a garden-variety Brompton, but rather, a man whose ambitions had honed self-centeredness into arro-gance and determination into ruthlessness.

"You don't need Miss Brompton's money, apparently," Phillip said, "so why court scandal by forcing yourself on her?"

"She would have come around," Johnny said as casually as if his horse would have won the match, given another furlong. "She will come around. The law is on my side."

He was too smug, too sure of himself. If Phillip remained in his presence, he'd pummel Brompton flat. Hecate wouldn't appreciate the drama, but the feel of Phillip's fist plowing into the Canadian Casanova's chiseled jaw would have been delicious.

"The law is not on your side," Phillip said, "and more to the point, *the lady* is not on your side. She doesn't need a husband, and you don't need a fortune, so for the sake of all concerned, leave her alone."

Brompton rose and stretched, not a care in the world. "What business is it of yours? The matter is one for the Bromptons to resolve, and if they don't resolve it to my satisfaction, I will see to it that Edna and Eglantine are no longer received, Portia and Flavia are pariahs, and Isaac and Charlie must resign from their clubs. I can do it too. I've had ten long, cold years to study on the matter."

He sketched an elegant bow and sauntered off into the darkness.

Phillip debated joining Hecate in her room, but if she needed one thing more than to be free of her strutting cousin, it was a good night's rest. He returned to the summer cottage and pulled off his boots, but didn't go to bed. Instead, he fell asleep on the terrace, his fitful rest interrupted when the first cold drops of rain pattered down from a starless sky.

~

Hecate awoke with the leaden limbs and foggy mind of one who'd barely made a start on a serious lack of rest. Exhaustion upon waking was nothing new, though. She lay in bed, listening to a pattering rain and rummaging in memory for the source of the foreboding that weighed on her heart.

Johnny. Wretched, rubbishing Johnny.

The recollection of his hands on her wrists, his lips on her cheek, had her throwing back the covers and slogging from the bed.

"Of all the harebrained, witless, presuming..." She considered her reflection in the cheval mirror and saw a woman as angry as she was weary. The Bromptons had had their fingers in her pockets forever. She'd learned to manage their perpetual demands, learned to impose schedules and budgets and even some manners on them.

Johnny didn't intend to help himself merely to her money,

though. He sought to pillage her very personhood. Steal her freedom and her fortune, the knave. She'd always wished the Bromptons would develop some ambition, but not like this...

She dressed with particular care for a change and wrapped her usual bun in a pair of twining braids. She fastened her shawl with a pearl brooch and dabbed a bit of scent on her wrists and beneath her ears.

"Battle-ready," she muttered, giving her appearance one last inspection. A lady was to be composed at all times. Hecate had no desire to disguise the pugnacious glint in her eyes.

To her surprise, Papa occupied the breakfast parlor. He picked up his coffee cup, flicked a dismissive glance over her, and sipped.

"Good morning, Papa."

He waited a moment before replying, for which Hecate wanted to dump his drink over his head. "Wet morning," he said. "Isn't your horse race today?"

Was he gloating? "One hopes the weather will clear off, but the course is flat. Safe enough even if the ground is damp." Hecate helped herself to eggs and ham, though another silent, brooding meal with Papa was not how she'd like to start her day. She took the chair one seat away from him.

She would have preferred Phillip's company, his quiet steadiness, his subtle humor, his calm.

"The weather will oblige you," Papa said, pouring himself more coffee. "All of creation orders itself according to your whim. Your mother enjoyed the same undeserved good fortune."

Hecate considered taking a tray to the conservatory, but all too often, retreat had been her tactic of choice with Isaac. The result was incessant bullying and whining.

"Mama wanted to present you with a son. She was denied that pleasure. Please pass the honey."

Another slight delay, then the honeypot was thunked down a foot from Hecate's plate. "Is that what she told you? She was trying to present me with a son? If nothing else, the blood of an accomplished liar runs in your veins."

Hecate stirred honey into her tea. "She also told me that you assured her you were marrying her because you esteemed her above all women and would expire for lack of her love. You swore her money was of no moment whatsoever. If Mama was mendacious, then I carry the name of an even more accomplished liar than she was."

The breakfast parlor acquired the sort of quiet that made the rain against the windows loud by contrast. Hecate did not confront Isaac in the usual course. If they had to communicate, they did so in writing, through the solicitors, or through other family members.

Hecate didn't hate Isaac—he'd suffered significant disappointments in life—but she neither liked nor trusted him. He was cold-blooded in a way the rest of the family was not and driven by bitterness as much as greed.

"Tell me, Hecate. Will you try to lie your way out of your betrothal to Johnny?" Papa put the question almost pleasantly. "I would enjoy seeing you try. I, who watched you sign the settlement agreements just before I signed them myself. I, who know for a fact that Johnny will be more generous with that money than you have ever been."

Hecate sipped her tea, feeling an old, rancid sense of betrayal. "Did you summon Johnny from Canada?"

Papa took a slice of toast from the rack and helped himself to the raspberry jam. "Why would you think such a thing? The man spent ten years making his fortune through luck, skill, and determination. Now he's come home to you, just as he promised he would. Another woman would be touched by and grateful for such devotion, particularly a woman of plain appearance and few accomplishments."

Eins, zwei, drei... "I begged Johnny to take me with him. He patted my shoulder and wished me luck. I cannot marry a man who has never proposed to me."

"Your memory fails you. Johnny proposed very prettily. You

accepted, but understood that he wanted to bring his own means to the union. You respect that about him. I do, too, and so will all of Society."

Hecate picked up her fork and understood that Papa was at least partly justified in his anger. Mama might well have hoped to present him with a son, but she'd also capitulated to the lure of her sea captain out of sheer despair. To be Isaac Brompton's daughter had been vexing and painful.

Mama must have suffered the torments of the damned as his supposedly barren wife.

"I am not marrying Johnny," Hecate said, spearing a bite of eggs, "who never did me the courtesy of a proposal, much less seek permission to court me, much less send me a single *billet-doux*. Believe whatever other fancies you please, connive with Johnny however you wish, but know that I will not marry him."

The silver lining in that declaration was that, but for Phillip, Hecate might be considering a negotiated truce with Johnny. Promises to Isaac notwithstanding, Johnny, as Hecate's husband, would guard Hecate's fortune for the simple reason that any settlements would make a part of that fortune his.

He would not champion her interests, but he would champion his own, and that could work to Hecate's benefit.

In the same moment those thoughts flitted through her brain, she rejected them. Putting up with her family, she'd learned to be pragmatic to a fault, to think always of the long term and of the larger picture. The larger picture was, when Johnny had frittered away *his* portion of her money, he'd come after *hers*.

"Don't marry him, then," Papa said, biting off a corner of his toast. "Have your tantrum, show your ingratitude. Give the gossips yet more to titter and laugh about. Johnny will simply present the signed documents to a court of law and bring suit for breach of promise."

Hecate took another bite of eggs, which needed salt. "He'll look a fool if he takes that route. Men don't sue for breach of promise."

"Society expects the Bromptons to flout convention. Johnny can legally bring the claim and even prevail. You are not well liked, and more than one gossip will be delighted to see your reputation tarnished by scandal."

Litigation, particularly between family members, was grist for gossip in itself. Johnny would make a convincing jilted suitor, and Papa would abet him every step of the way.

Hecate put down her fork. "You'd drag the whole family through the expense and spectacle of a lawsuit?"

Isaac dusted his hands over his plate. "Of course not. All I want, all I have ever wanted, is my daughter's happiness. But she's head-strong and misguided, unnaturally preoccupied with financial matters rather than raising a family. Along comes a handsome fellow of significant potential with the fortitude to court her, and she sees the error of her ways. Ten years on, though, and the situation has been left too late. She chooses money over the worthy man, even to the point of putting the family through litigation. One fears for her wits."

The problem with the Bromptons was that they not only built castles in Spain, they described those edifices so convincingly, that others began to believe in them as well. Impressive fabrications of dishonesty and subterfuge, built on a foundation of lies.

Phillip, trying so hard to learn Society's ways, would recoil from scandal.

But he would not recoil from Hecate herself, would he?

"Then I suppose we will entertain the gossips in the well-estab-lished Brompton tradition," Hecate said, "but you can expect your allowance to cease the instant Johnny goes to the courts."

"There, you see? My dear daughter can think only of money. An unnatural woman. Fortunately, I anticipated that response and have saved accordingly. I cannot say Edna and her brood or the others have shown similar foresight. Johnny tells me he's prepared to deal gener-ously with them. They are family, after all."

To hate Isaac would only allow him purchase on Hecate's soul he did not deserve, but she had underestimated him.

"You are saying that Johnny will claim my fortune through marriage or by an award of damages. Either way, I will lose control of a substantial part of my money." And of her freedom. Marriage obliterated that freedom outright, but scandal circumscribed a single woman's existence just as tightly. No invitations, every outing a gauntlet of stares and whispers, employees leaving without notice, merchants declining orders...

Hecate put another bite of eggs into her mouth. *I am too tired for this.* "Am I to be given any time to adjust to the potential change in my circumstances?" Either way, marriage or scandal, her circumstances would change.

"Time to pout, you mean? That is up to Johnny. I assume he'll want to make a favorable impression at Horse Guards, look up some old friends, and generally take Town by storm before he resorts to any drastic measures. Reconcile yourself to a humbler existence, my girl, because you can sulk and fume all you want, but your tyranny over this family has ended."

Johnny would spade the turf of public opinion, in other words. He hadn't waited ten years for his chance only to bungle the race a few yards shy of the finish line.

"Excuse me," Hecate said. "I have lost my appetite."

"Making a sudden dash away from the breakfast table?" Papa mused. "I wonder what that could portend?"

Mean, vile, nasty man. Hecate left at a dignified walk and nearly plowed into Phillip two yards down the corridor.

He steadied her with a hand on each arm. "Hecate, good... What's wrong?"

The concern, the immediate realization that something was amiss, undid her. She pitched herself against his chest as the first hot tear trickled down her cheek.

"They ruin everything," she said, "and now they have found a way to ruin me."

❧

The ruddy blighters had driven his Hecate to tears. Phillip set aside his rage and ushered her into the nearest parlor, closing and locking the door behind them.

And to blazes with what Society would say about that. The Bromptons as a family were unlikely to be abroad much before noon, and several of them would start the day in beds other than their own.

"I'm sorry," Hecate said, sinking onto a tufted sofa. "I'm tired, and I miss you, and I'm upset."

Phillip passed over a handkerchief and sat beside her. "This has to do with Johnny?"

"And Papa. They've outmaneuvered me, Phillip. Stolen around my flank while I was planning horse races and menus." She dabbed at her eyes with the handkerchief, and Phillip was angry all over again.

"They are your family, the people to whom you should be able to turn for aid in all circumstances." And they had reduced her to tears and apologies.

She folded up the linen and speared him with a look. "Like your family has been there for you?"

Lord, they'd upset her badly. "When Tavistock learned of my existence, he put matters right as quickly as possible. That is how family ought to behave. Who upset you at breakfast?"

"Papa. I don't want to call him that. Isaac. He wouldn't admit to colluding with Johnny, but he intends to support Johnny's claim on me right up to the courts and beyond, if necessary."

When dealing with a fractious beast, Phillip usually took the approach of first deducing what inspired the animal to bad manners and contrariness. Herd politics might play a role. A tummy ache, fear, inexperience, or a simple need for time to absorb new surroundings could all come to bear. Rarely was an animal difficult for no discernible reason.

The Bromptons were driven by money, the lack of it, the lust for it. Sorting out their motivation took no effort at all. "They are after your fortune."

She nodded. "And I would wish them the joy of it, except that in their hands, the money won't last five years. Charlie and Eglantine's children will come of age as paupers, Uncle Nunn's beautiful estate —his memorial to his lady wife—will collapse from dry rot, and Portia and Flavia will become spinsters."

And Hecate cared for those people, even as she loathed the man her mother had married. "You are like a yeoman," Phillip said. "Nature has dealt you blow after blow, but if you don't get out of bed each morning and strike back against the incessant rain, falling markets, and crumbling pasture walls, your family will suffer, and all those folk in the cities will have no bread at any price. So you get up, face the day, and carry on, tending your patch."

"They are my family, Phillip. If I marry Johnny, the money will be frittered away. If I don't marry Johnny, he will bring suit for breach of promise and demand my fortune in damages. Papa apparently has some papers I unknowingly signed that qualify as settlement agreements. I can repudiate them, but I've had ten years to do that and haven't. I'm sure Johnny will make that point to a very sympathetic jury."

"And then Johnny will fritter away the funds without *even* marrying you."

Phillip had dropped off to sleep last night the first time, anticipating shared pleasures with his beloved. In his worst imaginings, he could not have conjured waking to this mare's nest of intrigue, greed, and arrogance.

"I'm sorry," he said. "You don't deserve this, and it's certainly not your fault."

Hecate rested her forehead against his shoulder, bringing him a bracing whiff of her rosy scent. "Thank you. The words help."

Words could make no difference, though, to the misery pressing in on her from all sides. Phillip put an arm around her shoulders.

"You could marry me. Spike their guns, steal a march on the invaders." Not how he'd wanted to propose, but Hecate needed to know she had the option.

She straightened, staring hard at the rain dripping down the window. "Marry you."

Phillip waited, his heart sinking when she shook her head.

"That would only embroil you in the whole mess," she said. "Johnny can sue me just as easily if I'm married to you, more easily, in fact, because my perfidy—throwing him over for a marquess's heir—would be obvious."

Well, damn, but her logic was irrefutable. "Brompton said something last night about taking the matter to the court of public opinion. Said he'd ruin the young ladies, blacken Charlie's and Isaac's names, do worse to Edna's and Eglantine's reputations. Was he boasting, or can he achieve those ends?"

"He will turn on Isaac in an instant if he thinks that will support his objective, and Isaac will turn on him." Hecate rose and went to the window. She made a lovely, sad picture in the watery morning light, and she'd done something different with her hair.

"I am afraid, Phillip. I have been afraid for most of my life. Afraid Papa was angry with me, afraid the other girls wouldn't like me, afraid my family will create a scandal I cannot make go away with my money. I am so tired of being afraid, but Johnny is ruthless, and Isaac is mean. A word in the wrong ears, an innuendo in the clubs, a wager left for all the gents to see on the betting books... Johnny and Isaac can and will wreck the lives of innocents to get what they feel they deserve."

And then they'd make those lives a misery anyway, in all likelihood. Hecate could limit the damage somewhat, but she'd need solicitors and bankers and endless guile to do so.

Phillip slipped his arms around her from behind. "My father wrote a codicil to his will. If I ventured away from Crosspatch Corners, if I set foot outside my rural backwater, I'd lose the home I dearly love. I convinced myself, eventually, that I wasn't the venturing sort, because believing that of myself was the only way to preserve contentment."

"I'm not the only person cursed with a vile wretch where a doting father should be?"

"No, but my point, Hecate, is that the codicil was unenforceable. The legal particulars hadn't been observed, and the condition was vague, and so on. And yet, I let my entire life be limited by the fear of losing my home. I understand the burden placed on you, and I will share it any way you allow me to."

Don't send me away. Don't banish me. Please not you too. Rather than beg—and burden her with importuning—he held her. She turned and wrapped her arms around him.

"It's as if Johnny went away to Canada and came back a different man. I wanted to go with him. Wanted the simple solution of being an officer's wife, far from polite society and grasping relations. He gently refused, and advised me to remain unwed as long as I could. I would have sworn he meant that advice kindly and not for his own purposes. But why refuse me then, only to demand my hand now?"

"Are you wealthier now?"

"Considerably. I am good at investing and not averse to an occasional risk."

Had Phillip fallen into that category for her? A little deviation from good sense and decorum? Would she talk herself into believing that description if left to fret long enough over her perfidious cousin's scheme?

"Johnny cannot file his suit tomorrow," Phillip said, stroking Hecate's hair. "He'll have to ingratiate himself with Society first, spread the appropriate rumors, be seen to pine for you from afar. We have some time."

Hecate burrowed closer. "Time for what?"

"I will acquaint Tavistock with the situation, and he is connected to half the peerage through his step-mother. If Johnny thinks to fire the first shot across Mayfair's ballrooms, he will find himself late to the battle."

Hecate drew back. "You'd do that?"

"I would beg in the street to aid your cause, my dear, and it's my cause as well." Why did she find it so difficult to grasp that others could be as loyal to her as she was to her blighted family?

"London is deserted for the nonce," she said, resuming their embrace. "Everybody will have left for the grouse moors and the shires. Johnny can get to work, but Parliament sits, he'll probably stick with that pining-from-afar bit. The whole business is ridiculous."

"I agree, but the threat Johnny poses, to you and to your relatives, is all too real. What if I compromised you?"

Hecate again shook her head. "That doesn't give me grounds to refuse Johnny. I suspect his ultimate strategy is to get me to hand over my fortune before the case is heard. To settle out of court."

"Though scandal arises the instant suit is joined?"

"Precisely—scandal arises and attaches to me, while he is the wronged party sacrificing his dignity on an altar of last resort. He will back me into a corner, offer me a modest sum to subsist on, promise to look after our impecunious relations, and then break his word. I cannot recommend Canada to anybody if this is the effect it has on a man's character."

"Canada is unlikely to offer the Bromptons much of a character if darling Johnny is typical of the brood."

Hecate offered a wan smile. "I love you. I love that I can talk to you, that you don't fly into the boughs when serious thought is warranted, love that you don't blame me. I should have seen this coming."

For the love of gamboling lambs. "No, you should not. Johnny and Isaac counted on ambushing you. We have merely to devise a counter-ambush of equal effect."

"I have no idea what that would even look like."

"We will start with an alert to Tavistock and his bride. They might have some ideas. Until then, you comport yourself as a woman of means without marital impediments."

She leaned into his embrace. "Thank you, Phillip. I want to hope this will all turn out to be another typical Brompton imbroglio, but Johnny is very determined, and Isaac is very bitter."

Phillip wanted to ask her: *What of your other father, the one who even now demands regular reports on your activities, who bides one long, hard day's journey to the west?* A sea captain could doubtless spirit Hecate out of the country with little fuss, and then how would Cousin Johnny react? Hard to sue a woman when you had no idea where she bided.

Could Phillip leave Lark's Nest for Hecate's sake?

The answer surprised him: Yes, and he could, in part, because Tavistock and the good folk of Crosspatch Corners would look after the property conscientiously in his absence. They'd find him a suitable buyer if need be, all the while claiming to have no notion of his whereabouts.

Though Tavistock was a sibling of short acquaintance, he was already family.

"The rain has let up," Phillip said. "I will take that for a good omen."

Hecate stepped back. "Some fool planned a horse race for today. Will you be among the competitors?"

"DeWitt's colt will win. Roland has terrible form, but tremendous speed. I will take the opportunity for a hearty gallop anyway. I don't want to talk about horse races, but I suppose we must carry on as best we can."

"You won't spend the morning clearing some ditch or mending wall?"

"Not while the ground is this wet. I apologize for last night. I awoke as you were leaving."

"We are both tired. Just a few more days, but, Phillip..."

Ah, she would think of that. "No more nocturnal visits to the summer cottage?"

She turned from the window. "Not under the present circumstances."

Because such visits were scandalous and also because the result might be Phillip's cuckoo raised in Johnny's nest. Hecate would never put a child at risk for the fate she'd suffered herself.

"I understand." Phillip kissed her cheek, and they shared a smile. "I love you too, Hecate. Very much, and these barbarians will not part me from you, try though they might."

In point of fact, her menfolk were not barbarians. They were polite society's idea of gentlemen, while Phillip was at heart a farmer dressed up in lord's clothing.

The distinction brought him no comfort whatsoever.

CHAPTER FOURTEEN

"Johnny hasn't a chance," Edna said, sounding pleased as she leaned out over the balcony along the gallery, field glasses trained on four galloping horses. "That chestnut of his is all flash and no dash."

Hecate agreed. The weather had obliged with a lovely afternoon, the ground only slightly softened by the overnight rain. The riders had exploded down the Nunnsuch drive, twelve in number. Two were immediately straggling behind, six others had bunched in the posture of jockeys hoping the leaders would falter, and four others had knotted up in the lead.

Phillip, DeGrange, Johnny, and DeWitt still led the field as they thundered back up the drive. DeWitt's bay was an unruly fellow, punctuating his strides with audible flatulence and tossing in the occasional buck, which might be why DeWitt hung at the rear of the leaders. The colt also had an odd way of going, nose low, rather than stretched forward to the utmost. DeGrange was on a black mare who looked to be all business. Excellent form, no frolicking.

Phillip's gray gelding lacked elegance, but he had also settled into a punishing pace with the look of a horse determined to rise to a challenge.

Johnny's chestnut, coat matted with sweat, was laboring badly, and a mile yet remained of the course.

"Johnny will win," Hecate said. "Sheer ambition will carry him across the line."

"Ambition doesn't condition a horse," Edna said, setting down her field glasses. "He had to have bought that nag in Portsmouth or London. Perhaps he leased the animal in Reading. In any case, a town hack isn't up to country miles."

The horse was trying, staying ahead of Phillip's gray by half a head.

Or was Phillip allowing Johnny to hold the lead because the last mile always told the tale?

"There goes DeWitt."

The big bay named Roland lengthened his stride without any apparent signal from his rider. The pack veered into the park and cut a wide swath along the creek as Roland passed DeGrange's black. The black might have been at a sedate canter for the swift work Roland made of overtaking her.

"There's our winner," Edna said. "That bay has been merely gamboling, for all his strange way of going. I'm glad I didn't oblige Johnny by betting on his chestnut. I fear Portia will be a few pence poorer for her choice of champion."

The riders clambered up one of Nunn's prized ha-has, pressing on to the open terrain flanking the formal garden.

"The chestnut is done," Hecate said as Johnny applied his crop to quarters lathered in sweat. "The jumps have finished him."

"The distance has been too much for him too. I tell you that's a town horse. Matching white socks are fine for Hyde Park, but—there goes DeWitt again."

The battle was now between Phillip and DeWitt, between experience and youth. DeGrange hung on in third place, while Johnny whaled away on his chestnut to no avail.

They cleared a final stone wall, Johnny's chestnut stumbling on the landing, while the onlookers gave a cry of dismay. The chestnut righted himself, no thanks to the nincompoop sawing on the reins, and gamely trailed after the other three.

Fifty yards from the finish line, DeWitt all but threw away the reins, and the bay surged forward to take the race by two horse lengths. The spectators by the finish line whooped and cheered, some throwing caps into the air or holding their flasks aloft as Phillip took second and DeGrange third.

Johnny crossed the finish line, still whacking his horse.

"Bad form," Edna said. "If you plan to marry that one, stay away from him when he's been drinking."

Sage advice. "I don't plan to marry him."

"Isaac says otherwise."

"Johnny says otherwise, too, but he hasn't courted me, and he has given me cause to take him into serious dislike."

Not an admission Hecate had planned to make. She headed for the steps that connected the gallery balcony with the garden terrace. Edna followed, field glasses in hand.

"Oh dear." She put the glasses to her nose.

Even from this distance, Hecate could see what gave Edna cause for concern. The first four riders had dismounted, and Johnny was bent on scolding his mount, smacking it about the quarters with the crop. DeWitt snatched the crop from him, Phillip took the horse, and a fine display of masculine pride—and stupidity—looked to be in the offing.

"Brompton men," Edna muttered, "can seem to embody the best of the cavalier while occasionally exhibiting the worst of the cad. The combination grows tiring."

Hecate glanced over at her in some surprise.

"I loved my husband," Edna said, "but widowhood among the Bromptons has been challenging, and I fear Portia in particular takes too much after her papa's side of the family. She's set her cap for Lord Phillip, you know."

"One suspected as much."

"He, who probably can't recite the royal succession or manage the steps of a pavane, thinks her silly and vapid, and he's not entirely wrong." Edna wasn't admitting failure, but she was admitting something unflattering to her maternal efforts.

"She's young," Hecate said, wondering why Edna had never discussed the girls with her before. Both of them sought husbands, and Hecate had a wide circle of acquaintances as a result of her charitable work.

"She's all Brompton," Edna said. "She and Johnny would suit, though one shudders to consider the offspring. They'd come into the world trying to pick the midwife's pocket. DeGrange has joined the affray."

As Hecate and Edna made their way across the garden, DeGrange had offered Johnny his flask, slung an arm around his shoulders, and half hauled him away from where DeWitt stood, looking ready to apply the crop to Johnny's flanks.

Grooms took the winded steeds away, and the rest of the field straggled over the finish line. Henry Wortham, in great good spirits, brought up the rear on an enormous, shaggy plow horse. The spectators obligingly cheered each competitor, Henry receiving a loud ovation, and then the crowd drifted toward the tents Hecate had set up in the middle of the park.

"I like these events the best," Edna said, "where the village and the manor meet on equal footing. I suspect they appeal to Nunn as well."

"Because he knows the role he is to fulfill," Hecate said slowly. "You are right. He can be the gracious host, welcoming all to his lovely property, and nobody will expect him to be more than polite."

"I like Nunn," Edna said. "He hasn't succumbed to the family penchant for pouting, for all that he's short on charm. His very lack of guile makes him a novelty among Brompton men. Will you marry Johnny?"

"I don't want to. He has threatened scandal and worse if I balk. Claims I signed settlement agreements ten years ago, and Isaac supports that contention. They will doubtless produce documents with a credible facsimile of my signature on them, but, Edna..."

"It's exhausting," she said, "having to scheme and plot and plan simply to exercise the judgment an adult ought to enjoy regarding her own affairs. If I haven't thanked you for your generosity before, I am thanking you now."

Better late than never? "Isaac claims Johnny will be far more forthcoming with my fortune than I have been."

"Then Isaac is blinded by ambition. Johnny has the look of a fellow returning from exile. He has scores to settle. I don't recall him sporting such a prominent streak of ambition as a youth. He was always out of doors, watching birds and listening for their songs. He's apparently outgrown his boyish pursuits."

"Don't they all?" Though Phillip hadn't. He was still drawn to the out of doors, still fascinated by nature, horticulture, and wildlife. She suspected he would be even in great old age, when he'd become one of the fierce venerables who could fashion a stone wall that would stand for decades.

"Are you tempted by what Johnny offers?" Edna asked, an odd wistful note in her voice as the Earl of Nunn himself rang the bell drawing guests to the buffets under the tents.

"Of course not. Johnny offers nothing but misery. He's arrogant, has a mean streak, and wants what he has not earned." And yet, he was beautiful, charming, virile, confident, likely knew all the dance steps, and would be welcome in half a dozen clubs.

"Some people are like that," Edna said. "The more they have, the more they want. Others earn an honest fortune and appreciate how much luck and timing determine any man's fate. I must see that Portia and Flavia make a proper fuss over the Corviser boys."

"They strike me as decent fellows."

"Decent, though their prospects are humble. Portia could manage either of them blindfolded."

Meaning Edna could manage either one with less effort than it took to tie on her slippers. "And Flavia?"

A wistful look came into Edna's eye. "She is too sweet for her own good, when she isn't purloining my fripperies in an effort to stand out from her sister. A wise man would be drawn to that sweetness, but when have we ever enjoyed an ample supply of wise men?"

On that philosophical note, Edna passed Hecate her field glasses and strode forward with a jaunty wave in Mrs. Roberts's direction.

Phillip approached, looking windblown and delectable. "Miss Brompton, I hope you watched the battle for honor and glory?"

"I cheered only for you and Herne."

"DeWitt has been conditioning his colt. Roland will earn him some coin this autumn and more in years to come. How are you?"

They could have this conversation out of doors, with a veritable crowd in attendance, but Hecate was desperately aware of how careful they had to be.

"Johnny behaved badly. Even Edna remarked it, and she is not one for speaking ill of handsome, wealthy, single men."

Phillip aimed a look at the men's punchbowl, where the jockeys had congregated, tankards and glasses in hand.

"Johnny has recovered his dignity, or what passes for it. I dread to think of him navigating the Canadian woods, if he's that intemperate toward his horseflesh. Any halfway sensible mare would put him permanently into a ditch for behaving so badly."

"And yet, he's supposedly a successful fur trader. Perhaps he comports himself more prudently in the wilderness."

"He must, or he'd be dead."

The prospect did not engender much sorrow. "I wish he'd stayed in Canada."

"As do I. Will you share a plate with me?"

She wanted to share the rest of her life with him. She set aside Edna's field glasses. "Best not."

Phillip nodded. "DeWitt suggested the riders repair to the swimming hole after they've eaten and enjoyed neighborly congratulations. DeWitt and I have been using it to spare the staff the bother of heating bathwater for the summer cottage."

Precisely the sort of innate consideration and common sense Hecate could not expect from Johnny.

"Don't drown him," she said, "and don't let him accidently drown you."

"Sound advice." Phillip should have offered her a slight bow and strolled off, a man who'd given a good account of himself in the saddle and offered suitable courtesies to the family antidote. Instead, he studied the sky.

"I miss you, Hecate. That the Canadian Conniver has laid his dastardly mischief at your feet makes me want to haul him bodily onto the nearest merchantman and see him kept below deck until the ship docks in Halifax."

"Or in hell. If nothing else, Johnny's scheme has made me realize that I am angry, Phillip."

"With me?"

How could he think that, and where did he get the courage to ask such a question? "Never with you. With what I have allowed myself to become. I threatened to cut off Isaac's allowance if he continues to collude with Johnny. He sneered at that sally and informed me he's been saving in anticipation of Johnny's arrival, or of my eventual comeuppance. He *can* save, and yet, I've been yielding to his importuning for years, thinking economies are beyond him. How typical of the Bromptons to manipulate me so easily into doing for them what they could do for themselves. How typical of me to capitulate."

Phillip's gaze shifted from the clouds to Hecate. "Isaac bamboozled you. I suspect Charlie might also be capable of pulling a greater share of an adult load, but between his mama's boldness, his wife's adoration, and Nunn's inherent reticence, Charlie remains successfully immured in his randy youth."

"You don't think my anger is misplaced?"

Phillip touched her arm. "I think your anger might well be your salvation. Any other woman would have tossed the lot of them into the Channel long since."

The old refrain—*but they are all I have*—came to mind. Hecate had been wrong about that. True, she had her Brompton connections, but she also had a fortune. She could well lose the fortune precisely because she'd been so tenacious about holding on to her Brompton connections.

"I have never regarded wealth as anything other than an obligation," Hecate said. "I like my comforts within reason, but all that money... Have you ever longed for more acres to farm?"

Phillip offered his arm, an acceptable display of manners, and Hecate took it. "Not more acres, though I am considering adding a conservatory. Lark's Nest is good land and more than enough for my needs. My challenge becomes to do the best possible job I can by the acres I have. That's sufficient to occupy any man's ambitions, or it should be."

"Not for Johnny." Hecate allowed Phillip to escort her to the buffet. "If he's so successful, why is he going to such lengths to get his hands on my money?"

"Some people are never satisfied. They lack for nothing except contentment, and I do not envy them. Shall I fill you a plate?"

"Please." Not because she was hungry, though she was, but because every moment spent with Phillip was a moment stolen against a fate she seemed doomed to meet at Johnny's handsome hands.

◦～◦

Phillip watched Hecate quietly directing yet another social event while the Earl of Nunn allowed himself to be harangued by the vicar's wife, the occasional neighboring squire, and Mr. Jonas, a solicitor who'd retired to the neighborhood to be near his daughter. Nunn wasn't a jovial lord of the manor, but he was gracious within the limits of his character.

"Come along," DeWitt said, tugging Phillip's arm. "We've recovered from our exertions, digested our sustenance, and drained half a barrel of ale. Time for the dashing competitors to swim off the stink of our labors."

Hecate listened to some old grandpa maundering on about the misadventures of his youth. She'd doubtless heard the tale before, and yet, her smile was genuine, her expression serene.

"I'm losing her," Phillip muttered. With each passing hour, she was shoving her own wants and needs into some mental warehouse where she stored a lifetime of longings and dreams, even as she kept an eye on the punchbowl, the tipsy bachelors, the buffet, and the weather.

For the sake of the greater good—or the Brompton version of the greater good—she'd surrender to Johnny's scheme.

"Beg pardon?" DeWitt said as a shout of laughter went up from Henry Wortham's vicinity. "You came in second."

The greatest loss would not be her money. She'd been parting with that for the sake of various Bromptons since girlhood. Married to Johnny, she'd lose her freedom.

"Is scandal really such a force in polite society that it must be avoided at all costs?" Phillip asked as he accompanied DeWitt in the direction of the summer cottage. "I understand the devastation of foot rot. A whole herd can be destroyed in a season. Potato blights are just as destructive, and they tend to hit the poorest of small holders the hardest. A failed harvest puts hardship on a whole nation. But a tide of whispers and slander? How does one measure that damage?"

DeWitt was quiet until they reached the steps of the summer cottage terrace. "The damage looks like this: No offers for the family's unattached young ladies. No posts for the young men. No mortgages on the family's properties as the investment opportunities magically disappear. No credit, when many a respectable family lives on credit. No invitations, when who is invited where by whom is the currency of social standing. The servants begin to drift away, and the agencies no longer send the best candidates, if they send any."

"Like a neglected estate," Phillip said, "a slow spiral into an ever-deepening pit."

"That pit is financial, social, emotional, logistical... Say you want to rent out your town house to raise some capital, but the only tenants willing to look at it won't pay what you're asking and won't respect the premises. You want some new clothes made up by the fellow you've long patronized on Bond Street. He informs you that, sadly, he's unable to take any new commissions for at least three months. Try the lesser shop around the corner, though he's also unable to take your business."

If Hecate brought such a fate on her family—the blame would fall exclusively on her, never on dear Cousin Johnny or scheming Cousin Isaac—she'd have no allies or supporters with whom to fight back.

Except for Phillip, who was still trying to master the quadrille in the odd, private hour. He'd taken to stealing away to the portrait gallery after supper. He practiced the steps in solitude, the disapproving eyes of the Brompton rogues staring at his stumbling progress.

"I wish we'd left last week," DeWitt said. "The situation here grows complicated."

"We might not make it past the finish line," Phillip said. "If Hecate accepts Johnny Brompton's suit, I will not answer for the consequences."

The day was shifting from afternoon to a long, lovely summer evening, and Phillip endured a wave of homesickness. Not for Crosspatch Corners in particular, but for a life made simple by geographical limitations. As long as he'd kept to himself and tended his acres, he'd been safe from heartache.

"Come swimming with us," DeWitt said. "You stink as badly as I do."

"Worse," Phillip said. "A four-mile course was a romp for Roland. You've been conditioning him."

"He loves to run." DeWitt's pride in the horse was evident in his tone. "Speed is in his blood. The whole time I was away, he wanted to be about his job—galloping like the wind—but nobody was on hand to sort him out. He'll have more endurance for being allowed to grow into his frame before he's permitted to compete, but the native speed has always been there."

Had this conversation taken place in spring, before Tavistock had upended Phillip's life and Hecate had stolen his heart, Phillip would have taken the bait DeWitt so kindly dangled. A good long natter chin-wag about training a promising colt would have been enjoyable. The highlight of the day.

"Be off with you," Phillip said. "I will leave the hale-fellow-well-met nonsense at the swimming hole to you. You're the professional thespian."

"Don't say that too loudly. If you, as the ranking guest, disdain our company, Henry Wortham and his ilk will take it amiss."

Phillip had been very nearly of Henry's ilk until recently. "Then I will put in an appearance for the sake of Henry's pride, but charm is beyond me."

"One doesn't expect miracles, my lord. That's part of their appeal."

Phillip accompanied DeWitt down the path to a widening in the stream below the arched bridge. A bend on the stream's course had made for a stretch of deeper, slower water and obscured the location from the sight of the house or summer cottage.

Private enough that Henry Wortham was already parading around as God had made him.

Henry, a truly magnificent specimen in the altogether, made a clean dive from a handy rock and came up gasping. "Ruddy cold. My cods will be the size of raisins."

"They'll match your brains, then," somebody replied.

"Still bigger than yours." Henry splashed water at his detractor, and others peeled down and joined Henry in the water. A four-mile gallop had taken the starch out of most of them, and when the numbers began to thin, Phillip shed his clothes and waded in.

The water was luscious. Just cold enough to be refreshing, though the swimming hole itself lacked the dimensions to accommodate much more than a casual dip. Phillip scrubbed off, made use of the towels provided for the occasion, pulled on shirt and breeches, and found a place beside Henry on the grassy bank.

"How fares Mrs. Riley?" Phillip asked as several yards away, a still shirtless Johnny began to hold forth about some howling, half-man/half-beast creature rumored to inhabit the Canadian woods.

Johnny Brompton when drunk, perhaps.

"Midwife says Mavis is coming along nicely, and the baby's doing well too. I brought them the flowers. Didn't stay, just passed them over the threshold. I think Mavie was pleased. My ma sent over a quarter ham, and the basket from Nunnsuch could double as a cradle."

Hecate had doubtless chosen it for that reason. "But you're at a loss for what to do next?"

"Aye. Mavis is a hard worker, and I know not every man will take on another's get, but Mavie is also smart. Smarter than most village girls. Her pa was a vicar's lad, and they had books. She'll want a smart fellow like her William."

Henry spoke of books as Portia or Flavia might have referred to ducal invitations. "You aren't stupid, Henry." Though a man could be reasonably intelligent and still utterly stumped in matters of the heart.

Henry shoved damp hair from his eyes. "Ma put the manners on me, and I can read the London newspapers, but I'll never be like him," he said, jerking his chin in Johnny's direction. "He's a gent. A proper gent, and now half the village will be eating out of his hand. He listened to Mrs. Vicar go on about her knee and laughed at old Jonas's jokes. He's a better earl than the earl, and he hasn't even studied for the part."

No, he was not, but he might well be a better actor than DeWitt. "Johnny Brompton has no designs on your Mavis, I can assure you of that." Would that he had.

"He's a fool, then. Mavie is worth ten of the twittering misses from Town, meaning no disrespect to my betters. Brompton has something the ladies want, though, and he knows it."

Did he? Most young ladies were shrewd enough to see past handsome looks and flattery. They wanted manners from a fellow, true, but also genuine consideration, respect, affection.

"He will always be more enthralled by himself than he will be with any lady," Phillip said. "You don't appear to be afflicted with much vanity, for all that you're a fine figure of a man."

To comfort another frustrated swain felt good. Henry's cause was far from hopeless, despite his gloomy outlook.

Henry stared at his hands, great calloused paws capable of tremendous hard work. "I'll never have hands like his, not if I slather them with lanolin and wear gloves to bed every night. Mavie knows that."

"What Mavie knows is that you are a hard worker, just as she is a hard worker. Weed her flowers."

"Beg pardon?"

"An enterprising lady will have flower beds, a spice garden, a vegetable garden. We've had a good rain recently, and the weeds will get ideas. Stay ahead of them and use those calloused hands to tidy up Mrs. Riley's garden."

"I was weeding pretty much as soon as I could walk." Henry ceased studying his hands and peered off to the west. "Won't be dark for nigh two hours."

"Please give the lady my regards if your path should happen to cross hers. Make a fuss over the baby."

"Willa has her ma's red hair," Henry said, rising. "She's the prettiest baby you ever did see, my lord."

"I'm sure she is. You might also take a look at Mrs. Riley's henhouse while you're in the vicinity."

"Right. Nothing stinks like a neglected henhouse." Henry collected the rest of his clothing and strode off, a man intent on courting his lady one shovelful of chickenshit at a time.

And Henry would probably succeed in his aims, while Phillip...

He rose, tired in his bones, but restless in his mind. If Hecate hadn't the heart to fight Johnny Brompton, then the battle was Phillip's to win. The objective was to send the blighter packing while preserving Hecate's freedom and as much of her fortune as possible.

That money was hers, and she'd be a better steward of it than the Canadian Cad would be.

Phillip hoped to sidle off along the stream bank without having to make small talk with Johnny, but that wasn't to be.

"Why didn't you tell me DeWitt's colt is fit enough to win the Derby?" Brompton asked, getting to his feet and pulling his shirt on.

"The last time I saw Roland go," Phillip replied, "a half mile's effort left him winded. That was several months ago, and DeWitt has apparently had him in work since then." Mr. Dabney, a former jockey who now ran the Crosspatch Corners livery, was doubtless advising on particulars.

"Perhaps I'll buy that colt." Brompton did up his buttons and shoved his shirttails into his waistband. "Make him a wedding present to my bride."

"I'm sure every lady longs to have a flatulent horse for a morning gift, or perhaps giving a new wife a gift she can't use is the fashion in Canada?"

"You're saying I'd be giving the horse to myself, and you'd be right. I do not like to lose, my lord."

Oh botheration. Phillip gathered up his jacket, cravat, and waistcoat. "Is that how you justify cheating?" A gentleman would never have posed such a question.

Phillip had had a bellyful of trying to impersonate a gentleman.

"You realize I could call you out for such a question?" Brompton shrugged into his waistcoat and tied his cravat in a loose mathematical, for years the only fashionable knot Phillip had known.

"You are doubtless a dead shot," Phillip said, "veteran of the wilderness, former soldier, erstwhile fashionable scion, et cetera and so forth. I did not refer to the horse race, but rather, to your tactics with Miss Brompton. If you consider assault in the garden and blackmail to be anything but cheating, then I and every other gentleman present should be calling you out."

Hecate would disapprove. Phillip would disapprove, too, just as soon as he located some gentlemanly scruples.

"Not blackmail," Brompton replied, draping his jacket over his arm and starting down the path. "Hecate is free to reject my suit. If she does, I will console myself with recourse to the courts, and she will again be free to negotiate with me regarding adequate compensation for my disappointed hopes."

"You're going the wrong way," Phillip said.

Brompton bowed and twirled his wrist. "My tactics will be effective, despite your disapproval of them. We'll even invite you to the wedding."

"She won't marry you." Except that Hecate well might, because then she could check the worst of Brompton's excesses and make some provision for her rackety family.

"We shall see." Brompton sauntered along, the picture of manly splendor.

"You are going the wrong direction," Phillip said. "The stable is over there." He nodded to the westering sun. "The manor house is up the path that way, and the summer cottage is across the park to my left."

Brompton looked momentarily nonplussed. A trick of the slanting sunbeams perhaps, or maybe the man had been far gone in dreams of unearned wealth.

"I'm taking a constitutional," he said, "to contemplate my rosy future, despite today's defeat in the saddle. I bid you good evening, my lord, and congratulate you on having come in second. No shame in that. In fact, you'd be well advised to get used to it."

Phillip took the path in the other direction, though the whole exchange made him want to go for another swim and scrub himself thoroughly all over again. That, or go best out of three with Brompton.

At a fork in the path, he was reminded of a moment about two and a half miles into the race. The front foursome had rounded the village green and were crossing a neighboring estate before making the final run up the Nunnsuch drive.

Brompton had checked his chestnut, who'd been in the lead at the time. At that point, the race was a matter of maintaining the pace, getting a good distance to the jumps, and saving back something for the final stretch.

Brompton had yielded the lead to DeGrange as they'd approached the crossroads that would lead back to Nunnsuch. Phillip had a sneaking suspicion that Brompton had neglected to review the course. He'd relied on old knowledge from boyhood and a general description of the course to see him safely around.

A farmer paid dearly for failure to prepare. If his equipment was poorly maintained over winter, his team in bad weight come spring, his blades dull, his ditches choked with weeds, he paid and paid and paid.

Phillip turned his mind to how else Brompton might have failed to prepare for his assault on Hecate's freedom. Therein might lie a means of ambushing the scoundrel and bringing about his eventual defeat.

The problem occupied Phillip through his nightly dancing practice in the darkened gallery, though what could more clearly portend failure than a man stumbling about in the dark, with no music, no partner, and no plan?

CHAPTER FIFTEEN

"I do believe if Henry Wortham set his mind to sweeping a lady off her feet, she would be well and truly swept." Portia kept her voice down, though only a few other guests were whiling away the middle of the evening in the library.

"Henry's form did rather give me pause," Flavia replied, moving her peg on the cribbage board. "He could model for Hercules or Perseus. One of those famously fit fellows. Lord Phillip is nearly in Henry's league for muscle."

"Not for height. DeWitt has some fine attributes." Gavin DeWitt wasn't bristling with muscle like Lord Phillip, nor was he on the grand scale of a Henry Wortham, but he was lean and strong, and he moved with a sort of unconscious grace. "Well-muscled quarters. Boots Corviser, by contrast, clearly owes his fine shoulders to his tailor's skill."

She and Flavia shared a smile. They'd been spying on the male of the species at the swimming hole since their first summer at Nunnsuch. Somebody had obligingly left Mama's field glasses lying about, and enjoyable old habits died hard.

Flavia picked up the deck and shuffled expertly. "They weren't boys, those fellows we saw today."

"Boys make more noise."

"And they haven't well-muscled quarters. Or chests, or arms. Do you suppose Mr. DeGrange boxes at Jackson's?"

The question was meant to be casual, but Portia knew Flavia better than Flavia knew herself. "Do you fancy him, Flave?"

"He cleans up nicely, but Mama saw him first."

Portia hadn't spared DeGrange more than a glance to inspect his forbidden parts. She did that not because those parts were of any special interest—they were the most ridiculous appendages God had ever fashioned on a human body—but because any opportunity to investigate members of the opposing team, as it were, must not be neglected.

"Hecate has assembled a decent crop," Portia said, picking up her cards. "Not stellar, but decent. Then along comes Cousin Johnny to give the other fellows a run for their money."

"He was horrid to his horse." Flavia rearranged her cards, frowning at her hand. "I was embarrassed for him. He's apparently up to something where Hecate is concerned, else Lord Phillip would not have spoken to him so severely."

The talk of dueling had been interesting. "Why do you suppose Johnny didn't call him out? Johnny was a soldier. He'll be a better shot than any farming courtesy-lord-come-lately."

"Johnny always had more sense than the average Brompton. Witness, he went to Canada when everybody knew Napoleon was the greater threat to England. It's your crib, Porry."

"Right." Portia began the round, though her mind wasn't on the cards. "Lord Phillip is apparently smitten with Hecate. One must admit the obvious."

Flavia peered at her across the board. "They would suit. He's the steady sort. She is too."

"Steady is dull. I grant you, having Hecate's fortune about has been helpful, but I cannot imagine anything more tedious than life as a farmer's wife. I suppose one plucks chickens when one isn't birthing little farm boys and goosegirls, but crops, weather, weather, crops... I'm not sure I'd wish that on even Hecate. We might give Johnny's aspirations a slight nudge, Flavie."

"What of Hecate's aspirations? I don't gather she's as fond of Johnny as she used to be."

"When she tires of Johnny, she can disport with Lord Phillip all she pleases to, assuming Johnny allows her out of the house. She needs some excitement in her life, and Johnny is just the fellow to see that she has it."

Flavia held a twenty-four-point hand, which put her over the finish line. "Excitement is fine for a lark, but for a marriage... A fellow one can rely on, who esteems one, and has a kind heart strikes me as the better bargain."

Dear Flavie was hopelessly sentimental. "Johnny is rich, and all Hecate cares about is money. They'll get on quite well, if Hecate can be made to see reason. Let's get up a game of whist. I lost sixpence on today's race."

Mr. DeGrange was reading a paper over by the French doors, Boots Corviser was idly inspecting the offerings on the sideboard. Cousin Isaac and Mrs. Roberts were at the chessboard, and Mrs. R looked to be on the road to victory.

"Did you bet on Johnny?" Flavia asked, organizing the deck and setting it aside. "I bet on Mr. DeWitt. You can have my sixpence, but I promised Mr. DeGrange I'd partner him at whist this evening."

When had she done that? "I suppose one of us ought to keep an eye on him if he's playing Mama's gallant. Thankless job, and you are very good to take it on. Don't wait up for me."

Portia would have risen, but Flavia put a hand on her wrist. "Porry, what are you planning? This business about sparing Hecate the tedium of a farm life isn't a charitable impulse."

Portia looked around and saw nobody even close to eavesdropping. Nobody had gone up to the mezzanine either, which was where Uncle Nunn shelved the plays and French novels.

"That scheme with the notes almost worked last year, Flave. If we were more careful, we could pull it off this time. Get Hecate and Johnny sorted out before the London matchmakers can seize upon him this autumn."

Or before Hecate could seize on Lord Phillip, who was apparently more than willing to become her captive.

Flavia put the cribbage pegs back in the starting holes. "I'm glad we failed last year. I could have ended up married to a man who cared for me not at all."

"I would not have let that happen."

Flavia made the same face she used to make when Portia insisted the younger sister always take the smaller half of any shared biscuit.

"You would have been a viscountess, Flavia. Any other sister would be thanking her lucky stars to have found herself in such a situation."

Flavia was quiet for a moment, while Portia was mentally composing notes and choosing where to lure the soon-to-be-happy couple.

"I don't like it," Flavia said at length. "Hecate has supported the whole family for years, and now Johnny wants her money, too, just like the rest of us. He's not smitten with her. He'd have mentioned her in his letters if he had been, and he'd have written more than once or twice a year."

Flavia was at her worst when she was trying to apply logic to facts. "He was busy making his fortune so he was worthy of her."

"Then he shouldn't be underhanded in his courtship, accosting her in the garden and threatening scandal if she won't have him."

"We have only Lord Phillip's word for that version of events, and honestly, Flave, what would either of us know about how smitten fellows behave? Charlie is supposedly smitten with Eggy, and he's forever sowing wild oats nonetheless."

Flavia's brows drew down, portending a prodigious attempt to reason through that conundrum. The house party had a mere handful of days left to run its course, and Portia could not afford to wait on Flavia's dubious skill with cogitation.

"Let's not think it to death," Portia said, patting Flavia's hand. "If you are partnering Mr. DeGrange, I suppose that leaves me with Boots Corviser."

"Or Mr. DeWitt," Flavia said. "He was on the terrace when I came in."

"I wonder how much he won on today's race. Perhaps we should relieve him of a few pence in the interests of keeping him humble?"

"Fetch him," Flavia said, "and if Mr. DeWitt won't join us, we'll press Boots into service, though he looks none too steady on his pins."

Portia had no interest in a tipsy whist partner, so she repaired to the terrace, though Mr. DeWitt had apparently found elsewhere to end his day.

Time to plead a headache, then, and find a private place to practice imitating Hecate's precise, tidy hand.

～

Phillip had run through the whole prissy, prancing sequence of the quadrille for the third time, which he could do only slowly and because he allowed himself to stop and mentally review each sub-pattern before embarking on it.

"*Chassé jetté et assemblé, en avant en arrière...*" He'd asked DeWitt to help him with the pronunciation, because unlike the ladies, he'd not be carrying a fan that helpfully listed the steps. He'd be relying on the prompting of a caller, and thus a grasp of proper French pronunciation became imperative.

"Phillip, what are you doing?" Hecate stood framed in the doorway by the light of the corridor sconces.

"Making a cake of myself," he said, lowering his arms. "I regularly entertain the Brompton ancestors with my stumbling. You are sworn to secrecy."

She hesitated on the threshold, and that broke his heart. A week ago, she'd been willing to steal into his room by the light of the moon. Now, she looked both directions before slipping into the gallery and closing the door behind her.

"I promised you a house party without quadrilles."

Phillip approached her. Hecate's tone had been hard to decipher, but it had been far from warm. "I wanted to surprise you. Were you looking for me?"

She moved away before he'd come within embracing range. "I sought solitude, and this place reliably provides it."

"Johnny doesn't come here, you mean." Phillip stood near the door, feeling as Henry Wortham must when faced with the conundrum of wooing a lady he'd gladly die for. What next steps? Were there *any* steps that would lead forward?

"Johnny... accosted me again." Hecate crossed her arms and stalked to the French doors. "Rather, he could have. I was intent on counting table linens, because the buffet at the grand ball will require nearly all we have. Mrs. Roberts has offered to lend us some of hers, but I don't want to put her to the trouble... I was in the linen closet, and there he was."

That Hecate would spend her evening counting tablecloths when a housekeeper or chambermaid should have been tasked with the job was more reason for heartbreak.

"You were trying to hide," Phillip said, "as I've been hiding here of an evening. Did he touch you, Hecate?"

She shook her head. "No. He simply stood in the doorway, letting me know without a word that I was trapped. He offered to assist me, I waved him away, and he sauntered off."

"But first," Phillip said, taking up a lean on the door's opposite jamb, "he waited a moment, emphasizing your peril and his power. Let's step outside, shall we?"

Hecate passed through the French doors and into the summer night. Phillip followed, and when she took one of the padded benches beneath the eaves, he sat beside her.

"Johnny has you spooked," Phillip said, wondering if he dared take Hecate's hand.

"I should have known better than to be alone in a linen closet, Phillip. I'm not thinking clearly. A man who will force himself upon me within shouting distance of the house is a man who trusts that I will not bellow with outrage when he makes further advances."

What was she saying? "Have you decided to accept his suit, then?" Phillip had been steeling himself for that possibility without admitting it, but saying the words brought forth rage, despair, bewilderment.

Old emotions, long familiar to a boy who'd been rejected by his own father.

"I have mere days, Phillip, before Johnny gallops for London, where he will start his campaign to rob me blind. He will be subtle and thorough."

"Sly and sneaking."

"He means business. He has convinced himself that his ten years in the New World entitle him to get his hands on my fortune, and he will have documents, as well as Isaac's support in the clubs, Charlie will probably cheer him on too. Years ago, Johnny told me to remain single if I wanted to keep hold of my money. Simple, sound advice, though now I see that he wanted me unwed so my fortune would remain available to him."

Phillip's beloved was talking herself into surrender. "He won't stop at plundering your fortune, Hecate. He will use the threat of litigation to force you to the altar."

She sniffed and nodded.

By the light of the moon, Phillip saw a skein of silver on her cheek. "Damn and blast." He took her in his arms, and she came to him willingly.

"I hate to cry. Crying solves nothing. There is no such thing as having a good cry."

Phillip fumbled for his handkerchief and passed it over. "I cried when I returned to Crosspatch after my first foray into London. I felt like a soldier who'd survived his first battle. I realized even then that by leaving Crosspatch, by braving the wilds of Town, I'd lost something. An innocence, a purity of perspective. But I'd gained wisdom and strength, and I'd made the acquaintance of the most fascinating lady."

"Phillip, don't."

He stroked her hair, a terrible sense of parting cleaving his heart. "She was all starch and propriety, but also... fierce, kind, determined. She got me through my first formal dinner, and that gave me hope. This lady was devoted to her charities and had single-handedly established a sailors' home that was a model of its kind. Her family was an unceasing trial to her, and yet, she never played favorites or complained of the burdens they placed on her."

"Hush."

He could not hush. If he was to lose her, he at least deserved his third-act soliloquy. "Come with me to the hay meadow, Hecate. If, when we leave there, you want me to depart from Nunnsuch, I will yield to the press of business or whatever fiction polite society resorts to when making a hasty exit. Johnny does not deserve you, he will betray your trust over and over, and you do not love him."

Worse yet, Johnny did not love Hecate.

"I used to be fond of him, but now I cannot even esteem him, except as one esteems an enemy's artillery, but he will turn his guns on my family, on women and children. I am well acquainted with how that feels, Phillip, to be too young and too female to mount an adequate defense against Society's assaults."

"So you will bear Johnny's assault on your freedom instead?"

"It might not come to that. He can't know the whole extent of my fortune. I am vastly wealthy. I might be able to buy him off and still have enough left to care for my sailors and cousins."

"It will come to that, and worse. He will insist on consummating the vows, over and over, and you will have no choice but to yield to him. Your family knows this."

"Don't say that."

What *could* Phillip say, then? What did he know to be true, despite his rural, backward upbringing?

"Hecate, what sort of family demands the sacrifice of your personhood, your means, and your happiness? I know, believe me, I *know* the pain of familial abandonment. I was deemed unfit for my father's notice. My mother had to sneak away from Town to see me for a few hours. The betrayal and bewilderment cut to the bone, but people who treat you thus aren't worthy of the name family."

Phillip kissed Hecate's temple and bit back more frustrated lecturing. Johnny dared hatch this scheme only because the Bromptons, led by Isaac himself, would rally to his cause. The very generosity Hecate had shown them justified their resentment of her, and thus she was without allies.

"Marry me," Phillip said. "Marry me and be done with the lot of them."

Hecate shook her head. "You came to me because you wanted to acquit yourself well in polite society. If I elope with you, and Johnny goes to the courts, my scandal becomes yours. Tavistock's fledgling brewery will be bankrupt before he sells the first barrel."

"He has vineyards in France, a dozen other properties. He would not want to see you yoked to that scoundrel."

Hecate sat up. "Perhaps true, but your brother married down, Phillip. He fired his solicitor under a cloud of gossip. His father was not well liked. Tavistock will be tarred with the same brush that will end your foray into polite society. The young Misses DeWitt, his sisters-by-marriage, will be hard-pressed to find husbands. You want this to be a simple choice for me between my heart's desire and my worst nightmare, but the situation is complicated."

Phillip wanted to say that Hecate was exaggerating, seeing doom where only passing clouds cast shadows, but he recalled DeWitt's description of scandal's impact on a "good" family. Financial, social, and emotional ruin.

"If am your heart's desire, come to the hay meadow with me. You have not capitulated to the scoundrel yet. I'd ask you to hold out at least until the end of the house party."

"Days." She swiped at her cheek with her fingers. "Mere days, and then... I must be ruthless, Phillip. Much depends upon my ability to be ruthless."

Phillip wished she'd for once be *selfish*. What neither of them had admitted was that buying Johnny off would not serve. He might content himself with a year or two frittering away Hecate's money, but then he'd be back with the same threats of litigation, the same signed settlements to wave before a judge, until only marriage and complete control of Hecate and her fortune would placate him.

"I was never prepared to be ruthless courting Society's favor," Phillip said. "I told myself I'd make a reasonable effort, and if they tolerated me, I'd have done my part for a brother who has done much for me. Perhaps if a situation requires ruthlessness from one who is tenderhearted by nature, then ruthlessness is unlikely to succeed."

Hecate sighed and rose. "Phillip, I found you dancing alone in the dark. You've taken to wearing rings and lace. I've caught the scent of some Parisian fragrance wafting from your person when I know you'd rather be singing a haying song, naked from the waist up, making fodder for your cows. In your fashion, you are certainly being very determined if not ruthless. Johnny will destroy what progress you've made, and I don't want that—that, too—on my conscience. We are faced with the simple, frustrating fact that we cannot have every-thing we want."

She sounded like the old Hecate, the veteran of London's ball-rooms, the Antidote Heiress, no longer of any interest to the gossips and pleased to find it so.

Phillip stood as well. "Why are you responsible for the whole, conniving clan? Why have they no responsibility to you?"

"They are all the family I have."

"Then you are sending me away?" Another banishment, another exile, this one permanent.

"I am asking you to consider leaving before Saturday's ball.

Johnny might make some sort of announcement, force my hand, declare that he's finally come home to finish the courtship he started years ago. I won't have to agree to a proposal. He'll start the rumor that I already have. He wants my money badly."

"Not as badly as I want to spend the rest of my life with you."

Hecate said nothing and dabbed at her cheek with Phillip's handkerchief.

"You mean well," he said when it became obvious that silence was her refuge. "You are attempting to manage the whole situation for the benefit of all, but I have been ordering my own affairs for years, and I tell you... *I choose you.* I will always choose you, and I will await you in the hay meadow until dawn."

He kissed her cheek and took the steps down to the garden terrace. He'd likely sleep under the stars by himself, an appealing prospect as consolations went because the ache in his heart would fill the whole starry firmament.

He retrieved an old cloak from the summer cottage and made his way over the arched bridge. As he struck out for the field, he realized that Hecate was wrong about one thing.

The rackety Brompton cousins were not all the family she had. She had him, and through him, every connection Tavistock claimed, and she had the Earl of Nunn on her side. So to Nunn, Phillip would go, as shortly after sunrise as was decently possible.

~

Hecate hadn't told Phillip the worst of her latest encounter with Johnny.

Johnny had looked her over, inspected her visually, his glance lingering on her mouth, her bosom, her hips, *there.* His gaze had been confident and covetous, as if she'd been a fancy horse or a rare vase. The object itself mattered little, but absolute dominion over it, in all regards both public and intimate, counted for a great deal.

She'd stopped by the nursery before seeking the silence and

solitude of the gallery. The boys had been asleep, and she'd stood for a quarter hour at the foot of their beds, silently lecturing herself about what their lives would be like if she refused to yield to Johnny's suit.

His pawing and rutting, his frittering away of what money Hecate could not hide from him. He was simply another Brompton, worse than the rest. Canada had changed more than his youthful appearance, and not for the better.

Hecate rose from her bench on the gallery balcony and for once made a choice without weighing particulars and considering risks. Phillip had offered her tonight, and for the next span of hours, she could have her heart's desire.

She found him lying on a spread cloak in the same place where they'd made love before, his shirtsleeve pale against the night shadows.

He was on his feet, hand out before Hecate had left the darkness of the hedgerow. "You came."

"I tried not to." She kept walking until she was bundled against him. "Tried to be sensible and logical. I failed."

"But you couldn't leave me here alone in the dark. That means something, Hecate."

It meant she was a fool doomed to a miserable marriage. For herself, she could accept that choice—she'd been practicing self-denial and sacrifice for years—but the decision wrought misery on Phillip, too, and that broke her heart. He'd lost so much and borne his lot not simply with stoicism, but with a determination that had turned banishment from Town into victory in the shires.

Victory over anger, sorrow, and loneliness.

"Please, love me," she said. "Make love with me."

"I do and I shall." He led her to the cloak spread over the scythed grass. The meadow still bore the sweet, verdant scent of haying, an echo of their previous night under the stars.

The progression was the same—shoes, stockings, and dress set aside. Phillip's waistcoat and shirt followed—he'd already pulled off his boots and stockings—and then Hecate was on her back, wearing only her chemise.

She reached for Phillip, torn between a desperate yearning for haste and an equal determination to memorize each moment.

"Don't think," Phillip said, rising over her on all fours. "Be with me."

Good advice. Hecate mentally banished Johnny—that felt marvelous—and filled her senses with the man in her arms. Phillip's kisses ran the gamut from tender to carnal to reverent. By the time his breeches were off and Hecate's chemise had been tossed she knew not where, she was mad for him.

Mad, without any thoughts other than to join with him and to visit upon him as much pleasure as she humanly could. Phillip was apparently willing to comply with that scheme, because he made no protest when Hecate pushed him onto his back and straddled him.

He stroked her hips, his smile mischievous. "In this, I am yours to do with as you will."

Hecate traced a nail around his nipple. "Not in all things?"

"Not in all things. If you commanded me to stop loving you, I would be powerless to obey."

His reply, too honest, too mindful of larger realities, inspired Hecate to begin the joining. She had never made love in this position—perhaps none of her previous partners had been confident enough to allow her this degree of control—and she liked it.

Phillip was by no means passive, and at any moment, he could have taken command of the situation, but he didn't. He remained beneath her, the two as one heart, following her lead and taking indecent advantage of an arrangement that left both of his hands free.

His caresses to her back, breasts, hips, and arms were diabolically sweet, his counterpoint to the undulations of her hips relentless. She fought to prolong the pleasure, to give it back to him twice over, to climb yet higher before she fell.

"Let go, Hecate."

"I want to hold on."

"Hold on to me. Let go of everything else."

As pleasure welled, the poignance of his words—she must let him go if she was to preserve everything else—gave her passion desperation. For this eternal moment, she would yield all she had to him and cleave only to him. She soared for a progression of instants—into ecstasy, freedom, and oneness with Phillip—and then she was drifting down into peace.

Thank heavens she'd accepted Phillip's invitation to return to this meadow. Thank heavens he'd been generous enough to offer it. But for Phillip, she'd have gone her whole life without the sumptuous experience of truly *making* love.

Such glory, such vast, magnificent...

He withdrew and spent in the seam of their bodies, and Hecate's peace suffered a hairline crack. If she was to be blessed with children, she wanted them to be Phillip's children. She tucked close to him, unnerved by the thought.

Phillip dragged his coat over her and wrapped her close. "Rest now. I have you."

What calmed her heart when she would have gone a-sorrowing for what could never be was the warmth of that coat, which bore the lavender fragrance she associated with Phillip, and the consideration of the gesture.

One man loved her and loved her well. One man saw exactly who she was and yet regarded her with tenderness and care. That was wealth. That was good fortune.

"I love you, Phillip Vincent."

"Then I am content. My love will always be yours."

Phillip had spent a lifetime inuring himself to mere contentment. The subtle reminder of loss was plain to Hecate.

"You'll leave in the morning?" She could not have asked the question looking him in the eye. But she was sprawled on his chest, secure in his embrace, her eyes closed.

"If I leave tomorrow, I will return in time for the grand ball, Hecate. I want Brompton to know when he steals your happiness that

I see his larceny for the heinous dishonor it is. Promise him nothing further until then, or he will use your new promises to more easily wreak the havoc that he could previously attempt only on the strength of old, dubious documents."

More sound advice. Phillip was right—if Hecate accepted a proposal from Johnny, his breach-of-promise suit would no longer have to rely on those old settlement agreements Hecate supposedly signed.

"Don't stay for me," she said. "Look after your own interests, Phillip."

He kissed her crown. "I have been looking after my own interests since I was breached. I'm not about to abandon that office at this late date. Sleep now and know that I love you."

She slept, and when she awoke to a lone robin twittering in a misty gray light, Phillip yet slumbered beside her. At some point, they'd pulled on enough clothing to be decent. Hecate rose and toed into her heeled slippers, then gathered up her stockings and stays. Her hair was a loose braid down her back, a sensation she hadn't known since childhood.

Phillip remained asleep when she kissed his cheek and didn't stir as she made for the hedgerow. When she reached the path, she broke into a jog. She ran all the way to the bridge, lest she lose her nerve and instead run away with Phillip.

CHAPTER SIXTEEN

Phillip kept his eyes closed while Hecate slipped away. He watched, unmoving, as she ran up the path and disappeared into the darkened shelter of the trees. Only when he was certain she would not return did he sit up and finish dressing.

The woman he loved was holding on by a thread, and her parting words to him had been to look out for himself. Hecate believed Phillip was intent on securing Society's good opinion, and she'd had grounds for that conclusion.

Rings, lace, French perfume, *chassé jetté et assemblé, en avant en arrière...*

Those gestures had been not for the sake of Society's esteem, but rather, attempts to be worthy of Hecate Brompton's hand. Cousin Johnny doubtless had a *jetté* worthy of Almack's.

What did Phillip have?

A farmer's stamina and determination, his calluses, his passion for nurturing the land and beasts, his ability to work hard toward a good harvest even when fate seemed destined to starve him and everybody he loved.

The early morning mists began to dissipate, and Phillip realized he had something else to fall back on, another farming trait. Hours spent walking behind a team of plow horses, more hours spent waiting for a mare to drop her foal, yet still more hours contemplating rainy days that could destroy a crop or save it...

A farmer had time to *think*, to consider, to mentally try on ideas and refine them until nearly every problem gained an eventual solution. Clear those acres, divert that stream, fallow that field, cross those two strains of sheep...

Phillip sat in the hay meadow as the sky lightened and the avian chorus greeted the day, and he thought.

About a cousin coming back from Canada, a man changed for the worse.

About Henry Wortham, discounting his own many gifts, to focus on Johnny Brompton's arrogance and his elegant gentleman's hands.

About Johnny Brompton, casually declaring himself off on a constitutional and suggesting Phillip accustom himself to *coming in second*.

Phillip pulled on his boots and rose, startling a flock of sparrows from the nearby trees. He had mere days to work with, days when Cousin Johnny might be lurking in broom closets or accosting Hecate behind hedges.

"Not bloody likely." His sorrow and anger had sprouted into seedlings of determination, and they would bear fruit that could poison Cousin Johnny's schemes.

Phillip cut across the dewy field, his thoughts interrupted by the sound of hoofbeats. The Earl of Nunn was out for his early morning hack, riding the acres he only half knew how to manage.

Phillip planted himself in the middle of the path.

Nunn drew his bay to a halt. "Lord Phillip, good morning. You have grass in your hair."

"An occupational hazard of farming. You had the ha-has repaired because Hecate laid out the racecourse over three of them."

"And because a crumbling ha-ha is an invitation for sheep to wander. I'm told my timing was unfortunate, given the progress of the haying."

"Who told you that?"

"Henry Wortham, after yesterday's race. I thanked him for his honesty, though I realized when I gave the order I was putting the safety of the jockeys and their mounts ahead of the harvest."

The horse shook his head. A beast with fewer manners would have snatched at the reins.

"You did not want to put Hecate to the effort of designing a different racecourse."

Nunn looked bored. "She has more than enough on her plate. I'll bid you—"

Phillip put a hand on the reins, which was doubtless seventeen gentlemanly felonies at once. "She will marry that arsewipe if I can't find a way to thwart him. She thinks she has no allies, that if she turns her back on Johnny's threats, not a single Brompton will stand with her."

Nunn cued the horse to move to the side, and Phillip turned loose of the reins.

"Hecate has, and has always had, my highest esteem," Nunn said. "You know why I haven't been vociferous in my support, and I suspect Hecate knows as well."

"How could she know when you excel at disdaining all you survey?" Phillip asked. "How could she, when you've been in regular contact with her father, but never once asked if she'd like to be in contact with him as well? She sees the post coming and going here at Nunnsuch. Do you truly think she hasn't noticed the correspondence you've sent to Bristol?"

Nunn's pained expression suggested he'd contemplated that very possibility. He swung off his horse, loosened the girth, and ran the stirrups up their leathers.

"You are determined to interrupt the most pleasurable hour of my day," he said. "I admit your rudeness is in good cause. Mrs. Roberts has been quite clear on my responsibilities toward Hecate. Edna herself has suggested I take a hand in matters where Johnny is concerned. She claims his intentions are less than respectful, though she's doubtless alluding to his intentions toward the family fortune rather than toward Hecate herself."

"Hecate *is* the family fortune," Phillip said. "But the only family member to truly treasure her is apparently sitting on his fundament in Bristol and awaiting an engraved invitation to take a hand in matters. I need details, my lord. Time is of the essence, and if that blunt statement offends your polite sensibilities, I do not give one hearty goddamn in apology for my rudeness."

Nunn looped the reins through the throatlatch of the bridle, ensuring that even if the horse grazed, he could not get a foot caught in them.

"Home," he said to the horse, gesturing in the direction of the stable. "Go on, go home, and enjoy your oats." He stepped back and brandished his crop playfully, and the horse obligingly trotted off. "I'm not a farmer, but I fancy myself a decent horseman. Air your questions, my lord, and I will do my best to answer them."

"First, your assurances that you will make plain to Hecate that she has your support."

"I will discreetly assure her of my loyalty." Nunn went the opposite direction from his horse, who had disappeared around a bend in the path. "Next question."

Phillip's interrogation lasted until they reached the arched bridge, where they tarried under a rising sun.

"You could take my coach," Nunn said when Phillip had learned the essentials necessary for the moment. "Not very stylish, but comfortable."

"That will attract attention. I arrived on horseback, and I will leave on horseback. I want Johnny to see me departing."

"Oh, very well. Reject the only aid I am in a position to offer."

Nunn's dignity and stubbornness put Phillip in mind of Hecate. "Not the only aid. The sooner you talk to Hecate, the better."

"After breakfast, assuming you allow me to return to the manor in the next hour."

Phillip watched the water moving beneath the bridge, mentally inventoried the revelations of the past hour, and pushed away from the bridge stone railing.

"No more questions. Keep an eye on Johnny, a close eye. He's accosted Hecate twice and assaulted her at least once."

Nunn whacked at his boot with his riding crop. "I will alert the staff and put in a word with Mrs. Roberts. She has no patience with knaves."

"Then I'm off to have a chat with DeWitt about the loan of a fast horse. My thanks for your time, my lord."

Nunn smiled, a surprisingly charming departure from his usual hauteur. "Now you turn up mannerly. Be off with you, and we will look for your return before Saturday evening's entertainment."

Phillip parted from the earl on the bridge and made straight for the summer cottage.

∼

Hecate had slipped into the house through the conservatory, changed into a day dress, and repinned her hair. She relied on the good offices of the butler to assure her that Johnny was yet abed and likely to remain so for some time. Last evening had devolved into a sort of whist championship, and Cousin Johnny had partnered with Portia to sweep the field.

The brandy decanters had been vanquished thereafter, and two footmen had been needed to assist Master Johnny to his bed.

"He'll waken with a devil of a head," the butler observed. "One would expect a former soldier to know better. Even Mr. Charles Brompton remarked his cousin's excesses."

"Canada has not been a good influence on Johnny Brompton," Hecate replied. "If you would keep me apprised of his movements, I'd appreciate it."

"Mrs. Roberts has made the same request, miss, and I expect for the same purpose. Mr. Johnny will not set a foot out of his apartment without you knowing it before his door has swung closed." The butler bowed and decamped with that blend of dignity and dispatch typical of his station.

An ally. Two, if Hecate counted Mrs. Roberts. A heartening thought. Hecate's next destination was the breakfast parlor—love-making under the stars had left her famished in body as well as heart —though she nearly collided with Mr. DeWitt when she reached the top of the steps.

"Mr. DeWitt, good morning. You're up early. Will you join me for breakfast?"

DeWitt went to the window and watched a lone horseman canter down the drive on a big bay.

"I will happily accept that invitation," he said. "Lord Phillip has been called away on urgent business. I am to convey his regrets to you, though he assures me he will return for the final ball."

Hecate abruptly sank onto the wide windowsill. Not a window seat proper, but only for lack of a cushion.

"His lordship has left? I trust all is well in Berkshire?" She'd told Phillip to go, and perhaps he'd decided he was hers to command in that detail too.

"He did not confide particulars, other than to ask for the loan of Roland and to assure me he'd return. Lord Phillip also impressed upon me the need to ensure that you are not pushed into any pantries or china closets by your charming Cousin Johnny."

Another ally? Phillip disappeared into the lime alley, lost from sight. "You have no idea where he's gone or why?"

DeWitt took the place beside her. "He's returning on Saturday, and not just so Portia can have her way with him."

Hecate had a sense of having come into the middle of a play, and not the play she was expecting to see. "I beg your pardon?"

"Portia has a plan, involving notes and secluded corners and convenient discoveries. I was on the terrace outside the library last night when she mentioned the generalities."

Why must the Bromptons always be so, so... Brompton-ly? "Have you any specifics?" Phillip would come back in time to do the pretty at the grand ball and find himself embroiled not only in scandal, but in scandal and matrimony.

"Flavia would know the particulars. I caught only part of the conversation."

"You will please resume lurking on terraces and at keyholes to the best of your ability, Mr. DeWitt. Portia tried such a scheme last year and nearly ruined Flavia's reputation as a result. Fortunately, I overheard the maids whispering about a locked linen closet, used a hairpin to good advantage, and thwarted the scheme fifteen seconds before Mayfair's biggest gossips would have arrived to seal Flavia's fate."

"I gather the gossips were not in the script?"

"Portia was supposed to find a certain viscount in unseemly proximity to Flavia and to promise silence in exchange for coin. She hadn't counted on other young ladies and their chaperones taking an interest in the young man's whereabouts, or noticing that he was absent from the ballroom as the supper waltz approached."

DeWitt rose and held out a hand. "Poor planning, just as she ought not to have been plotting her reprise near open windows. I've worked with directors like her. Frequently in error and seldom in doubt, as the saying goes. Shall we to breakfast? One wants fortification against the challenges of the coming day."

Hecate allowed him to aid her to rise, and she found him a good conversationalist over breakfast. When a footman brought her a note informing her that Lord Nunn requested the favor of her presence in his study, DeWitt made it clear he would escort her abovestairs as well.

Not merely an ally, then, but a bodyguard, simply because Phillip had requested it. "You and Lord Phillip are friends," she said as they left the breakfast parlor. "Not merely neighbors?"

"Phillip is a few years my senior, and I have no brothers. My father was making the transition from merchant to aspiring gentry, and what he knew best—business—was not what I needed to know to become the first bona fide DeWitt country squire. Phillip knew. He somehow just knew, and he was patient with my questions."

"Who taught Phillip?" And what could Nunn possibly want that was of enough moment to justify an after-breakfast summons?

"The staff at Lark's Nest, from the boot-boy to the steward to the dairyman and the goose girl, were and are devoted to him. They became his family and his champions, and the neighbors did as well. He is our Phillip. For years, he was our Mr. Heyward, a bit singular in his habits, but always willing to lend a hand or a team or a plow. London doesn't deserve him, and if Mayfair fails to appreciate him, then all of Crosspatch Corners will decry polite society's folly."

What would that be like, to have a whole village shaking its figurative finger at Mayfair's hostesses? How would it feel to know that same whole village offered an unconditional welcome, no matter how far or long Phillip wandered?

"This is Nunn's study," Hecate said, stopping outside a paneled door. "Thank you for your company, Mr. DeWitt."

DeWitt bowed. "Phillip will return, and until then, I am to let you out of my sight only if Mrs. Roberts, trusted staff, or Nunn accompanies you. You'll summon me when you've completed your business with the earl?"

Hecate wanted to say that Phillip had overreacted, that Johnny wouldn't force himself on her, but she recalled all too clearly that insulting, assessing stare he'd turned on her twelve hours ago.

"I will summon you. Go linger near open windows and lurk at keyholes."

"While avoiding the near occasion of locked linen closets." He waited until Hecate had knocked and been admitted, and he was still lounging across the corridor when she closed the study door.

∾

"One cannot find proper rest in the country," Portia said, dropping a third lump of sugar into her tea. "The wretched birds, the bellowing cows, the neighing horses... I forget what sheep do—something that begins with a B—but it's most unpleasant to the ear. They all make such a racket, and then the sun is so disgustingly bright and at such an unspeakably early hour. I vow my head will never recover from this enforced rustication."

Flavia, who had made it out of bed and even changed into a morning dress, regarded her from the escritoire by the window.

"Drink your tea, Porry. Whether we are in Town or the wilds of Hampshire, you are never fit company until your third cup. Though as to that, what were you thinking, sampling the brandy last night?"

Portia had done more than sample the brandy. She'd allowed Johnny to be a bad influence, at which he apparently excelled. Between them, they'd downed a considerable portion of Nunn's library stock.

"A nightcap aids with sleep," Portia said, stirring her tea. "Any dowager admits as much. If you must scold me, please keep your voice down."

The maids had come and gone, but they had a way of circling back with a fresh pot or flowers or some other excuse to eavesdrop on their betters. Portia sipped her tea and wished she'd thought to ask one of the maids for a headache powder.

But then, Mama would doubtless get wind of that request, and an interrogation would follow.

"You deserve a scolding," Flavia said. "I know Johnny is a cousin of some sort, but he's also a grown man, and we don't really know him that well. If Mrs. Roberts hadn't assured me she'd remain in the library for the duration, I would have been kept awake until all hours watching you make a fool of yourself with Johnny."

Portia tried a bite of toast. "I did not make a fool of myself. I merely kept up with him. I took one sip for every two of his—his rules —and won sixpence off him. I took very small, almost invisible sips, Flavie, so don't be a nag."

Had Mrs. Roberts been there the whole time? Lurking on the mezzanine perhaps. The evening's details were a bit hazy.

Flavia regarded her with something that looked very like pity. "You undertook a drinking contest involving strong spirits and an unattached gentleman. Portia, that will not serve."

Portia's conscience, when last she'd consulted that tiresome article, did not care in the least that Flavia had turned up puritanical at this late date. Flavie had no sense of adventure and was doomed to live a dull life. Portia's inherent shrewdness nonetheless admitted the rebuke was deserved.

If Johnny got to boasting in his clubs, if he let the wrong words slip over cards with fellow former officers...

"I'll give him back his sixpence and swear him to secrecy, but honestly, once I get him compromised with Hecate, he will be forever in my debt, and you will think me the greatest genius ever for putting him there. Besides, Johnny is almost as aged as Mr. DeGrange. Tippling with him is nearly like tippling with an old uncle."

Flavia spread jam on a croissant and did so without creating the usual cascade of crumbs. "We saw Johnny and Mr. DeGrange in the altogether, Porry. They are nobody's doddering uncles, and you have been foolish."

Portia set aside the tea tray, flipped back the covers, and pushed to the side of the bed. "I'm foolish because I engage in the occasional minor diversion? Foolish because I make the smallest inconsequential wager when ruralizing at the family seat? Flavia, I despair of you. We are no longer schoolgirls, and gentlemen like a woman with a bit of dash. We will be in our *third Season* next year, and you know what that means."

Flavia bit off the end of her croissant and munched placidly, like the silly cow she was. Three Seasons and no offers was tantamount to ruin, only without the adventures.

"Porry, you are apparently intent on getting Johnny compromised with Hecate, so why does it matter if he likes a woman with a bit of dash? You don't need to attract his notice. You plan to solve all his problems by discovering him in *flagrante linen closet-o* with the family heiress. Instead, you have given him the worst sort of gossip—true gossip—about *you*."

Portia steeled herself for the rush of pain that always followed upon rising after a bit of indulgence. She stood, and the pounding in her temples became the afflictions of the damned.

"Please don't make me cross, Flavie. I will say things I regret if you make me cross."

"You should be regretting what you did last night, Portia. I found you asleep in the window seat on the landing."

"No, you did not. I'd recall that if you did." A vague wisp of memory, of cold glass at Portia's back and Flavia undressing her, tried to intrude.

"You doubtless waved off the maid who was to light you up, and that will have caused talk belowstairs."

Flavia was beginning to sound a lot like Mama, and Mama lately had taken to sounding like Hecate.

"I hate the countryside." Portia's mind, still a bit foggy—from excessive fatigue, of course—lit upon a consoling thought. "Perhaps I need a tonic."

"You need a spanking," Flavia said, rising. "Let's get you dressed."

A spanking, like a naughty girl. On any other day, that comment would have been merely the sort of annoying observation Flavia was prone to, one of a hundred petty vexations Portia brushed aside in a morning.

"Don't be insulting, Flavia. If I'm currying favor with Johnny, I'm doing it for you and Mama. When he has control of Hecate's fortune, you will thank me for humoring him last night."

Flavia disappeared into the dressing closet and emerged with a muslin day dress at least three years out of fashion. Little better than a schoolgirl's rag.

"You fancy Johnny because you know you cannot have him," Flavia said, retrieving Portia's half-empty tea cup from the tray and passing it over. "I grant you, he's a splendid specimen, and he can be charming, and cousins do marry, but Johnny is apparently set on gaining the family fortune."

Portia finished her tea, unable to dismiss Flavia's observation entirely. "Johnny has dash and daring, two qualities one does not often find among the Mayfair tulips. All that time in the wilderness honed his courage, no doubt."

Flavia took the empty tea cup from her. "Shall you wash, Porry?"

Portia took a sniff in the general direction of her armpit. "I'll have a bath later. I want to do one more draft of my notes."

Flavia held out a hand for Portia's nightgown. Flavia would have made a good lady's maid, which was a cheering thought. When Portia was married to Lord Phillip, she might keep Flavia around as a sort of unpaid companion. Many spinster sisters dwelled with a married sibling and made themselves useful despite having neither husband nor children of their own.

"If you are done with your tray, make use of the toothpowder, please," Flavia said, folding up Portia's nightgown and placing it beneath the pillows. "All in your ambit will thank you, and you might consider ringing for some parsley."

"Don't be half-witted. Chewing parsley makes me bilious. Have a look at my notes. Tell me what you think. They're in the drawer of the escritoire."

Flavia obliged. She was a better speller than Portia, but she apparently found nothing to correct.

"You will lure Johnny to the gallery?" Flavia set the notes aside. "On the night of the ball, the gallery will be lit. It's a public room with lovely views from the balcony. Half the shire will be milling around there at some point in the evening."

"Which is why I've asked for Johnny to post at eight of the clock, before the guests start to arrive, when everybody will be rushing around, making last-minute preparations, servants everywhere. Our mistake before was not waiting until enough witnesses were on hand."

"But the gallery? If Hecate is admiring Great-Uncle Nunn's

portrait, and Johnny is across the room, perusing the painting of him and Emeril in their regimentals, nobody will find that in the least compromising. Johnny and Hecate are cousins, and she's on the shelf."

Flavia, in the venerable tradition of blind hogs, had a point. "Hecate wouldn't ask Johnny to meet her in a linen closet." Portia tried to sort through other possibilities, but Flavia's nattering, the bright sunshine, and the hopeless, infernal birdsong conspired to rob her of her powers of concentration.

"Let's do your hair," Flavia said. "A loose braid to start with and a low bun."

"Like a governess?"

"Your head pains you." Flavia picked up the brush and ran her thumb across the bristles. "You are always cross when your head pains you. I thought only of your comfort when I suggested the style, Porry."

Portia took a seat on the vanity stool. "Go gently with that brush. You are correct. The fresh country air has given me the worst head."

Portia was admiring her reflection in the cheval mirror—a tot or three of brandy really had very little effect on a lady's appearance, after all—when it occurred to her that Hecate's bedroom had no parlor. Flavia was always borrowing things. If Johnny was lured to Hecate's bedroom, and Hecate was inspired to visit the same location, and Flavie—accompanied by Portia, of course—took a notion to borrow something from Hecate's jewelry box at the opportune moment...

"You are looking a little more the thing," Flavia said. "Still a bit pale, but fashionably so."

"I am, aren't I? Fashionably pale. Well done of me."

"You've had an idea. What are you planning, Portia Ariadne Brompton?"

Not even Hecate resorted to using Portia's middle name. Perhaps Flavia would make a poor choice of unpaid companion after all.

"Whatever I plan, whatever I do, I am doing it for the greater good of the Brompton family, meaning I do it for you too, Flavia."

Flavia took the vanity stool and pulled the ribbon from the end of her braid. "I know you will think badly of me for saying so, but I don't like to hear you telling fibs. You want Hecate out of contention for Lord Phillip's hand, and that means foisting Johnny off on her. She won't like that, Johnny won't like being manipulated even if he does get her money, and Lord Phillip... He won't marry you, Portia. He's not the sort to be duped by notes or schemes."

"Perhaps not, but he's the sort who will do the right thing by a lady's reputation when the decision has been taken from his hands. The trouble with you, Flavia, is that you lack ambition and imagination. One can manage with only one or the other, but I have both, and I intend to use them."

Flavia muttered something about having a little humility, but Portia elected not to hear her. Flavia meant well, but she truly was rather limited. Portia had until Saturday night to talk her sister 'round.

All the time in the world, when it came to convincing Flavia to comply with a scheme.

~

"Hecate, good morning. Do have a seat," Nunn said, on his feet and very much on his dignity by the study's windows.

To Hecate, Uncle Nunn had been a fixture, the patriarch harrumphing and scowling over the familial landscape, not malign, but certainly hard to warm up to. Morning light revealed him to be human, aging, perhaps even tired.

Good God, I can't lose him too. Not now. A wife would be a little check on Johnny's excesses, but Nunn's consequence would have some real influence. Clubs would reject Johnny, hostesses and bankers would do likewise if Nunn asked them to.

"You are wondering why I intruded on what will be a very busy morning for you," Nunn said, clasping his hands behind his back. "I began my day in the company of Lord Phillip, and he has delegated to me certain tasks."

That Phillip would assign the earl a few chores was unsurprising —Phillip had been inspecting Nunnsuch at close range for more than a week—but that Nunn had apparently accepted those orders without protest was astonishing.

"We haven't done our quarterly review of Nunnsuch's books," Hecate said, the only reason she could come up with for Nunn's summons.

"Our quarterly tutorial on the care and feeding of a pretty country manor, you mean. I have managed to save back a few pounds again. This pleases me inordinately, but Lord Phillip had a different discussion in mind."

Nunn was shy. Hecate had deduced as much years ago. He dealt fairly well with his lord of the manor duties, when he could circulate in a crowd, making small talk for a few minutes here and there, never risking more than boredom or bad jokes. He was equally capable of managing a private discussion, where formalities need not apply.

He loathed, though, the settings in between—formal suppers, where he could not escape the scrutiny of the whole table, or breakfast parlor meals, where anybody raiding the sideboard could aim verbal darts in his direction.

Phillip was shy too. What had these two shy, reserved men found to discuss that concerned Hecate? "Whatever you have to say, Uncle Nunn, just tell me. The way this week has gone, I would not be surprised if you announced a decision to take holy orders and move to Sweden."

Nunn propped a hip on the windowsill, his gaze on the vast park. "Lord Phillip was insistent that I make my support of you known, though I have little enough to offer. You have been all that has stood between this family and ruin—between Nunnsuch and ruin—for years, and you don't deserve the treatment your Brompton relations have in mind for you. Whatever is in my power to do on your behalf, you have only to ask."

Lord Phillip had been insistent? When had he done this insisting, and what on earth was Uncle Nunn about? "Not all of my Brompton relations are plotting my doom. This marriage scheme is Johnny and Isaac's doing. I know that."

Nunn rose and took the place not behind his desk, but in the chair next to Hecate's. "I doubt Isaac had much to do with concocting the business. He's lazy by nature. My late countess pronounced him born to pout and sulk, but he's certainly complicit with Johnny's maneuvers now that mischief is afoot. Perhaps an old scheme of Isaac's inspired this new scheme on Johnny's part. I am sorry."

The apology likely cost Nunn considerable dignity, but it amounted to an admission of defeat, an acknowledgment that Johnny's machinations would achieve his desired goal. Hecate might have reached that conclusion—though last night had given her reason to rethink the whole situation—but Nunn's astonishing declaration of support was all but obliterated when he proposed to give up without a fight.

"You owe me no apology, my lord. Let's have a look at your books, shall we? I have not been shut up in the tower of Johnny's choosing yet, and you might have a project or two in need of financing."

"We soldier on, don't we?" Nunn said, gaze on the late countess's portrait hanging behind his desk. "Lord Phillip is likewise not one to give up. If you must look at the books, feel free. Lord Phillips has recommended Henry Wortham for the post of understeward, and with what I've set aside for the past few quarters, I can afford to create the position. Dear old Mr. Jamison can retire to Bristol as he has longed to do, just as soon as Henry learns to dress the part." Nunn rose and fetched a ledger from shelves behind the desk. "The quarterly summary, for your review."

Henry was an inspired choice, one Hecate should have seen, but she'd given up expecting Nunn to listen to her on any but financial matters. She perused the earl's summary figures and mentally compared them to last year's totals for the same period.

"More income," she said, "and fewer expenses."

"You claimed that marling and irrigating and so forth would bear fruit eventually. In fact, those suggestions have born peppers and potatoes and a lot of other garden produce. We can haul our surplus to Basingstoke and Reading in a few hours. The roads are better than when I was a youth, and both towns have grown enormously. I have become something of a gentleman farmer, despite myself."

"And the reduced expenses?"

Nunn's hands were behind his back again. "I don't really care that much for Town. The hostesses are forever pairing me with silly women half my age. The old coach is quite serviceable, though Edna despairs of my sense of fashion. I'm not riding to hounds enough to matter, so why keep a dozen horses whose sole redeeming attribute is a willingness to jump the occasional stile? When one sets out to look for potential economies, one is more likely to find them."

Particularly when those economies had been mentioned every quarter for years. But that Nunn would implement them quietly and wait patiently for the results...

There was hope for Nunn and for Nunnsuch. "Are you doing this for Charles and Eglantine?" Hecate asked. They would certainly benefit, as would their children.

Nunn nodded toward the countess's portrait. "I do it for her. Her likeness hangs behind my desk so she can look over my shoulder as I tend to the estate. I ride the bridle paths she took such delight in, and when I at last join her in the celestial realm, I intend to be welcomed with open arms, rather than with the sort of scold only my dear countess could deliver."

Not the motivation Hecate would have guessed, but entirely consistent with what she knew of Uncle Nunn. "You loved her that much?"

"I *love* her that much." Nunn resumed his seat. "She would be displeased with your situation. If there's anything I can do, Hecate, any influence I can bring to bear, you have only to tell me. One hoped you were aware of my perspective on recent matters, but Lord Phillip was very severe with me. He cited an excess of discretion on my part, an unwillingness to show any favoritism lest the family have another reason to take you into dislike."

Nunn's logic was sound, but his confession—that's what this was —nonetheless hurt. "I wasn't looking for a full-page advertisement in the *Times*. You might have said something to me. An occasional word of encouragement. Some sort of acknowledgment."

Hecate's throat had acquired an ache. Perhaps the result of sleeping under the stars, more likely the result of Phillip seeing what needed to be done and doing it.

"I am offering encouragement now, albeit too little and too late." Nunn seemed to hold a silent exchange with his late wife's portrait, then he rose and went to the safe reposing behind a landscape of Nunnsuch manor and withdrew a packet of documents.

"Your young man has quit the premises," he said, resuming his seat. "He has promised to return, and I cannot vouch for his destination, but I suspect he's gone to Bristol."

"Is he taking ship?" The ache in Hecate's throat was spreading downward, toward her heart.

"No."

"His father forbade him to see the world. Phillip was a virtual captive to the old man's whims, but he managed... Phillip managed to make a paradise of his prison."

Nunn considered the papers in his hand, some of which were yellowing, all of which were covered in a tidy script. "Not a paradise, but one takes your meaning. He found joy and purpose despite the ill will directed at him. Does the name Edward Ross mean anything to you?"

This extraordinary conversation had just exceeded all bounds. Hecate managed a nod. She would have popped to her feet, bounced a curtsey, and claimed a pressing appointment with the housekeeper, except that she did not trust her legs to keep her upright.

"Mama mentioned him." With love. Mama had always mentioned him with love, on the few occasions she had brought him up, or Hecate had found the nerve to ask about him. "I hope Mr. Ross fares well."

Please do not let him be dead. Please not that.

"I must ask you to hear me out," Nunn said. "My intentions were good—I consider Ross a friend, always have. I introduced him to your mother, in fact, which Isaac lists among his many grievances with me. I have tried to act as a friend would act, but I also have an obligation to you, and Lord Phillip went very spare with me for neglecting it."

Uncle Nunn maundered on for a good quarter hour, unburdening himself at the measured pace of a man trying to maintain his dignity in the midst of a fraught topic and mostly succeeding. Hecate listened, and by the time he finished, she was no longer crying. She was instead wondering why Phillip had gone to Bristol and whether he'd truly come back to her.

Though, really, sorting Phillip out was not the most pressing problem.

"I will understand if you cease speaking to me," Nunn said. "You might well move to Paris and leave the lot of us to muddle on as best we can. I would request, for the sake of your young man, that you delay your departure until this house party has concluded."

"Isaac has likely told Johnny of my patrimony."

"And Johnny will threaten to make the matter public at the time least convenient to you," Nunn said. "I doubt polite society will take notice. Old news regarding a woman long gone to her reward, and Isaac has doubtless cried in his brandy often enough in the clubs."

A comforting and likely accurate perspective. "Johnny has other leverage over me, or so he claims."

"Read these," Nunn said, passing her the folded missives. "You have resources Johnny hasn't accounted for, in me, in Lord Phillip, and in those letters. Mrs. Roberts is staunchly in your camp, and my guess is Edna will at least affect neutrality. I cannot speak for Charles, but Society regards him as little more than a chattering tailor's dummy with an overdeveloped interest in opera dancers. I daresay Johnny isn't ready for the forces you have at your disposal."

Hecate took the letters, and Nunn rose.

"Read them here," Nunn said. "You will not be disturbed. Take as long as you like, and then the letters are yours to do with as you wish."

He pressed a hand to Hecate's shoulder and departed, and that gesture—avuncular, personal, consoling—was yet another source of amazement.

Hecate moved around to the desk and settled into the more comfortable chair. She debated for another quarter hour whether to do as Nunn had bid her and read the letters. They were from her father, who might well have married and sired six other children. Who might not have recalled Mama as fondly as she had her Edward.

Hecate glanced at the dates, which started a month after Mama's death and continued, the most recent being less than a month old. Most of them began in the same general manner:

My dear Nunn,

Your epistle of the nineteenth brought me much joy and no little worry. As proud as I am of my dear girl, I am anxious as well. How I wish I could aid her, and how appreciative I am of every word you relay that acquaints me with her circumstances...

The closings were all of a piece as well.

No daughter was ever so well loved, or so poorly served, by her father as my Hecate, and yet, I beg you for the next missive, as soon as you find it convenient to write...

. . .

There *was* such a thing as a good cry, such a thing as tears that acknowledged heartache and accorded it the respect it was due. Tears that admitted the truth and gave that truth dignity and meaning.

Tears that strengthened resolve and illuminated the way forward.

Hecate gathered up the letters and returned them to the safe, where neither moth nor rust nor conniving cousins could destroy them. She went to the door and found Mr. DeWitt at his ease in the footman's chair several yards down the corridor.

"Mr. DeWitt, might you locate my uncle and tell him I'd like to speak to him?" Tears had made Hecate's voice deeper, but she had never enjoyed such clarity of purpose. "I have a question to put to him, and I will await him in his study."

"You've been crying." This conclusion apparently displeased Mr. DeWitt. "Did Nunn give you the sharp side of his tongue?"

"He finally gave me the truth. Please fetch him, Mr. DeWitt. I will not set foot outside his study until you do, and then you and I can go for a stroll in the gardens, and you can tell me more about growing up in Crosspatch Corners."

"More about Phillip, you mean?"

She smiled, because even the thought of Phillip gave her joy. "Of course about Phillip."

CHAPTER SEVENTEEN

"You cannot assist me to dress for the ball, Mr. DeWitt." Hecate allowed a note of exasperation to underscore her words.

Gavin DeWitt had become her shadow in recent days, sitting through last-minute menu reviews with Cook, trundling along through the wine cellars when Hecate conferred with the butler. DeWitt had just finished patiently waiting through a discussion with the stable master regarding where coaches should park when half the shire showed up for tonight's ball.

When DeWitt had been unable to escort her—to the parlor after supper, for example—Mrs. Roberts had taken up the duty. She'd admonished Hecate to keep her bedroom door locked at all times and not to venture down to breakfast until Mrs. Roberts or Mr. DeWitt arrived to escort her.

"As it happens," DeWitt said, "my years with the theater mean I am an expert lady's dresser. I am also accomplished with cosmetics, of which you have no need."

Hecate reached the top of the staircase and turned for her room. "A man of varied accomplishments. Now I need you to turn invisible, because for the next ninety minutes, I will be in my bedroom, having a short lie-down, and then outfitting myself for the evening. If this is how royalty lives—no privacy, a retinue hovering at all times—it's no wonder poor old George went mad."

DeWitt strolled along beside her, damn his longer legs. "Comfort yourself with this realization, Miss Brompton: Wherever Lord Phillip is, whatever task he's about, he is half mad worrying for you, and his anxiety is justified. Darling Johnny has been lurking behind potted lemons, loitering on balconies, and making a general attempt to keep you in his sights to an alarming degree."

Hecate stopped outside her door. Johnny had been comporting himself like some lovelorn adolescent, or a villain intent on a kidnapping. He'd watched Hecate at meals, maintained a brooding distance from her over pall-mall, and taken a seat for piquet and whist that allowed him to stare at her over his cards.

"Phillip said he'd be back in time for tonight's ball," Hecate muttered, extracting the key from a pocket. "He has less than two hours before the dancing begins." She twisted the key and pushed the door open, stepping back to allow DeWitt to inspect her room before she set foot therein.

Had she not lived her whole life among Bromptons, she would have thought the measure excessive.

"What have we here?" DeWitt posed the question to Flavia, poised before Hecate's open jewelry box, a gold bracelet winking from her wrist.

"Nothing of any moment," Hecate said, though Flavia had managed to get past a locked door, and then she'd had the presence of mind to relock the door before embarking on her larceny.

"I can't undo the clasp," she said, holding up her hand. "One puts the bracelet on one's right hand, the better to display the pretty bauble, but then one's left isn't equal to the... I wasn't stealing it. Please believe that."

"Where is your familiar?" DeWitt asked, opening the wardrobe and moving dresses aside.

Flavia looked confused. "I am not a witch."

"He means Portia," Hecate said. "Did she accompany you?"

"Porry is having a lie-down. She's on her last nerve, and Mama isn't helping. I'm to waken Porry on the half hour so I can help her dress and do her hair. The maids always annoy her, and Mama's lady's maid won't look in on us until Mama's ensemble is complete."

DeWitt moved aside curtains and peered under the bed, then had a look on the balcony. "No Portia. Shall I escort Miss Flavia to her room?"

Flavia fiddled with the clasp, pink staining her cheeks. Ashamed because she'd wanted to look pretty and sophisticated for a change.

"I think not," Hecate said. "Flavia and I can chat while I get off my feet for a bit."

"Don't harangue me," Flavia said, apparently giving up on the clasp. "I never steal. You know that. I only borrow, and then I put everything back."

"Mr. DeWitt was just leaving, and I know you're not a thief, Flavia." A dupe, yes; a thief, no. "Mr. DeWitt, I will not go down to the buffet until you rap four times on my door. Give me at least an hour."

He bowed and withdrew, sending Flavia the sort of look headmasters reserve for recidivist pranksters. Hecate locked the door after him, because he'd linger in the corridor until he heard the mechanism catch.

She gestured to one of the chairs by the empty hearth. "You are welcome to keep the bracelet, Flavia. You have the delicate bones for an article like that, while I do not."

Flavia stared at her wrist. "You should be scolding me."

"Everybody scolds you. I know how that feels." Hecate took one of the worn chairs and waited for Flavia to do likewise. "No matter how hard you try, they criticize the results. If, by chance, you manage something perfectly, they warn you against showing off."

Flavia looked up. "I don't do anything perfectly."

Hecate wanted to howl on behalf of her younger self and on

Flavia's behalf. "You keep a complicated set of signals straight at one game of whist after another."

"That's cheating." Flavia resumed trying to free herself from the bracelet. "Porry says nobody misses tuppence, but we win a great more than tuppence sometimes. We never just enjoy a hand of cards anymore. I used to like whist."

"Is that why you've been partnering Mr. DeGrange lately?"

Ah, a smile. A sweet, genuine, slightly bewildered smile. "Mr. DeGrange is kind and funny, and he's only ten years older than me. He's not silly, but he's not serious either. Porry claims he's merely gentry. Gentry live in the country, and I hate London's coal smoke and bustle."

Flavia got up to pace, which a lady did not do and which Hecate was prone to doing when vexed by an investment.

"One cannot think when the noise in Town never ceases," Flavia went on. "Don't tell Porry I said that. Porry claims a third Season is a disaster, but Mr. DeGrange says ladies should be allowed to thoroughly examine what's on offer, not be rushed to the altar before they've had a chance to avail themselves of Town's diversions. Porry declares that's nonsense."

Porry says, Porry claims, Porry declares... "Portia Brompton has never, to my knowledge, been appointed the arbiter of truth in any regard. She is often in error, frequently bullheaded, and unrelentingly selfish. Mr. DeGrange is quite well fixed. He tends his acres conscientiously, and his grandmother was a copper heiress. She left him significant means that he's invested wisely. I would not have added him to the guest list if he were merely agreeable."

Flavia sank back into her chair. "Portia was wrong. I knew it. Porry is often wrong, but one cannot tell her that, or she flies into the boughs, and then one must apologize for having done nothing wrong, or she pouts. Nobody can pout like Portia."

Edna, Isaac, Eggy, Charlie... They could all give Portia a run for her pouting money. "You are not her nanny, Flavia. Tell her she's mistaken, decline to partner her at whist, and bide here at Nunnsuch if you don't choose to go to Town. Uncle Nunn could use the company, truth be told."

Flavia tucked her feet up and curled her arms around her knees. "I can't. Portia is all I have. Mama is off on her intrigues and scheming with Eggy, or doting on the little boys. If Portia turns her back on me, I'll have nothing and nobody, or worse, Porry will decide I need to be taught a lesson. She used to do that. Hide my dolls. She tossed one of them to the rag-and-bone man once because I wouldn't give her my pudding."

What a horrid thing to do. "And yet, you are loyal to her."

Flavia shrugged. "You are loyal to the Bromptons, and then Johnny struts home from Canada, and the lot of us can't wait to see him snatch your fortune from you. I think it's horrid myself. You aren't doting, but you are fair and generous, and you have a head for figures. Porry says Johnny will be more generous than you are, but she's determined to marry Lord Phillip. She won't be the one wearing last year's bonnets when Johnny leaves us all to starve. I'd really rather not wear your bracelet, if you don't mind."

She held out her wrist, and Hecate undid the clasp, though the links had snagged on the lace of Flavia's cuff. Freeing her took some delicate maneuvering.

Hecate held the skein of gold up to the slanting beams of evening light. How many of her own figurative dolls had the Bromptons tossed to the rag-and-bone man? How many of her years, her best efforts, her good intentions?

Her fortune was the least of it.

"I like Lord Phillip," Flavia said.

"I love him. Is Portia intent on getting compromised with him?"

Flavia tucked herself into a smaller ball. "I never said that."

Hecate waited, mentally castigating herself for having overlooked the one family member who never gave her any trouble.

"Eggy vows I'm nearly simpleminded," Flavia said. "Mama warns me that I'd best work on my charm and wiles, because my brains and fortune will never impress a man. Charles says he might be able to foist me off on one of his older friends. Portia has a use for me, sometimes."

Hecate had been five years younger than Flavia was now when the Bromptons, abetted by a lot of crooked solicitors, had decided that she, too, had a use.

Damn them for that and for what they were doing to Flavia. "You are pretty, Flavia. More attractive than Portia, and that bothers her exceedingly."

Flavia looked up, her expression suggesting the dressing bell had sounded an hour early.

"You learned the quadrille in three days flat," Hecate went on. "Lord Phillip, an intelligent and determined man, is still struggling with it after weeks of practice. You would doubtless be a dab hand at the ledgers, and I cannot find another Brompton who will even glance at them. You have seen Mr. DeGrange's good qualities without even knowing he possesses a fortune, and that will matter to him a great deal."

Flavia worried her lower lip. "You are really rich, aren't you?"

What had that to do with anything? When had that ever had a blessed thing to do with what mattered?

"Yes and no."

Flavia stared hard at the gold winking in Hecate's hand. "I wish I could be like you, wealthy enough that I don't have to marry. Don't have to be pretty. Don't have to charm all the bachelors in hopes one of them will take me off the Brompton charity rolls. I could work at your sailors' home—I'm good with a needle."

This was as much enthusiasm as Flavia had ever shown about anything, and Hecate was reminded again of all the enthusiasms the Bromptons had criticized, ridiculed, and shamed her out of.

And now they wanted to take Phillip from her, too, and foist Johnny off on her?

"Flavia, if that's what you want, then I will make the arrangements. You can have a cottage in Chelsea—Miss Blanchard adores her cottage—devote yourself to charity, and leap over the whole Mayfair madness."

"You'd do that?"

"I wish somebody had done that for me." Wished she had done it for herself, but like Phillip, she'd accepted a sentence passed upon her by those unqualified to render judgment.

Flavia set her feet back on the floor and smoothed her skirts. "Porry plans to compromise you with Johnny so Lord Phillip will be left for her. She might choose Mr. DeWitt instead. I saw Mr. DeWitt first, but when Portia makes up her mind..."

"She'd leave you with no one?"

"No one but her, though to be honest..."

"Right. No sister at all might be an improvement over a sister like that. How is this compromising supposed to work?"

Hecate had a general idea—DeWitt had mentioned that Portia was plotting more mischief—and Flavia supplied details consistent with prior offenses.

"Thank you for telling me," Hecate said. "You'd best go waken Sleeping Beauty, and I will have a word with Uncle Nunn."

"What about?"

"A topic we aired in theory several days ago that now must be dealt with in earnest." Hecate stopped Flavia at the door, pulled her into a hug, and then slapped the bracelet into her palm. "Keep it for luck."

Flavia hugged her back and slipped into the corridor, where Mr. DeWitt waited, already attired in his evening finery.

～

"Porry, hold still, or your coiffeur will be lopsided."

"This vanity stool is an instrument of torture, and lopsided is fashionable. A curl or two cascading over my milk-white shoulder. Can you try that, Flavie?" Mama claimed Lord Phillip would be returning for tonight's ball—where had he got off to, and how did Mama know that?—and the usual ringlets would not do.

Schoolgirls wore ringlets. The future wife of a marquess's heir was entitled to more sophisticated styles.

"I can try." Flavia, still attired in chemise and dressing gown, began unbraiding the plait she'd just made. "We will be late for the buffet if you don't soon make up your mind."

"The buffet is only for family and guests. We don't need to be punctual. Besides, you are going to be late anyway, remember?"

"Because I'm to discover Hecate and Johnny at five minutes past the hour... Where did you decide I'm to discover them?"

"Must you pull my hair?" Portia took a fortifying sip of punch, though if Hecate had allowed any wine into this batch, Cook had used a very subtle hand. "You, accompanied by Eggy, at least, and possibly Mr. DeGrange and Mr. DeWitt, will find Hecate and Johnny in the warming pantry beside the formal dining room."

"Because I heard strange noises coming from there and don't want to risk my hems in the vicinity of an angry tomcat?"

"If you can think of something better, feel free. Strange noises ought to arouse curiosity, and because the formal dining room isn't in use tonight, the warming pantry is the perfect place for a pair of servants to canoodle. Private, small, dark..." Only one door.

Nobody expected Flavia to be very clever or worldly. She could make a convincing job of anxiety over strange noises.

"And I'm to pull this off when you've left me less than forty-five minutes to dress and do my hair?"

"You're quick, and I will tarry a moment to help you." Portia considered her reflection and assessed the progress Flavia was making. "That is rather good, Flavie. I look quite Grecian."

"If you're not to look completely undone, you need more pins. What exactly did your note to Hecate say?"

"That Johnny is willing to see reason, and they need to have a private discussion if they are to resolve matters to her satisfaction. *Ouch.*"

A light rap on the door interrupted the scold Portia would have delivered. "See who it is. Mama or Eggy wouldn't knock, and Hecate had best not think to interrupt our preparations with one of her lectures about moderation and decorum and whatnot." Though perhaps Hecate was already in possession of her note—the butler himself was to deliver both notes—and wanted Portia to oversee the buffet or something equally tedious.

Flavia went to the door and came back bearing a single folded, sealed page. "For you."

Portia broke the seal and considered her reflection in the mirror. Quite sophisticated. Alluring even.

"He's back," Portia said, scanning the few words on the page. "Lord Phillip has returned. This invitation must be from him."

Flavia sat on the hassock by the hearth to don her stockings and garters. "What does it say?"

To share or not to share? Poor Flavia would never receive notes from gentlemen begging the favor of her company...

"'If a certain young lady would see fit to join a certain lonely fellow in the earl's study at a quarter to the hour, much interesting conversation will ensue. Ever thine.'"

"No signature? How do you know it's not from Shoes or Boots or Johnny or Mr. DeWitt?"

"They would not dare make improper advances toward me." Johnny might. Delicious thought, to sample the charms of Hecate's prospective husband before Hecate had the honor. But no. Johnny had already received his summons to the warming pantry. Not even Johnny could manage two assignations in twenty minutes.

Not well, at least.

How droll. Assignations everywhere. "I'm off to the earl's study by way of the maids' stairs. You'd best stop dawdling, Flavie. In thirty minutes or so, you must interrupt a torrid embrace between our cousins."

"I can tell time, Porry. You need more pins in your hair, or that arrangement won't last through the first set."

"Do not, I beg you, scold me when all of my hard work and planning are about to bear fruit. You see before you the future Lady Phillip."

Flavia curtseyed. "You see before you a woman in a hurry. Best of luck, Porry, but do be careful. I've not heard that Lord Phillip has returned, and that note could be from anybody."

"You have no feminine intuition. Of course it's from Lord Phillip. He's learned that Hecate intends to accept Johnny's suit, and thus he's making the most sensible match available. He's the logical sort, and he and I will get on splendidly. Besides, Berkshire has been terribly lonely for him."

Flavia shed her dressing gown and took up her stays. "You are privy to gossip I haven't heard."

"I am, and if you were any sort of sister, you'd congratulate me on my impending success."

Flavia gave her an odd look, one that revealed a certain resemblance between Flavia and Hecate. "Congratulations, Portia, on your impending success. When your enjoyable discussion has concluded, please do remember to secure your coiffeur with more pins."

Portia gave her reflection one last inspection. "If all goes well, I will need to put my entire ensemble to rights after my *conversation* with Lord Phillip."

She swanned out of the room, leaving Flavia looking puzzled and forlorn in her shift. Poor, dear Flavie was doomed to frequent bewilderment and little adventure. Fortunately for her, she could wield a hairbrush competently and mend a hem in a trice. That was something.

Not much, but something.

Portia let herself into Uncle Nunn's study without knocking. A gentleman stood by the window in formal evening attire, his back to her.

"You were expecting me?" she asked, trying not to sound nervous, though a little nervousness was to be expected. The fellow turned, and she found herself in unexpected company. "What on earth are *you* doing here?"

Johnny strode across the room, looking splendid and annoyed. "I might ask the same of you. Did you set this up?"

"I most certainly did not. How dare you accuse me of such an underhanded scheme? I have no need to lure gentlemen into assignations."

He prowled closer, until he could look down his nose at her. "That's not what the Corvisers say."

"A pair of nattering ninnyhammers, and how dare you accuse me of scheming when you accosted Hecate in the garden, and she rejected your advances?"

Johnny's gaze strayed where a gentleman's ought not. Portia let him look and even took a deep breath because men were too stupid to know that was a ploy.

"Hecate plays hard to get," Johnny said. "What else should I expect from a woman who's been on the shelf for half her life?"

"You should expect gratitude," Portia snapped. "If a handsome, well-heeled man of substance favors her with that much attention, she ought to be grateful." Hecate would be grateful eventually, though Johnny had exactly fifteen minutes to get himself down to the warming pantry, unless the butler had failed to deliver that invitation.

Johnny smiled, and his annoyance turned to a wicked, wicked sort of allure. "Little Portia is all grown up. My gracious."

Portia debated with herself for one more deep, deep breath—Hecate did not deserve to marry such a fine specimen—and then she seized Johnny by his lovely broad shoulders and took possession of his mouth.

She felt the surprise go through him—she'd ambushed the former soldier—then he wrapped his arms around her and began kissing her back. He tasted of brandy and forbidden fruit, and Portia almost wished she wasn't about to become engaged to Lord Phillip.

She pushed herself closer. Gather ye rosebuds while ye may...

The verse had no sooner popped into her head than she heard a slight scraping sound. Then Johnny shoved her away—he was the one breathing deeply now—and stood at attention.

"I can explain," he panted. "This is all her fault."

∼

Hecate had turned the house-party assemblage loose on the buffet a quarter hour ago. A few guests from distant parts were already arriving and milling about in the foyer. Uncle Nunn, accompanied by Mrs. Roberts and Mr. DeGrange, had gone up to his study not five minutes ago, and Hecate's nerves were in a state.

"Where can he be?" she muttered to nobody in particular.

"Beg pardon?" Mr. DeWitt materialized from the alcove at the top of the main staircase. He was a credit to his tailor and to the fine country air of rural Berkshire. Not as muscular as Phillip, but lean, elegant, and rangy.

"Where is Lord Phillip? You assured me he'd return in time for the ball. The receiving line will be assembling in the next twenty minutes, and no Lord Phillip."

"Unless I'm mistaken, he has traveled to Bristol, made certain arrangements while there, and will complete the journey... Ah, the prodigal returns," Mr. DeWitt said, peering out the window. A large coach was tooling up the drive, a rider cantering before it on a stout bay colt.

"That's your Roland?"

"And your Lord Phillip, unless I miss my guess."

Hecate's emotions coalesced into pure relief. Whatever else the evening held—Johnny's mischief, Portia's machinations, Hecate's own schemes running amok—Phillip was safe, and he'd kept his word.

"I dearly wish," Mr. DeWitt said, "that somebody would smile like that when I arrived at a formal occasion in all my dirt."

"He'll arrive fashionably late," Hecate said, "meaning he'll take a few minutes to spruce up at the summer cottage, then join the festivities." Phillip handed his mount off to a groom, and the lumbering coach pulled up to the front steps. "You will please greet Lord Phillip and tell him I expect him in the ballroom in thirty minutes."

"That would require that I leave your side. I know not where Johnny lurks, but as the long-lost cousin newly returned from the perils of the Canadian wilderness, he'll take a place in the receiving line, meaning he has an excuse to accost you here. That alcove is a few short steps away, and he could have you against the wall in the time it takes you to say, 'Unhand me, you brute.'"

"Phillip is coming in the front door." One did not attend a formal ball in dusty riding attire. What was he about?

A lone gentleman climbed down from the traveling coach—who took a traveling coach to a neighborhood ball?—and then Phillip was through the door, past the butler, and marching up the steps. The dozen or so guests already in the foyer watched with varying degrees of curiosity as he ascended.

His gaze lit on Hecate, and the relief in his eyes was obvious.

"Is that Lord Phillip?" Edna, the hostess of record, chose then to swan forth from her sitting room. "I daresay he's in want of a wash."

Eggy appeared at her elbow. "He does look a bit road weary. Did you send him away, Hecate? Is he here to create an untoward scene?"

Must Eglantine sound so pleased? "He's here, and for that, I'm grateful. One worried." Phillip looked exhausted, but... confident, pleased. Not despairing.

He gained the top of the steps and bowed. "Miss Brompton, good evening."

"My lord, a pleasure." Hecate curtseyed as Charles joined the gawkers.

"Not done," Charles said, "to anticipate the receiving line, bring half the dirt of Hampshire with you, and trudge up the steps in your boots, my lord. Hecate, offer to send his lordship a footman. The staff can't be expected to manage bathwater, given the general pandemonium, but even a basin—"

"I'll not have it!" Johnny strode up the corridor, Portia trailing at his side, and Nunn, DeGrange, and Mrs. Roberts bringing up the rear. "The whole business was a complete travesty, concocted by an overwrought spinster with ambitions above her station."

"I am not a spinster," Portia retorted, "and if anybody is overwrought, it's you, Johnny Brompton."

"My, my, my," Eglantine said. "I do believe we are about to have an untoward scene after all."

"We already had an untoward scene," Nunn said, his tone sufficient to freeze the punch in the bowls set up in the foyer. "I went to my study, thinking to share a quiet brandy with a pair of guests, and what should we come upon, but Portia nigh climbing Johnny's person, and Johnny aiding her ascent with both hands upon the lady's fundament."

"A unique approach to kissing," Mrs. Roberts added. "Very athletic."

"What it lacked in refinement," Mr. DeGrange observed, "it made up for in enthusiasm on the part of both parties. I see Lord Phillip has returned." He bowed courteously, and Phillip reciprocated. "My man will happily attend you, my lord, should you wish to freshen up."

"I'm not marrying her!" Johnny spluttered. "She manipulated me, she used me, she took unfair advantage."

Portia assayed a pitying smile. "Come now, Johnny. You needn't be coy. You did send me a note."

Phillip was looking amused. The other recent arrival waited on the landing, while Hecate hoped the guests in the foyer were catching every word.

"I sent you no note," Johnny said. "I vow I sent her no note."

"Feeling frustrated?" Hecate inquired pleasantly. "Cornered? Trapped? Without allies or advantages? Victimized through no fault of your own?"

Johnny's expression shifted from worried to puzzled to furious. "*You* did this? You maneuvered me into this situation?"

"She didn't maneuver you into kissing me," Portia said.

Johnny drew himself up. "I regret a momentary lapse of decorum, Miss Portia, but I am engaged to Miss Hecate. If that scene in the earl's study was of your making, then you will have to content yourself with my apologies. I am not free to offer for you."

Phillip took up a lean on the banister. "Oh, but you are."

Nunn looked from Phillip—dusty, weary, nearly bored—to Johnny, resplendent in his evening attire, doing a fine impersonation of the aggrieved hero, and standing militarily erect. The performance was only slightly marred by the odd angle of his boutonniere and the smudge of pink lip color on his cheek.

"Lord Phillip, you will please elucidate particulars," Nunn said.

"That fellow," Phillip said, nodding at Johnny, "was doubtless planning to make a grand announcement at tonight's gathering, one intended to further entrap Miss Hecate Brompton into marriage. He might not have announced a betrothal per se, but he'd have made plain that the lady had given him permission to court her, will she, nill she."

"One wants to be forthright about a courtship," Johnny said, while Portia glared daggers, and Hecate longed to smack him with her fan.

"Does one want to be equally forthright about his identity?" Phillip mused. "It might be the case that Johnny Brompton signed settlement agreements at Isaac's urging years ago. I am less connived that Hecate signed anything binding, and I am utterly certain that you are not Johnny Brompton."

The ensuing silence was brief and absolute, followed by general babbling.

"He's daft," from Johnny.

"I suspected as much," from Edna.

"How marvelous," from Eggy.

"I say," from Charles. "I do say. How extraordinary."

Hecate had only one question. "My lord, do you have proof?"

Phillip pushed away from the banister and faced Johnny—if indeed that was Johnny. "He's supposedly a trapper inured to the elements, accustomed to battling the forces of nature for months on end, and yet, he cannot tell east from west when the sun is nearly touching the horizon. His hands are those of a clerk, not a hardy back-woodsman. He is inordinately preoccupied with who comes in second, as a younger brother would be when overshadowed by a more impressive sibling. In the middle of a racecourse laid over the grounds of his family seat, he became lost. This is not Johnny Brompton."

"I am Johnny. I am."

"Give up, Emeril," Phillip said, not unkindly. "If we compare Johnny's letters with those of his younger brother, we'll see that Johnny's penmanship at some point came to resemble Emeril's exactly. Nunn, you have the letters?"

"Every one, going back ten years."

"I am Johnny, I tell you. If I don't have sufficient calluses to suit his lordship, then I will have to plead months of idleness while I made my way home, and even in the wilderness, we use compasses."

"Calluses don't disappear that quickly," Nunn said. "Shall you pen us a little missive, whoever you are?"

Flavia had at some point taken the place beside Mr. DeGrange. "No need for that. Johnny has a scar on his shoulder where Emeril accidently ran him through with a wooden sword. This fellow has no such scar."

DeGrange patted her hand. "Been engaging in a spot of bird-watching, my dear?"

Portia's mouth was hanging open.

Hecate wanted to dance a jig. "Thank you, Flavia, for putting us in possession of yet more evidence proving that Emeril, rather than Johnny, came home from Canada."

"The settlement agreements are real," Emeril said. "The signature is valid."

"But that signature," Phillip said, "is not yours, and there's the rub."

"Shakespeare," DeWitt murmured. "He has you, sir. You have no claim on Miss Hecate Brompton *whatsoever*, and you owe her a sincere apology, assuming she doesn't have you arrested for extortion or fraud or some other hanging offense."

Portia elbowed her way past Edna and Eggy. "You cannot arrest him. He owes me a proposal."

Emeril looked her up and down as if he'd never truly seen her before. "We're cousins."

"If royalty can marry cousins, so can we."

Hecate took Phillip's hand. "She has a point, and besides, Emeril, or whoever you are, your scheme was about to blow up in your face. I've signed over most of my fortune to Uncle Nunn."

Phillip kissed her cheek. "Well done."

Another general uproar ensued, and Hecate let it wash around her. She was content to stand hand in hand with Phillip, to be free of Johnny, of riches, of any expectations save those dearest to her heart.

"You signed it away?" Edna asked when the hue and cry had subsided. "Truly?"

"The money made me miserable, or I allowed you lot to make me miserable over it. I never wanted wealth, I didn't earn it, and Uncle Nunn will steward those resources as well as I could. I wish you all the joy of squabbling over it, but you will no longer vex me with your importuning."

Phillip took both her hands. "You're sure?"

"You were right: Family is as family does. Will you have me without my money?"

"Will you have me if I never learn to dance a quadrille?"

Hecate purely beamed at him. The joy was both roaring and quiet, enormous and intimate. "I will have you, my lord. Depend upon it."

Somebody cleared his throat.

Hecate looked past Phillip's shoulder to see an older gentleman—the fellow who'd brought the traveling coach—looking uncomfortable at the top of the steps.

"If somebody wouldn't mind handling the introductions, I would very much like—love—to make Miss Brompton's acquaintance. My lord?"

Hecate abruptly needed Phillip's arm for support. "Who is that fellow?"

"A prosperous Bristol merchant. Nunn has known him for ages. Let's find somewhere private so you can make his acquaintance without an audience."

"Let's," Hecate said. "Please, let's."

CHAPTER EIGHTEEN

The murmur of voices coming from the foyer was leavened by the strains of a string quartet. Nunn and Edna, abetted by Charles, Eggy, and Emeril, were greeting the stragglers, and Phillip was far from dressed for the occasion.

He should have been mortified, but he was too busy holding hands with his intended to care. He'd shepherded her and Edward Ross to Nunn's study, where nobody would dare intrude.

"Your mother," Edward Ross said, "was a force of nature. She appeared at first glance to be the demure wife of another London dandy, but her conversation was insightful, her humor uproarious, and her determination... You inherited that. You clearly inherited much that is wonderful from your mother."

Father and daughter had been talking for nearly an hour. Haltingly at first. Platitudes.

Thank you for receiving me.

You're looking well.

Have you always lived in Bristol?

Ross had been born in Dundee, and traces of the accent still flavored his speech. Until the last two changes, Phillip had ridden in the coach with him and learned much of his prospective papa-in-law. In appearance, Ross was tallish, solid, going gray about the temples, and imposing about the eyebrows. His blue eyes had likely always been fierce.

Ross read voraciously, and he'd shown a prodigy's facility with figures from a young age. He was known for scrupulous honesty in business and for driving a hard bargain. He did his own negotiating, leaving the lawyers to clean up details, and he was as yet unmarried.

By degrees, Hecate and her father were tiptoeing up to more difficult matters.

"Mama didn't mention you often, but she was always complimentary. Said I must not blame you and that someday, she hoped, I might make your acquaintance. I did not dare."

Ross rose and went to the sideboard. "I will presume to pour a round of brandy, to steady our nerves and, in my case, to celebrate. My daughter has acknowledged me more than civilly, and I..." He busied himself moving decanters about, back to Phillip and Hecate.

"I am celebrating too," Hecate said gently. "Phillip?"

"My rejoicing is without limit."

Ross collected himself and passed out the drinks. "I did not dare approach you. Firstly, I did not deserve to intrude on your life, and secondly, Nunn had assured me repeatedly that the Bromptons would turn any overtures from me to their own purposes should they get wind of them."

"They would have." Hecate took a sip of her drink. "They rifle the mail, listen at keyholes, lurk behind hedges... If only their enthusiasm for gathering information focused on something useful, like making investment decisions. Isaac loathes you."

"A man I would have pitied, except that he took out his bile on you, who were innocent of any wrongdoing. One wishes he'd gone to Canada."

Phillip sampled his brandy, a good vintage. "One wishes Emeril had stayed there."

Hecate smiled a wicked little grin. "Portia might well be the making of him."

Edward resumed his seat. They'd taken the chairs by the hearth, though no fire burned, and they were likely missing the promenade.

About which, Phillip did not give one hearty, Berkshire bedamned.

"Do you mind that I left Nunn in charge of the money?" Hecate had put the question to her father, suggesting she'd deduced a few pertinent details.

"The money was always yours to do with as you wished. Your mother invested the initial sum in the cent-per-cents, as conservative a place to put funds as any, but as you grew a bit older, she asked for your suggestions. You were reading the paper long before you should have been allowed to, and when you mentioned the tulip craze, she realized you'd been nosing about Nunn's library as well. She began to heed your suggestions, modestly at first. By the time your mother left us, we already knew you had inherited at least some proclivities from me."

"You and Mama corresponded?"

"Nunn's countess facilitated our correspondence and then bequeathed the responsibility to Nunn when she grew ill. Your mother and I saw each other once a year in the spa towns—I lived for those three weeks, my dear, and I suspect she did too. After your mother's death, I permitted myself an annual sojourn to London. I, too, lurked behind an occasional hedge, Hecate. Thank the merciful powers you enjoy a gallop of a morning. I hope you won't judge me for spying."

On the whole, interminable journey from Bristol, Edward's sole concern had been that his intrusion into Hecate's life would make her situation worse. Phillip had assured him it would not, but only she could say if knowing her father would make her situation better.

"Shall I leave you two some privacy?" Phillip asked. "I'm told I need to make the close acquaintance of a large washbasin, the sooner the better."

"Stay," Hecate said. "Please."

Edward considered his brandy. "I have no secrets from you, my lord. I've carried too many secrets for too long and would rather have done with such measures."

He was making a request and trying to maintain his dignity while doing it. Phillip sympathized, but the plea was Hecate's to answer.

"I cannot acknowledge you as my father," she said, "not openly, but you are a dear friend of Uncle Nunn's, and you share with me an enthusiasm for investing. My favorite charity is a sailors' home, in which you are sure to take an interest."

Edward nodded once. "I've seen it. Lovely establishment. Your residents cannot stop singing your praises."

Another hedge Edward had apparently lurked behind.

"Mama mentioned that you take good care of your pensioners," Hecate went on, "and that a life at sea can leave a man distant from his family and with few friends ashore. She said you owned merchantmen."

Ross nodded. "A few."

He likely owned a fleet, and Isaac Brompton doubtless resented him for that more than for poaching on marital preserves Isaac had abandoned.

"If we were to take on a joint project," Hecate said slowly, "a sailors' home in Bristol, nobody would remark our continued acquaintance."

Phillip wanted to kiss her, for her kindness toward a father who'd kept his distance for too long, for her genius, for her courage.

But then, he always wanted to kiss her.

Edward stared at her. "A sailors' home?"

"Britain loves her seamen," Hecate said. "We respect our soldiers, but our sailors... Wellington will always be venerated, but we love Nelson. We still pray for his soul. We name our children after him. I would be honored to advise you on the establishment of sailors' homes in Bristol, Portsmouth, Liverpool..."

"And Berkshire," Phillip added. "You will always be welcome at

Lark's Nest, sir. I know nothing of sailors' homes or international trade, but I well know who is family and who is not."

Hecate squeezed his hand. Edward produced a handkerchief and found it necessary to admire the view from the balcony.

"Put him up in the summer cottage with me and DeWitt," Phillip said. "You were already sorting through possibilities, weren't you?"

"He is so... not what I expected. I expected a merchant prince, charming, willing to show me some sentimental fondness provided I did not ask for anything more than a passing smile from him, but he's..."

"Your father, to the best of his ability."

"And you found him for me."

"He wasn't lost, but I did want you to consider that the Bromptons are not your only option in terms of family. Nunn was forthcoming about your parents' history, and I could see Johnny's, or Emeril's, mischief wearing you down. Do we banish the scoundrel back to Canada?"

Hecate rose and deposited herself in Phillip's lap. "Life would certainly be more peaceful, and I do believe Portia intends to have him."

Phillip enfolded Hecate in a hug, his sense of homecoming finally complete. "I need a bath."

"I need you."

They enjoyed a moment of perfect contentment before Hecate resumed her seat and finished her brandy. "I should be in the ballroom."

"I have a suggestion," Phillip said, leaning over to murmur his next words in her ear.

Hecate listened, she smiled, she kissed him, and she sat back. "A fine plan. You see to Papa and pay a quick call on the swimming hole, and I will expect you both in time for the supper waltz."

She stood, squared her shoulders, and beamed at him. "Until tonight, and, Phillip?"

He got to his feet, prepared to hear that she wanted a long

engagement, that Lark's Nest would not do, that he had best not appear in riding attire on a formal occasion ever again.

"Miss Brompton?"

"Thank you. Thank you from the bottom of my heart and the top and all the compass points. Save that supper waltz for me, or it will go hard for you."

"Your servant, Miss Brompton." He bowed politely, she curtseyed, and Phillip watched her go with a gentleman's appreciative eye and a lover's besotted devotion.

~

"Canada will be wonderful, Flave," Portia said, taking yet another sip of the punch, though the libation continued to disappoint. "You'll see. Emeril says the forests are mindboggling and the summers spectacular. You've always liked nature more than I have. You'll come to love it, I'm sure."

Flavia's gaze was on Mr. DeGrange, who was partnering Mrs. Roberts. Portia had done the promenade with Emeril—begin as you intend to go on, after all—and he appeared to be reconciling himself to his good fortune.

"You're sure you'll live in Canada?" Flavia asked.

"Emeril has a good post in Toronto, or he did. He wanted to look in on us here in Merry Olde, but he'd taken to opening the mail that came through for Johnny, and Johnny barely sets foot in civilized surrounds anymore apparently. Likes life in the wilderness, if you can imagine such a thing. Emeril says that happens with the trappers. They become part wild themselves, and domesticating them again is nearly impossible. Are you listening to me?"

Flavia's expression had become preoccupied. Mr. DeGrange twirled by again, and Portia caught a sneaking whiff of an unpleasant notion.

"Of course I'm listening, Porry."

"Then you are coming with us? Many a spinster lives with a

married sibling, and Emeril says Canada is crawling with single men. Some of them, like Cousin Johnny, are even worth some blunt. You'll find a husband in no time, and I won't mind having you on hand until then."

A generous offer. Flavia would not hear a better one.

"That is very kind of you, Porry. Very thoughtful."

"I am kind by nature, and you are my only sister. This punch is awful."

"I fear I must decline your suggestion nonetheless," Flavia said. "My place is here."

Portia put the back of her gloved hand to Flavia's forehead. "Are you coming down with something? I thought I just heard you say you will force me to cross an ocean with only Emeril's dubious company to fortify me. Society has had its chance to appreciate us, Flavie, and they failed us."

Flavia fluttered her fan slowly with her left hand, then touched the tip with a single finger. *Come and talk to me*, followed by, *I wish to speak with you.* Did Flavia even realize what she was signaling? Probably not. Flavia wasn't much given to flirtation, and who would she flirt with when Mr. DeWitt was lurking among the dowagers?

"You and Cousin Emeril will manage splendidly," Flavia said. "You will be the making of him. He has wanted direction, and you can provide that."

"I can, can't I? Lots of direction. And as you've always done, you will help—"

Flavia snapped her fan closed. "I am not going to Canada with you, Portia. You will have grand adventures and see wonderful sights, while I bide in England, stitching samplers and sipping tea."

The sneaking whiff of an unpleasant notion had become the rank odor of betrayal. "Flavia Brompton, you cannot expect me to go to Canada all on my own. Canada lies across a whole, perilous ocean."

"You will have the company of your husband on that journey. I might have a husband too."

"Then bring him to Canada, for pity's sake. Flave, you must come with me." Surely the obvious did not bear repeating?

"No, I must not. You will have Emeril to sort out and marvelous summers to enjoy. While I... Mr. DeGrange has been importuning Mama for permission to court me, and I will tell her to allow it. He claims he noticed me last year, but expected I would look higher than mere gentry. He's very sweet, and not that old, and I was never one for adventures."

Oh, good Lord. Of all the... but then Portia recalled that Mr. DeGrange had always been punctiliously correct toward Mama, and Mama had not taken to smacking him with her fan, which was a sure sign she was in pursuit of a flirtation.

The punch abruptly sat disagreeably. "Flave, you cannot abandon me."

"We are not abandoning each other. We are growing up and taking our places in Society. You must promise to write to me, Porry, at least once a month. You will be the making of Cousin Em, I know you will."

God in heaven. Flavia and Mr. DeGrange. Hecate and Lord Phillip. Blind hogs on every hand.

"I cannot fathom that you'd betray me like this, Flavia. All I can tell you is, my door will always be open to you, and I hope you and Mr. DeGrange are very happy."

Flavia touched her arm. "Thank you for those good wishes, Portia. You will write to me?"

Portia had the sense that Flavia had stolen something from her—a future, a dream, an inheritance—but that was ridiculous. Emeril was handsome, ambitious, and a prodigiously good kisser, and Portia would indeed be the making of him.

"I shall write to you," Portia said. "Once a month might be a bit too much to ask when I'll be establishing my household and entertaining and furthering my husband's interests to the best of my ability, but I will write."

"Thank you." Flavia imposed a one-armed hug on her, and Portia nearly hugged her sister back. A whole ocean, vast forests, winters... Why must Canada be so deuced far away?

Portia sat up lest those thoughts lead to needless fretting.

Flavia hadn't reciprocated that part about *my door will always be open to you*, probably an oversight, but... maybe not. Her door would be Mr. DeGrange's door, and Mr. DeGrange did not appear to hold Emeril in very high regard at present. But then, Mr. DeGrange was mere gentry.

Portia rose. "The supper waltz approaches, and my Emeril has promised me... Oh, Flavia, *look at him*."

Flavia stood as well, her gaze on the grand staircase, where Lord Phillip escorted Hecate down into the ballroom.

"Look at *them*. She's radiant and he's resplendent."

"Mama would say he cleans up nicely."

"Mama would be *vastly* understating the situation."

Lord Phillip paused on the third step up and, before the whole of the glittering assemblage, kissed Hecate's gloved hand.

"Not done," Portia murmured, her heart genuinely fluttering. "A gentleman doesn't allow his lips... It's the outside of too much, Flavie, and Hecate is simply beaming at him."

"When Lord Phillip is courting his lady, it's apparently done and done well. I am promised to Mr. DeGrange for the supper waltz."

She swanned off as Lord Phillip gave the musicians leave to begin the introduction. The dance floor filled with couples bowing and curtseying, though Portia didn't see Emeril anywhere. She finally spotted him by the men's punchbowl and barely got him onto the dance floor before the introduction concluded.

～

"We must extract a promise from Nunn to always leave this meadow in hay or pasture," Hecate said. "Can one do that with a patch of ground?" How little she knew of the details of farming and how eager she was to learn them.

"One can," Phillip said, walking hand in hand with her beneath the full moon, "and because this ground rolls and has a slope to it, that might be the best use of these acres anyway. Ah, your minions have been busy."

Hecate had slipped down to the kitchen to whisper a request to Cook at the supper break, and Cook had hugged her. *Not done.* So much was not done and should be done. Frequently.

"Dawn isn't far off," Hecate said, settling onto the blankets that had obligingly been spread for them. "We have two hours at most."

"We have the rest of our lives." Phillip sat beside her and began removing his boots and stockings. "Now that you've had some time to ponder the matter, are you still pleased to have Edward Ross underfoot?"

Hecate had pondered the reality of having a father and would be pondering it for some time. She had also pondered—with unseemly relish—the pleasure of casting Isaac unto dear Uncle Frank's impecunious charity. Living frugally was so much easier on the Continent, after all.

"Edward Ross did the best he could," she said. "Part of me wants to rail against him—he left me among the Bromptons for so long, and their latest trap might well have ensnared me."

"You were losing your heart for the fight. I thought reinforcements might aid the cause. Something restored your independent spirits before those reinforcements became necessary."

Phillip was so modest, so pragmatic, and without airs. "Flavia, of all people. She has never given me a moment's difficulty, never complained of her lot, never spoken ill of anybody, and yet, her sister —her only sister—nearly got her compromised, treated her like an unpaid lady's maid, and expected a hound's loyalty from her. When I asked Flavia why she tolerated that treatment, she informed me that Portia was all she had."

Phillip looped an arm around Hecate's shoulders. "You will always have me, Hecate. Thunderbolts from on high, London gossips, scandal, penury, droughts, floods... None of it matters as long as I am by your side."

Hecate heard that for the vow it was and answered him with a kiss. Phillip was apparently in no mood to hurry, drat him. Hecate was in no mood to dawdle, and a delicious contest ensued.

She remained in possession of her wits long enough to give him the words in addition to the kisses and caresses. "You will always have me too, Phillip. *Always*, and you will have me right now as well, if you'd please be about it."

And nobody could *be about it* as Phillip could when he was determined on his objective. Hecate tried counting stars to distract her from the pleasure. She tried listening to the distant refrains of the good-night waltz drifting over the woods and fields.

She gave up, and gave in, and gave and gave and gave, until Phillip had sent her twice 'round the bend. When he would have withdrawn, she stopped him.

"Stay with me, Phillip, please. This time, stay with me."

He levered up on his arms. "Are you proposing to me, Miss Brompton?"

She tried to think. Didn't get very far. "We do this properly. I'm asking for permission to court you."

"Ah." Phillip seemed to be having trouble getting thoughts and words in harness together too. "Is a special license proper?"

"Very. Set you back five pounds, though."

"No matter. My beloved is a financial genius, and besides, that's the best use of five pounds I ever heard of. Kiss me."

The courtship commenced to the wild satisfaction of both parties, who were frequently wildly satisfied, even after the service at St. Nebo's in Crosspatch Corners, Berkshire, and the wedding breakfast at the Crosspatch Arms.

A dear friend of the family, one Edward Ross, late of Bristol, stood up for the groom, as did Lord and Lady Tavistock. The whole village stood up for the bride, and that, according to Lord Phillip's faultless sense of proper etiquette, was exactly how it should *always* be.

Made in the USA
Las Vegas, NV
05 October 2023

78600325R00154